Praise for ALL THE DEAD MEN

"Errick Nunnally's ALL THE DEAD MEN is a fang-filled rollicking mix of horror, noir, and adventure pulp. It's swift, smart, and packs an emotional punch. You'll want to join the church of Alexander Smith, if he'll have you."

—Paul Tremblay, author of A HEAD FULL OF GHOSTS and SURVIVOR SONG

"It's as if Richard Kadrey and Walter Mosley made a baby and they grew up to write ALL THE DEAD MEN. If brutal and original, hard-boiled horror-noir is your jam, grab this book. If it isn't...I feel sad for you."

—Christopher Golden, New York Times bestselling author of ARARAT and RED HANDS

"Errick Nunnally's All The Dead Men injects a generous dose of horror and a noir aesthetic into a gripping adventure of shapeshifters, vampires, and sinister magic. Alexander Smith battles his inner demon and the ghosts of his past while fighting the monsters targeting his family and preying on modern-day Boston. I can't wait for the next installment in the series!"

—Dana Cameron, award-winning author/author of the FANGBORN series

"Alexander Smith has quickly become one of my favorite werewolves. I read BLOOD FOR THE SUN in two sittings, and the only reason it took me three sittings to read ALL THE DEAD MEN is the fact that my kid insisted that I stop to feed him. In this second novel of the Alexander Smith trilogy, Errick Nunnally brings so much more to the page—more magic, more violence, more vampires, and more emotional complications for this fascinating fictional character."

—Michelle Renee Lane, Bram Stoker Award nominated author of INVISIBLE CHAINS

"Nunnally's potent combination of noir and horror made ALL THE DEAD MEN the best late night reading I've had in ages. Fans of both genres are going to love this dark and violent crossover."

—Tony Tremblay, Bram Stoker Award nominated author of THE MOORE HOUSE

"ALL THE DEAD MEN flows smoothly through horror, noir, and crime. A dark, delicious blend of genres that simply proves what I already know: Errick Nunnally knows how to tell a riveting tale. This is the second Alexander Smith novel I've read and I look forward to the next dozen books in the series."

–James A. Moore, author of THE SEVEN FORGES series and the SERENITY FALLS trilogy

"The best horror fiction takes reality, the things we know and accept as fact, and tips it just out of plumb…and ALL THE DEAD MEN does that with such skill and ease that you find yourself rooting for a monster. Fast paced, visceral and real, ALL THE DEAD MEN will grab you by the throat and not let go."

–P.D.Cacek, author of SECOND LIVES

"In ALL THE DEAD MEN, Errick Nunnally illustrates a version of Boston that's layered with magic and monsters, with a shapeshifting protagonist who might be the biggest monster of all. It's dark, rich, and utterly compelling."

–Toni L.P. Kelner, coeditor of NYT best seller DEATH'S EXCELLENT VACATION

"Alexander Smith is back and once again dishing out his unique brand of supernatural justice! Readers who like their hardboiled mysteries full of monsters and soaked in blood will rejoice!"

–Nicholas Kaufmann, Thriller Award-nominated author of CHASING THE DRAGON and DYING IS MY BUSINESS

"Errick Nunnally's ALL THE DEAD MEN is a cause for celebration—not just because it continues the story of Alexander Smith, the werewolf seeking redemption from BLOOD FOR THE SUN, but because *Any* new writing by Nunnally is a welcome event in my house. Nunnally writes in a precise and sumptuous style, instantly inviting any stranger or fan into his stories, no matter how complex they might be. More, ALL THE DEAD MEN is a triumph of careful plotting, excellent pacing, and satisfying world-building, all tightly controlled by Nunnally's talent. I can't wait to see what Errick Nunnally writes next, and where Alexander Smith's story continues."

–Paul Michael Anderson, author of STANDALONE and BONES ARE MADE TO BE BROKEN.

"Errick Nunnally is a must read for urban fantasy enthusiasts. The second book in the Alexander Smith series, ALL THE DEAD MEN, is like going to the store on your regular route but then surprisingly, and delightedly, passing through another dimension before being dropped at your final destination. It will entertain you to no end. Nunnally is a name you should get used to hearing."
–Gerald L. Coleman, author of THE THREE GIFTS epic fantasy series

"ALL THE DEAD MEN is poetic, visceral, and kinetic as hell. In Nunnally's masterful hands, the inhuman anti-hero who is Alexander Smith becomes terrifyingly real and touchingly empathetic. The energy never stops, making the book a breathless and gory feast for all lovers of urban horror and powerful prose."
–Chet Williamson, author of DREAMTHORP & ASH WEDNESDAY

"Action-packed storytelling at its utmost! ALL THE DEAD MEN launches you from one scene to the next with scarcely a second to catch your breath. Nunnally has perfected the supernatural thriller in his latest novel."
–Rena Mason, Bram Stoker Award® Winning author of THE EVOLUTIONIST, and THE DEVIL'S THROAT

Praise for BLOOD FOR THE SUN

"Despite his (Alex's) memory lapses, he's driven to solve crimes, especially those against children, to expiate his own past crimes. His inner dialog is fascinating as he tries to hold himself together when dealing with the police, the local supernatural underworld, an unfriendly pack of werewolves, his vampire foster daughter, a magical scientist, and more. In some ways, this is a standard dark urban fantasy mystery, but as damaged detectives go Alexander is a doozy barely able to remember enough to get by at some points, but strangely likable as he keeps plugging along without self-pity, just wondering at his condition and where it's going to lead him."
–Carolyn Cushman, LOCUS MAGAZINE

"…Built from the characters and their lives rather than a "what if" idea. The novel's rock-solid structure comes from all its components blending into a seamless work. BLOOD FOR THE SUN is a paranormal murder mystery, similar only in its subgenre to other books of that ilk. Its greatest fault is that it wasn't published sooner.

–J.G. Stinson, Foreword Reviews

Praise for LIGHTNING WEARS A RED CAPE

"Nunnally confronts the grittier aspects of the super-powered human genre and the result is a bruising thrill ride. LIGHTNING WEARS A RED CAPE is brutal, dynamic, and action-packed, but it's also an insightful glimpse into the hearts and souls of men and women gifted, or cursed, with the power of gods."

–Laird Barron, author of BLOOD STANDARD

"Errick Nunnally's novel is an action-filled world of god-like super-humans whose lives are complicated by their very human emotions. Filled with realistic action, a mix of ethnic characters that reflect the real planet we live on, I loved the movie created in my mind."

–Linda D. Addison, author of HOW TO RECOGNIZE A DEMON HAS BECOME YOUR FRIEND

"With LIGHTNING WEARS A RED CAPE, Errick Nunnally thunders into the superhero genre with an ensemble super-powered crime novel that combines dark drama, intimate character work, and breathless action. I hope this is just the beginning for the world Nunnally has created. An author with a bright future ahead of him!"

–Christopher Golden, New York Times bestselling author of ARARAT and THE PANDORA ROOM

ALL THE DEAD MEN

The second Alexander Smith novel

Errick Nunnally

ALL THE DEAD MEN
© 2020 Errick Nunnally
Cover design and illustration © Errick Nunnally

ISBN - 978-1-949140-22-4

Twisted Publishing
an imprint of
Haverhill House Publishing LLC
643 E Broadway
Haverhill MA 01830-2420
www.haverhillhouse.com

ACKNOWLEDGMENTS

First, I have to thank Owen Dean, Vikki Ciaffone, and Richard Shealy. A trio of editors that helped hammer this beast into shape. And many thanks to John McIlveen, of course, for driving the final nail to bring this book into your hands. As ever, a big thank you to the Mad Dogs— Chris, Bracken, KL, Javed, and TJ. They were instrumental in encouraging my efforts to create, when this book was written.

I've mentioned before that Alexander Smith has been a labor of love for me. The origins were born of my interest in urban fantasy—ugh, I hate that genre name. I prefer "horror thriller" or something. Okay, sure, let's go with "horror thriller." The horror thriller genre is one dominated by female authors and female protagonists. Often white. As much as I enjoy the genre, I wasn't seeing enough of myself or the world I was closest to. Write what you want to read. That's what became an idea that first found form in a three-page gouache and ink comic* that covered Alexander and Ana's first meeting. The writing was, shall we say, overwrought. I was in art school at the time and it was all about the art. If I'm recalling correctly, that was sometime around 1996. So he's been with me for that long. Fast forward to late 2014, the year of *Blood For The Sun*'s first publication, and I get a call from my uncle. It's about a cousin we were unaware of—living in the same neighborhood we all grew up in! An entire offshoot of the family right under our noses. Which isn't as weird as it sounds since the families of American descendants of slavery in this country have been under assault and broken up for centuries. This fellow had been doing genealogy research and found my uncle. Since all the raw info was electronic, my uncle contacted me to figure it out. Long story short, I learned that our common ancestor, a great-great grandfather, had escaped slavery, became a decorated soldier after the Civil War, and received what he was owed. That last part was apparently a rarity. So he was a badass. It also turned out that he'd married a woman of mixed descent, from African-American and Moswetuset lineage. If "Moswetuset" feels familiar on your tongue, it's also a place within, and doubtless the root of the name for "Massachusetts," the state I grew up in. My great-great grandmother? A black woman surviving and raising a family in post-Civil War America? She was badass too. Considering some of the smug Puritan descendants I went to school with, I wish I'd known this stuff then. Because my lineage trumps whatever claim they have on being the earliest Americans, for sure. Anyhow, my petty revenge fantasies aren't the point. If you'll recall, Alexander's father is an escaped slave who marries a native woman in Canada. When I got this news about my family's history, I was shocked. In a good way. Because until that moment, I'd had no idea of my family's heritage beyond my grandfather. It had been like being unmoored in time, separate from your own country's history, adrift. Next to my grandmothers' struggles with dementia and the like, I think not knowing my lineage fueled the background I developed for Alexander. It's simply stunning that it paralleled my own history so closely.

I'll need to dig that comic out and blog about it, one of these days.

DEDICATION

This book is dedicated to those of you who have failed miserably and still try, because the essence of humanity is defiance, particularly in the face of orchestrated adversity and failure. *Semper prorsum*.

IT'S ABOUT TO GET DARK

By Bracken MacLeod

If there's anything I hate in a novel (or film) series, it's when the next installment picks up as though the previous story never happened. No one has learned or changed from their prior experiences, least of all the protagonist. They are, at the beginning of each story, the same exact character we met last time. No matter how many beatings, bullet wounds, and blackouts they suffer, there's no lasting trauma. The new story is a hard reset. Maybe that character will note a scar, or a longing for a departed love interest, before launching right into a new adventure without a trace of a limp, post-traumatic headache, or regret. Classic episodic TV, like *Battlestar Galactica* or *Spencer for Hire.*

I like dark stories. I like consequences and seeing characters I empathize with struggle and maybe even fail. This is why I LOVE *All the Dead Men.* At the end of *Blood for the Sun*, Alexander (I won't spoil things if you haven't read that book yet—though you ought to; it's EXCELLENT!), has been through a helluva lot and he begins this story licking his wounds—he's a shape-shifter, remember—and feeling troubled by the unresolved trauma of his last adventure. So great! But as Christopher Golden's twin, Billy Mays, used to say, "Wait, there's more!"

This is a middle act!

That means, we're in the realm of rising tension and greater stakes! And loss. You see, you hold in your hands the middle book of a trilogy. And that means, maybe, just maybe, things aren't going to work out for Alexander in this one. Maybe, he's going to go through a lot more than the first book because this isn't you getting to know him anymore, but you getting to see him at his lowest. At the point where even the hero might break.

This is my kind of book!

Now, I may have spoiled something by telling you this is a middle act. But honestly, did any of you suckers really believe that Frodo wasn't coming back in Return of the King (the book, not the ding dang diddly movies!) or that Han Solo wouldn't get thawed out in Return of the Jedi? No, you knew that was how it was going to go (though both of them *should've* died in their third acts!), but still, you were a little worried, weren't you? Well, worry now. No one here is safe. And if you think Alexander is, maybe you need to investigate your understanding of "safe."

If we were to look at this book in terms of narrative structure, *Blood for the Sun* was Exposition and Set-up, and *All the Dead Men* is Confrontation and Complication. Or, as Chuck Wendig would put it, we've moved from "Holy Shit" to "HOLY FUCKING SHIT!" Or as he also puts it, we've moved from order to chaos.

This is the part of the story where, after they find their way home using rocks, at the insistence of their stepmother, Hansel and Gretel's father takes them out to the woods *again*, and this time the birds eat their breadcrumbs. This is the part of the story where C3PO has been blown apart, Luke loses his hand, and Han gets frozen in carbonite and given to Boba Fett, and at the end our heroes are staring out into space, wrestling with heavy lessons and an uncertain future.

This is the part of the story where things that once looked bad, but manageable, become unimaginably worse, to the point of crisis. This is where failures and setbacks happen. This is where the protagonist of the story really gets their lumps, and it looks like they are going to fall.

But we know that ain't gonna happen because Alexander is our hero, right? Don't be so sure. You already know that Errick Nunnally doesn't play by those rules that other writers in this genre do.

All the Dead Men is my favorite book in the Alexander Smith series so far, and you're about to find out why. It has real stakes. Alexander still has his personal obstacles, but now he also has something to lose that makes tension and danger (Errick's middle name) seem much more urgent. We believe that maybe things won't work out for him and Ana, even though their names appear in the inside flap copy and they're the big heroes of the first book.

Have you thought about what "safe" means?

Go get yourself a glass of bourbon and a candle, because things are about to get dark.

Bracken MacLeod
15 March 2020
Sudbury, Massachusetts

ALL THE DEAD MEN

CHAPTER 1

Then.

The last notes of the foot-tapping jazz of "The 'In' Crowd" blared from the radio and faded into the DJ's voice. After some insipid rambling, he introduced the Beatles' current hit, "Help!" I spun the volume knob on the dash and cut off the music, uninterested in hearing any more of the mishmash of genres that had been dominating the airwaves this summer. Maybe it was the American zeitgeist's response to the announcement of an official commitment to combat troops in Vietnam or maybe some other, larger cultural shift.

Hot air blasting through open windows made the loose hairs on my head tickle my ears. I made the familiar motion to tuck the errant strands in and realized once again that I needed to adjust the leather band holding my braided ponytail in place. I smiled, concerned with nothing, and felt alive while hurtling down the highway. Alive for too long, certainly. I had a plan for survival, and *it was working.*

At this moment, I was on my way to meet a ghost. Ted Rooster haunted the southern reaches of the forests around Mount Rainier. The message he'd left with my answering service had me thinking about him as if I'd just heard his voice the day before. He was one of mine, a damaged one, a boy I'd tracked to a sodden grave over a decade ago. Left for dead. Children are resilient, to say the least, and he'd survived his scoutmaster's prolonged sexual assaults right up to and beyond when the molester couldn't bear the secret anymore. Ted's volunteer leader, the betrayer of a child's trust, decided it'd be simpler to murder and bury Ted rather than do the honorable thing and dispose of himself, freeing Ted and any other boys his eyes fell on. Coward. The halfhearted strangling and burying of the boy with nothing but hope that his victim was dead was the best he could muster. The police already had the feckless human when I found Ted and dragged him out of that hole.

I flicked the radio back on and tuned in a different station. "Papa's Got a Brand New Bag" burned out of the tortured speakers in the early-generation Impala and I thumped the wheel in time with the funky drummer. The decade-old vehicle ran well and I was happy to have acquired it after crossing the border from Canada on foot. At the time, I'd had no particular reason to be heading south through the Pacific Northwest, and I'd been fortunate to have heard from Rooster at all. I hated the goddamned phone, but the answering service was helpful in ensuring that I got interesting cases to support my bid-to-stay-sane hobby. My little network was working.

Rooster grew up a natural survivalist. Very difficult for his parents to keep up with. I passed through the area from time to time and taught him what I knew about the woods. In return and to assuage his own idiosyncrasies, he kept an eye on the area—he couldn't bear another case like the one that had stolen his choices and defined the rest of his life. Roofs and running water became anathema to his altered nature; he was a natural protector and amazing tracker—for a human being.

Well before calling me, Ted had slid out of the forest on the trail of Kelsey Thomas, a girl who'd disappeared with her father some weeks before the beginning of summer. With nothing better to do, she became the reason I was going south.

He'd lost her trail in the city, one of the places Rooster tended to avoid and where his particular skills came up short. He was claustrophobic like he'd been forced to live beneath the stars his entire life. He never trusted the Boy Scouts again—not that he or anyone else had to worry about that particular troop leader. Bringing the boy out of the forest guaranteed that his scoutmaster went to prison for a long time. We both figured it was the least price a scoutmaster should pay for the extreme measures he'd taken to cover up his crimes. Regardless, the sentence wasn't for life and Rooster could always visit the sorry bastard if he felt like discussing anything.

For local media, Kelsey's disappearance was a big story until it wasn't. I found it consistently amazing how little coordinated attention was paid to these disappearances and murders. It seemed that only the children of the white and wealthy grabbed the national media's attention and brought the authorities out in coordinated force. And there were so many curious cases or just-plain-gone kids like Kelsey. It was a golden opportunity for me. Something I could distract myself with and keep the mental gears turning. A cornucopia, for sure.

The Impala chugged along and I had not a care in the world until I saw the little boy standing on the side of the road. As I passed, we locked eyes. We knew each other; I remembered him and he remembered me. I never knew his name and any guilt I felt at the sight of my victim's ghost got packed deep down with vigor. I didn't see him in the rear-view mirror and I grinned, happy to leave the unshakable memory behind. Though I saw him sometimes but no one else could, it wasn't nearly enough to rattle me too bad. I was becoming accustomed to the weird in my head.

Hours later, at dusk, I pulled into a spot on the edge of the forest where Rooster lived illegally. One might think he "camped," but that presumed he was leaving at some point. No, Rooster was there to stay until his dying day. Fine by me. It just meant a bit more effort on my part, more exercise for my brain. I slipped out of my clothes and into the transformation, dumping my weaker skin for the more durable stuff. It was a palpable joy, running into the steaming forest, luxuriating in the green.

There was no breeze, no way for Rooster to hide downwind. I criss-crossed the edge of the pine until I picked up his scent. Then I followed it in a zigzag pattern, noting where it got stronger, keeping all of my senses alert for where he might be waiting. It was a game we'd been playing for years, a long game. He'd yet to win, but he was getting better every year that I passed through.

I tracked him up to a sharp rise. A feint, I was sure, something to get me to expose myself. I hunkered down and skirted the base of the incline until I found his trail again. It doubled back more than once until I could smell him, strong in the air. I felt like I was right on top of him, but there was no other sign. I spun in a quick circle, eyes and ears alert. *Damn it to hell, I can practically taste him.*

"Does this mean I won?"

Rooster had a laconic, soft-spoken voice. He rarely used it, so he tended to sound hesitant. At this point in his life, I knew he was anything but. He was up a tree. Way up, I could see, now that I bothered to look. Ana had warned me about looking up more often, but I'd gotten cocky and let it slip.

I huffed and sat back on my haunches while he climbed down.

"First time," he said with a smile playing at the corners of his bearded mouth.

Rooster was short and well-muscled, the human equivalent of a badger. He was currently wearing just enough clothing to ward off any discomfort the forest might provide, but it was a particularly warm night and he was sweating by the time he hit bottom.

Speaking with a mouth better suited for destruction, I growled out, "What've you got for me, Rooster?"

"Pretty much what I told ya on the message." He spoke carefully, reciting facts. "This girl, Kelsey Thomas, nine years old, been gone for 'bout two months now. Her mom was murdered an' the cops 'spect her daddy. He was something of a big-shot businessman in the area; a lot o' folks knew him. I know he did it; all the evidence says so."

Rooster's brown eyes sparkled in his hairy, mirthless face. He was talking about a predator and it was raising his hackles. I knew he was disappointed that he hadn't been able to find them.

"Her room didn't look loved an' their home had that cold feeling to it, like it had been under a shroud. Nothing out of place, no personality. All appearances seemed manufactured. The mother had confided in a friend that she was…unhappy and that her husband was…touching their daughter. And had been for some time. That must be why he killed her; he must've found out she told or she'd had enough an' confronted him. I s'pose the friend got lucky, 'cause he didn't have time to get to her. Police been lookin', but they ain't doin' so good."

"You spoke to the friend?"

Rooster spread his arms and glanced to the side. "No, man, look at me. Who the hell would willingly talk to the wild man from the woods? I read the papers at the library."

Libraries were a nexus of all available information. Rooster was smart enough to know that. "Where'd you lose the trail?"

He chewed the inside of his lip for a moment before telling me. "'Round the edge of Rainier, west of here."

I nodded.

"Did you tell the police?"

"Anonymously. Didn't do no good."

"Tell me everything you know about the case and I'll start from the beginning."

It took Rooster the better part of an hour to recount all the details he'd uncovered. I had all the information I needed to start from scratch—the better to use my own head to work out the particulars.

"Find 'im, Alexander. He don't deserve no mercy."

I left the forest faster than I came in. With no need to be stealthy, I enjoyed the run, feeling the supernatural power coursing through my body and energizing my legs.

Back at the car, I decided I'd head to the Thomases' home first, under the cover of darkness. I could visit Mrs. Thomas's friend in the morning. I didn't want to waste any time, and my head buzzed with possibilities. This would be a good hunt, more than a puzzle. Either option kept my monster at bay; all the better for me. I had a long drive to get out of the national park lands and into Centralia. It would be the middle of the night when I arrived.

I pulled the car off the road into a secluded area about a half a mile from the Thomas home. When I'd driven by it, the place was dark and the neighborhood quiet. The area remained still and I didn't want to alarm any of the neighbors by letting them see a strange car nearby. No need to draw that kind of attention. The entire neighborhood was carved into the woods, a beautiful development with plenty of space and trees between lots. Private, plenty of places to hide.

Where the road curved and the wooded area thickened, I was able to hide the Impala from anyone not looking and slip into the woods straightaway. Without incident, I passed through several backyards, giving wide berth to those with dogs, until I came to the home in question.

It shared the same outward characteristics as all the others in the area. A ranch-style home, sloping roofline, with sliding doors set above a small concrete slab on what should have been a manicured lawn. The Thomas yard was going to pot fast. In this lush environment, the grass was more than twice as long as the neighbors' and the bordering green encroached, leaving a blurry line between where the trees ended and Man's dominion began.

There were no outdoor lights on, and after observing the dark home for a few minutes, I slipped across the lawn and took a close look at the sliding door. According to my nose and the appearance of the slab, there'd been plenty of foot traffic in and out. The investigators. How careful had they been when finishing up? I couldn't see any kind of alarm system or bracing bar inside. I tried the door and it slid open easily. People in these areas rarely developed the habits of inner-city residents who locked every door behind them.

Inside the home, I was just off the black-and-white-tiled kitchen. At the corner of the kitchen, a well-used pea-green electric stove was cornered against a yellow-speckled Formica countertop leading to a bulbous refrigerator the color of squash. I still couldn't get used to the unnatural color schemes introduced after the Second World War. Progress, indeed.

The air was stale and I confirmed Rooster's assessment of the décor. It seemed less a home and more a place where people stayed. I didn't bother with the lights; I could see well enough and, more importantly, I could smell even better. The mother had been murdered here in the kitchen. There weren't any bloody smudges, but they'd clearly done a poor job cleaning up. More scents lingered here than anywhere else, trapped in the house with the dead air. I could smell the old death and dozens of male scents. Guns, boot polish, tobacco and coffee. It was an olfactory blueprint for law enforcement around the world.

According to Rooster, Mr. Thomas had killed his wife with a butcher knife. Classic. A glance confirmed one missing from the knife block. The largest. They must've argued in the kitchen—or he caught up with her there—and he decided a course correction was in order. I decided it must've been an argument. The mother couldn't bear it and confronted him as far from the bedrooms upstairs as she could. Far too many men of David Thomas's ilk operated for years right under the noses of friends and family. Sometimes with tacit approval or an iron fist.

It looked like David had been sucking the life out of this home for years. Iron fist, then. Years of hidden atrocities that overflowed when confronted, revealing him for who he truly was. All the claws and teeth he'd kept tucked safely away bristled, and no one was safe. No human, anyway. I grinned to myself. Western society continued to produce the perfect fodder for my continued survival. David was going to be worthy of death.

There was nothing more of interest downstairs. What I wanted at that point was a clear scent profile for Kelsey and her father. Upstairs, fewer scents lingered. They'd focused much of their investigation downstairs. Thick carpet covered the stairs and the entire upper floor. My movements were disturbingly silent on the plush surface. There were four rooms. Three were bedrooms and one was an office and storage space. The master bedroom was messier than expected, considering the sterile state of the rest of the home. I peeked into the adjacent bedroom—clearly a guest room. It was neat and had been inhabited by Mrs. Thomas. Perhaps life in the grey zone had been off for longer than anyone knew. I wondered how long Mrs. Thomas had known about her husband's proclivities. The main bedroom must've become David's nest. I stood in the center of the room, breathing in the patriarch's scent with confidence.

Inside Kelsey's room, I sat on her pink twin bed. The room, sparse like the rest of the house, barely radiated much more than "this is a girl's room." I sat and breathed in Kelsey's identifying scents for a few minutes and looked for any clues that might help later on. What little theme there was in the room soon became apparent. Kelsey loved dogs. There was a dog calendar on the wall and a few stuffed ones on the bed. I peeked under the bed and in the closet. Nothing of note except a few books on dog breeds. I stood there for a few minutes more and then ran my hand along the wall at the top of the closet, just out of sight. Then I pulled the drawers of the dresser out one by one. On the back of the drawer third from the top, I found something. A piece of mesh thumbtacked to the back. Inside it, several sheets of folded paper with neat, girlish writing. Some were in pen, others in pencil. From the first page, I gleaned that this was Kelsey's version of a diary. At least, the kind of diary she wished her life reflected. I pocketed the papers and returned the drawers.

I poked around the office for a while, getting to know David Thomas, what he spent most of his time doing. He was a clown. In every sense of the word, to me, but only occasionally to the locals. Here and there, on shelves and walls, were photos of David at events, with clients. Faded color photos with various people of all sizes and shapes with conservative haircuts and pink faces. All white, of course, the better to hide in plain sight and get comfortable. In all of the photos, David looked plain. His hair was always cut and styled the same way, his clothes were similar in every photo. Looking at the repetition, I thought it might be hard for the police to circulate a photo of this guy for help. If he changed his look, he'd be a completely different person.

He ran a small business that served a wide area. A party supplier with all the entertainments, living and otherwise: ponies, clowns, balloons, games, popcorn machines—you name it. Sometimes, when needed, he slipped on the greasepaint and filled in, entertaining children in his lap. Parents trusted him. An upstanding businessman who provided parties for children? Gold. He got into schools, daycares, homes. Every job must have been like a victim interview. Since he needed to know the spaces he was working with, he would often have unfettered access. Children look to their parents for whom to trust, and there he was; being trusted. Society at large was unwilling to believe the extent that pedophiles would go to satisfy their needs. I knew how patient and dedicated predators could be to claim their prey. I wasn't surprised when a dangerous beast came in human shape rather than some other animal on the plains of Africa or from the depths of the ocean. Murderous creatures came from both of those places and everywhere in between, but none compared to what Man could do. Maybe one day, humanity would learn.

Downstairs, back near the kitchen, I didn't pause to think. I just slipped out the back and kept following the clues. Surely the police had the same information I had managed to glean from the Thomas home—excepting Kelsey's fantasy journal pages. They couldn't follow a scent trail like I could, however, couldn't use their other senses to pick up details that would go unnoticed. It would be dawn soon and I needed something to eat before going door to door and figuring out who really knew the Thomas family. At my car, I shed my clothes and then my skin to do a little hunting that didn't involve humans.

From what Rooster had told me, David Thomas's parents were deceased and he didn't have close family in the area. He was estranged from his only aunt and cousins. Telling, I think. Kelsey's mother, Sarah, however, was a somewhat different story. Her parents had been a hurricane in the area for the past two months; everyone knew them. They were back home in California, so that day I would work for them, that day I was a private detective. They'd hired me due to frustration that the police hadn't made much progress in locating their granddaughter or their daughter's killer. That was my story. With no legal constraints and nothing but time on my hands, I could learn more about David Thomas than they already had.

People still wanted to do the right thing; they wanted the world to be good and clean. And they were willing to talk to force the matter in this young and remote neighborhood where residents still neglected to lock their doors. I could use the authorities' lack of progress to pry open doors and mouths. I pinballed from home to home, inhaling a heady mix of potpourri, dogs, and children while absorbing story after story defining David and Sarah Thomas.

I learned that David was well liked and respected—an entirely different personality than the truth of him, the personality able to murder the mother of his child and steal his own daughter away to play with. Unsuspected, as *they* always were. He was handsome, helpful, and committed to building a successful business. His few employees didn't have much to say about him other than that he was fair and professional. He was the owner and manager; they did what he told them to do and it didn't involve becoming friends.

David Thomas was involved in the community, but not too involved. He never took the lead of his own volition, but occasionally he would be volunteered and he'd do the job good-naturedly. People liked that about him, liked that he'd pitch in when called. He seemed to know everyone, but few people knew him. What I did find were the couple's friends—some dating back to high school, neighborhood pals from way back. Through them and their guilt and loss and disbelief, David's life as an emotionally abused and wayward youth could be cobbled together. I was able to follow this bland trail to one of his estranged cousins, someone who knew David *before*.

Phil Thomas lived off the beaten path, to say the least. He stayed in a small trailer off a short, broken road. I stopped on the main road and took in the area. Tall, golden grass surrounded the trailer for hundreds of yards, getting thicker at a pine tree line in the distance. It would have been beautiful but for the pile of crap Phil lived in that had clearly been sitting in the field for some time. A smaller pile of discarded junk sat next to a rusted red pickup. Two dirt lines were scored into the grass leading to the truck.

Before I was within fifty yards of the thing, I could smell the weed and corn liquor, greasy food, and dirty humans. More weed and liquor than any one man would ever need for recreation. Phil lived with a pregnant woman topped with thin blond hair who looked like a hundred miles of bad road. Her five-year-old had the same empty look her mother did. The resemblance was stunning. When I met her pale, blue eyes, there was nothing there, no curiosity. The kid was barely alert. She picked over a ruined plastic bowl of corn flakes.

I wondered if I'd be back in the neighborhood for Phil one day. We spoke in the dirt patch of the front "yard" under a tattered awning tacked to the side of the trailer. Phil was shirtless and skinny, wearing tight jeans that flared at the bottom, a patch on either knee, and thick tan boots. An intricate belt buckle of tarnished pewter with a center of turquoise on a thick leather belt did little to hold the pants up. His long head was constantly in motion; dirty blond hair hanging down past his ears waved with every movement. I could smell cigarettes and gunpowder on him, but I didn't believe he was armed. That didn't mean the woman in the trailer wasn't. Or that she didn't have a weapon trained on me right now. I shadowed Phil and kept him between me and the trailer. It seemed to agitate him a little.

"Davey wasn't no angel, none of us were, but we wasn't so interested in some o' the things he was." Phil's thick horseshoe mustache danced when he spoke.

"Meaning?"

Phil spit and kicked some dirt at the wet spot. "Shit, I always swore I'd never talk about family like this."

"David turn out like anyone else in your family?"

"Hell, no! Man, you believe he's messin' with Kelsey, y'know, like that?"

I just stared at him and waited. Waited for the rusty gears in his head to turn and pull the curtain further back. It took time to unravel belief.

"Shit, man. That's... Shit."

"You were telling me what David was like when you were younger."

"Yeah. Yeah, we wasn't tight. Y'know? But we was cousins—by marriage—and we got together often enough. The usual goofy stuff as kids. Y'know?"

I didn't know, but it also didn't matter. Again, I waited, leaving dead air for Phil to fill.

"There was a couple times we found dead animals and he wanted to—I dunno—dissect 'em or whatnot. Weird shit. I remember one time he tried to get a few of us to do some really crazy dares."

"Like what?"

"Ah..." Phil looked around, avoiding my eyes.

I bent over and met his eyes, followed them, stayed in his field of vision. "Like what, Phil?"

Phil sighed and relented. "Man, he always wanted to stick his dick in something or watch someone do it. Girls, boys, whatever. He didn't bring it up often. Y'know?"

"No, Phil, I don't know. Explain." Phil gave me a hard look, the kind of glance that served as a warning. I resolved to take the easy way with him and reminded him that I was working for his aunt and uncle.

Phil spit. He liked to spit when he was thinking. "He never missed an opportunity to try and worm it in. Okay? Got a little reputation for it, for a while, then nothing. He cooled it. No one ever let him do it 'cause it was fuckin' weird. Right?"

"Yeah. How did his parents treat him?"

"Aaah, his mom was cool. But his dad was mean. Not mean like he beat him a lot or nothin' for no reason. Y'know? Just, like, cold. Never did much for Davey other than to tell him to do shit around the house or remind Davey that he was worthless. A real prick to his mom, too."

I heard the motor before Phil's eyes glanced over my shoulder. I looked and saw a black muscle car grind to a halt at the turnoff onto the road. I couldn't make out how many people were in the vehicle. Customers, no doubt.

I nodded at Phil. "Where'd David like to hang out when he got older, in his teens?"

"Aw, I dunno. We sorta drifted apart before then. Our moms wasn't draggin' us around no more, so we was doin' whatever we was doin.' All I know is he started runnin' away when he got older."

"Yeah? Tell me about that."

Phil chewed his lip, thinking, then spit. I hoped he wouldn't embellish too badly. "He'd disappear for a couple o' days before coming back. That I know of, he took off three times."

"Each time longer than the last?"

"Yeah! How'd you know?"

"I'm a private dick."

"Uh, sure, right." Phil's eyebrows creased.

"So, how long each time? Do you know?"

"Uh-huh. The whole family'd go on red alert. He's gone two days the first time. Like, four the next. And I think over a week the last time."

"Consecutive?"

"Huh?"

"Like one time after the other. Right away?"

"Oh, no. Second time was 'bout a year later. Third time I know of was more'n two years later."

"I see." *Practice runs, reconnaissance, the son of a bitch.* "You remember anything else that might help us find him?"

"Um, no, I don't think so. Anything else I can do to help my family?"

"Love your children instead."

"Instead o' what?"

I turned and left Phil with his busted-up trailer and waiting customers.

David had gotten smart, knew what his behaviors meant, how they affected people. He had started hiding his true self, making plans to become the man he was that day. David Thomas had been a poor kid who'd seemingly pulled himself up by his bootstraps, gotten married and started breeding like all the other humans around him. His entire history smacked of quiet focus. No college, just sheer determination and sweat. An elaborate camouflage for a dedicated monster, all this time festering and waiting. He was careful, and now his hide was coming undone and he could finally come into being. For all the good that did him. He was cut off from his established patterns, on the run. He had his little girl, sure, but that couldn't last, no matter how clear the illusions he kept in his mind. I began to suspect he'd eluded authorities and evaded detection for this long because he had a keen, narcissistic sense of self-preservation. The monster would most assuredly spin further out of control, if murdering his wife was any indication.

The more I learned about David, the more confident I

was that he was spiraling deeper into his true self. He had his daughter, Kelsey, his plaything, a toy he owned, something he'd created. Dear Old Dad, with nothing more to lose, finally had the opportunity to slip further into his fantasies. And David had experience hiding himself, had disappeared several times as a youth to live off the grid.

This had been the longest it had taken me, so far, to find someone. And the longer it took to find this particular bastard, the more time I had to think on the situation. None of this sat well with me. I tracked what was left of the missing Thomas family northward, through Centralia into territory I'd known to have been inhabited by the Nisqually. White men named the city "Yelm," after language believed to have something to do with heat mirages. I knew better but didn't dwell on it.

David Thomas appeared to be cutting a beeline north to more densely populated areas. He had a broad pattern I could discern: using a mix of lonely motels on the outskirts of towns and never staying longer than a day or two. He had to stop somewhere, though; I didn't think he'd drag Kelsey all the way into Canada.

I had to eliminate his old stomping grounds and calculate how far he'd have to go to stay unnoticed. How far and where. He needed a neighborhood both familiar to him and far enough away that no one would easily recognize him. I knew his service area—as did the police, so it was safe to assume he'd move beyond that. Probably somewhere inside fifty miles. Dense population. City. It'd need enough poor people to have generated the kind of economy David could exploit.

At a gas station near Graham, I picked up a map of the surrounding areas and spread it out on the warm hood of the car and went to work. Once I was certain I had a viable city, I started driving again. It took nearly two weeks of crawling through small cities like this and haunting the halls of motels and rest stops until I came up on the borders of Enumclaw. Another of many cities in the Pacific Northwest that got its name from the First People. Around the time white people began stealing these lands, my mother had told me a tale from the Salish who lived here, of two brothers transformed into thunder and lightning to battle the evil spirits who hailed from a nearby mountain.

I moved through the neighborhoods, eliminating street after street under the grey skies, looking for the areas that might help a man like David escape his childhood and his pursuers. More stalking, more patience, passing time to pick up his or Kelsey's scent. I came across hers first.

Kelsey was under constant stress, producing sweat and oils, wild pheromones, and shedding hair. He'd colored her hair, I learned, and not very well. Her health was rapidly declining and I knew she'd be a shell of a girl someday soon. What then? He'd be forced to discard her and move on to something new, perhaps. Her scent was turning into a sour mix of depression and anxiety. The flavors of betrayal. A betrayal so fundamental that there was no possible way for her to cope with it; she'd become the embodiment of hopelessness.

I wasn't sure where all this musing was coming from. I'd pursued others without this sort of analysis. I don't think I'd ever tracked anyone quite like David, a man who'd murdered his wife in cold blood, probably in conflict over the sexual abuse he was doling out to his daughter and other children. All for reasons only psychiatrists could pretend to understand. The rest of the race, when confronted with such flawed people, were content to assume they were simply insane. I knew better. These sorts were well aware of what they were doing and why it was wrong. They did it anyway.

The basest instincts called for an erasure of their existence, the better for everyone to move on without the toxic weight. In my case, this was a selfish solution, something to further my goals; I couldn't lie to myself about it. It was impossible to erase the mark that was left on these souls whose lives I affected.

Humanity seemed to be both taking a turn for the worse and making gigantic leaps forward. Vietnam, the resurgence of feminism, free love, civil rights, putting men into space, all the musical genres being played on the radio. Whatever it was that was happening in American history seemed to be occurring in conjunction with a rise in more humans preying on each other. Or waking them up.

Kelsey's trail supplanted David's in strength. It was her scent I began to follow more than anything else, picking it out of the damp air. It led to a cheap motel on the southwest side. The squat, single-story building sprawled for a few hundred feet along the parking lot and met the side of a brick townhouse. I found the room they'd stayed in, but it was occupied. I knocked on the door, simple enough. A short, fat man, shirtless, wearing striped pajama bottoms, slung the door open and poured hate out of his rheumy face.

"What?"

It was warm, but not hot enough for him to be sweating like this. I tamped down any curiosity about what he might be doing in the room and breathed in Kelsey and David's smells, ignoring the rest.

"Sorry, wrong room."

He smirked and slammed the door.

I made my way to the front entrance. The small foyer was made much tighter by the built-in desk creating a nook for the motel's keeper. The particulate stink of cigarettes and the occasional joint permeated the rug and walls. All around, the soiled march of many humans at the lowest point of their lives raked my nose as well. Behind the desk, a gatekeeper of the down and nearly out stared at a small black-and-white television on an abused folding table, ignoring my entrance, lazily dragging on a cigarette.

"Excuse me."

The rangy man, with a thick head of black hair, wore battered denim and a wildly patterned shirt stretched tight across his lean upper body. He eyed me while he stubbed out the tobacco and licked his lips, sucking the long mustache into his mouth briefly before speaking. His ugly face matched the photo and certificate behind the desk. Dennis Lacourte, Manager.

"What you want, boy, need a room for the night?"

"No. I'm here to ask you about a former boarder."

Laconic, he stood up, stretched and leaned into the desk, staring into my face.

"You ain't a cop."

"That's right."

"You best gimme better reasons to talk to you than just shufflin' in here, Tonto." He rubbed two of his fingers together.

I stared back, unimpressed, and considered my options. I wasn't prone to taking subtle racist jabs before I could crush a man's skull with my bare hands. I could pay the guy, I could argue, or I could walk away.

"Hey, you hear me, chief?" He snapped his fingers in my face.

Fourth option.

My hand cracked smartly across Dennis's cheek, turning his head. A red welt blossomed on his face and a curt exhalation of air from his mouth followed the blow. He stumbled to the side, grasping at the desk for balance. When he recovered, his long arm snapped out in a wide arc of a right hook. It looked like slow motion to me. I dipped my head at the blow and let his clenched hand slam into the hardest part my skull, just above the forehead. I heard fingers snap. He gasped and I popped him with a right cross into the center of his face. He flailed backward, knocking the television over and scattering other junk piled up back there. Blood gushed down into his mustache and started to paint the front of his ugly shirt. He pulled something from his back pocket.

I vaulted the desk and put my foot in the center of his chest, slamming him back into the wall again; a switchblade clattered across the floor. He lost his balance and tumbled to the floor, where I stepped on his remaining good hand.

"I don't believe we know each other, so you don't get to give me nicknames. How about it? Want to get to know each other better? Maybe we can be friends and I can come by for regular visits?" I leaned on his hand for emphasis. I'm not a true heavyweight, being just south of two hundred pounds, but a booted foot could grind bones to dust inside a hand. Especially those little sharp ones.

Dennis ground his teeth in pain and hissed through his teeth. "No, man, no! Okay? What the hell do you want?"

Still defiant. A little crease of frustration ran up the back of my head and I felt a wash of power like I'd been dipped in a hot bath. The manager's eyes widened and his breath started to come in short gasps. Where his skin was flushed from effort and abuse, he now turned pale. I thought for a moment that he was having a heart attack, but the accompaniment of the energy coming from my body made me think otherwise. I concentrated on it, and even though I still felt the heat, it tamped down a bit.

Dennis continued to squirm beneath my boot. His attention shifted for a second and I could see that the knife was within his reach. I drew one of the two pistols I kept at the small of my back and showed it to him.

"You want to fight some more?"

"No! Okay? No, man; I'm sorry." He sobbed a bit, snorting up blood and writhing like a worm on a hook. "I'm sorry. Just... What do you want from me?"

"There was a white man here, mid-thirties, light brown hair, with a young girl. About ten years old, short blond hair."

"Yeah, yeah, they were here!"

"What was he driving?"

"Huh?"

I leaned on his hand. "I don't like repeating myself, Dennis."

"It was a Rambler, man, white, kind o' beat-up! Okay?"

I doubted Dennis was the kind of freak who collected license plate numbers, so I wasn't going to bother to ask about that. I was curious about something else, however.

I let Dennis's hand out from under my foot and he curled around both of his aching mitts. I remembered the heat, the power bleed, and focused on it, feeling the room warm again. Dennis looked up at me, fear painting the corners of his eyes as he scrambled back to the corner, a small whimper escaping his lips.

This was a new and terrible feeling for me, this tingle of wanton energy crackling on my skin. A field of electric fear that fluctuated around me and terrified human beings? I liked it, thought it might come in useful someday. I took to the road with elevated spirits, eager to catch up with my prey.

Their trail now cut westward, toward Tacoma. I knew three things about the city: one, it took its name from the mountain white men had renamed "Rainier." Two, city hall was only just recovering from decades-long corruption. Three, when I was a young man, the whites here would not hesitate to round up and evict undesirable non-whites. They'd drive several hundred people out *before* burning their homes to the ground. Compassionate racists. In the 1890s, the discovery of gold farther north, near Seattle, took even more wind out of the city's sails. This would be a perfect place for David Thomas to fade into.

I started canvassing streets on the southeastern edges of the city, working my way inward. I knew what he was driving and my nose knew what they smelled like. Again,

I picked up Kelsey's scent. A corner market. David would need supplies. I wandered into the store and followed their trail. He made stops for all the basics, dairy, meat, fruits and vegetables. Then back out. Such a conscientious parent. I followed the cloud of what they left behind to a shitty apartment building four blocks north where the white Rambler was parked out front.

The sun fizzled on the horizon while I circumnavigated the building before sitting outside and waiting. The first time I saw them, Kelsey's hair had indeed been shorn to just beneath her earlobes and dyed, while David's had been buzzed short and hidden under a khaki ball cap. Not much of a change in appearance, but a completely different locale made them anonymous. David had been smart enough to not leave much photographic evidence behind, nothing significant for the authorities to share in their limited capacity.

The amount of madness going on beneath the cops' noses was staggering for their lack of communication. I was looking at scores of options for years to come, if things didn't change. For two nights, I watched David Thomas's comings and goings and determined which apartment they were in. He *always* had Kelsey with him. Either he didn't trust her or she didn't trust him. She couldn't; I knew.

It would've been easy to snatch Kelsey from her father—he couldn't stop me—but the solution wasn't supposed to involve traumatizing the girl further. I could call the cops. Or I could wait. David was bound to frequent the market down the street often enough that someone would notice. Sooner or later. Any of those options would've been too easy. None of them served my own purposes; I needed to be sated. To keep my sanity, went the usual argument.

I needed Kelsey's trust to get to her alone and move her somewhere safe before dealing with her father. Since he kept her close, that would mean a nighttime scheme. She had her own bedroom and it faced the alley. The two-bedroom apartment didn't have much of a lock; I could get in when I wanted to. I resolved to use a trick that had worked once or twice in the past: big, dumb dog. Shift to my alternate form, keep my lips over my teeth, and let my tongue loll. Adopt a few other dog-like mannerisms and fold my ears back. It often worked with younger kids; they were drawn to big, furry animals who needed a belly rub. Kelsey was a bit old for the routine, but clearly, she loved canines. Once I got her safely away from David, I could deal directly with him. Or so I thought.

The night I concocted my idiotic plan, David started in on Kelsey. This was his night. In my mind, I had two immediate choices: wait until David was finished assaulting his own kin or intervene violently. Despite my selfish need to do this work, I couldn't bear listening to what was going on inside that shitty apartment. Kelsey had been trained well; she didn't make much noise. But knowing what I did and hearing David's satisfied humming and smelling the telltale signs of sex pushed hard on the human buttons I had left.

I'll never know if David had been surprised or not, whether he knew the kind of smothering fear his victims did—the fear his own daughter knew. Never having seen his face when I seized the back of his neck in my jaws and dragged him from the room, there was none of that to remember. When I snatched him off of Kelsey and out of the room, the strong scent of fear hit my nose. His eyes must have faced his daughter, but she remained turned away from him. I do remember his naked form struggling feebly as my teeth sank into his neck. His arms and legs flailed as I hustled backward with him caught in my teeth. Teeth that pointed inward held on and ensured that whatever was caught had only a one-way ticket. He managed to snag the doorway and left scratches and most of his fingernails behind. In the kitchen, I twisted, crippling David. What remained twitched as I tore him to pieces, reveling in the rush of pleasure and calm his death brought to me.

Kelsey never moved, remained curled in on herself, a small ball on the bed, the remains of a child.

The only evidence I left of her father was a smeared trail from the room to the kitchen. David would never be seen again, much like his wife and several other victims. People he'd murdered inside and out, some gone forever.

I trotted back to Kelsey's room, where she remained as small as she could be. She whimpered a bit when I entered the room. I was likely the biggest "dog" she'd ever seen. I licked, lolled, and flapped my ears as I shook out my fur. I tumbled on the floor and panted while lying on my back. Waited. Waited for Kelsey to uncurl, to watch me, for her defenses to shift and include me. I rolled to my feet and nudged her foot with my wet nose, only to resume the clown act on the floor because I was too big for the bed.

Over an hour passed before she slid off the mattress and rubbed behind my long ears. Then she put both arms around my neck in a vise grip and squeezed with her face buried in my fur. She cried and smothered herself in my warmth. She told me I smelled like mint and wondered where her father was, if he were coming back. Until she slept.

It was immensely satisfying for me to be the savior, the comforter, with my full belly and head full of myself. And stupid. Stupid because Kelsey wasn't going to have me for the rest of her life. Not in the way she needed. I couldn't love her, couldn't raise her like I had done for Ana—I'd never do that again. This girl was well and far damaged. She needed the kind of help I couldn't provide. Not directly.

As she slept, I tucked her journal pages into her nightgown and delivered her to the nearest hospital. She'd remember me as a giant dog; my human form would likely be relegated to a dream. The authorities would find the apartment over time and wonder eternally if Kelsey's story were true.

Over the following years, I was able to make anonymous financial donations, getting her as much counseling and assistance as was available at the time.

Kelsey had an elusive, crackling quality to her, something sharp that lay in her psyche that drove her, kept her relentlessly alive, pushing boundaries. The kind of kid I kept some eyes on, someone who might be useful in my future, depending on how she turned out. I added her to my book in the earliest years of trying to keep track of my life. For a time, she became one of the bits and pieces irrevocably lost to memory.

In her teens, after she'd plunged off of my radar, society stepped in to betray her. She was committed as a juvenile, lost to her foster parents and dumped into the psychiatric system for over a year until I became aware of her again, flipping through the pages of my book, looking for something to do before I slipped over the edge. Selfish as I had ever been.

The mental hospital on the southeastern border of Seattle was centered on a sprawling estate with minimal security. Finding out which room she was being kept in was the hardest part. Once I knew, I was able to scale the building's wall, pry open the iron grate, and slip into her room in the dead of night.

Kelsey lay restrained on the bed, out cold. Her hair was longer and its true blond color, but thinning—like it had been when her father was abusing her. She'd matured into an attractive, young woman with a puckish nose and strong eyebrows. It was hard to tell through her abnormally pale skin and sunken eyes, and the somewhat distorted appearance of her body. She seemed to have a layer of water beneath her skin—strange weight gain. Her lips, full and cracked, were slightly parted and her breath was rancid. I didn't find much evidence of actual care in the room.

At the end of her bed, a chart was clipped to the bars there. I scooped it up and flipped through a few pages. They'd diagnosed her as schizophrenic. A far cry from the truth. I knew the kind of shit-show these institutions had been over the past several years. White men and their psychiatry had cut a swath of misery through the nineteenth century. The twentieth wasn't much better so far, just a more refined brand of bullshit. As society began its slog through the seventies, it bore witness to a resurgence in institutions such as these.

They had her personal effects scattered in a drawer next to the bed. Among them were the loose journal pages, a little thicker this time, and a small photo of her mother. I scooped out the few items and shoved them into my pockets.

I started undoing the straps on her ankles first. "Kelsey. Wake up, girl."

Her eyes fluttered open and struggled to focus. She squirmed and surprise showed on her face when her legs slid freely. I set to the straps on her wrists.

"Let's go; you don't belong here."

"Oh, God, it's you. Isn't it? It's you again. You, you, you...you again..."

"Alexander. My name is Alexander. Yeah, c'mon. Hold on to me; hold tight."

She put her arms around my neck in a grip weaker than her ten-year-old self had managed and I lifted her out of the bed. With her nose in my neck, she said, "Mint, mint, mint."

Bearing her slight weight, I took us back out the way I

came in and off the hospital's property.

It took a few weeks for her to recover from the experimental Thorazine cocktail they'd put her on after their dangerously mistaken diagnosis. With her faculties available again, she was able to recognize me in human form and catalog my personhood somewhere in her damaged psyche.

We had nowhere to be and not much in common. One day, the skies as grey as ever there, she started a conversation that must have been on her mind for years.

"Why have you helped me?"

I didn't have a good answer for that; my reasoning was flawed. "It's difficult to explain. I need to do things like this, stay...active to live."

"You don't care about me."

"I..." Was that true? I wanted to be honest and I wanted to be sure of my answer.

She gathered up the sheets on her bed and slid her feet to the floor, facing away from me. I heard the crinkle of her journal pages unfolding.

"You've read my journal pages."

"No. I never have. Not even the first time I found them."

Even from behind, she seemed surprised by this fact. I didn't want to invade her privacy in that way, not when I had no reason to do so. She dipped her head again and folded the pages up.

"They did. They photocopied everything and kept it in a file. The doctor thought having my possessions nearby might help."

I didn't have an answer for this situation, no counsel. My experience with psychiatric doctors was limited and biased. "It wasn't about whether I cared or not, Kelsey. Not at first. I cared enough to intervene, when I did, and to keep some tabs on you in the future."

"Why?"

The question hung there, nibbling at the edges of my conscience, an unstoppable question, open-ended and with endless answers. "I don't know. How I live is complicated. You have to live your life without me, care about yourself first. I can't be around all the time." At least that was the truth. What I did had a distinct purpose for me, but I couldn't deny the interpersonal messes it created; the emotions involved were volatile and one-sided. I didn't even want to try and explain the memory lapses I'd been having recently, the chunks of time I'd been losing.

Kelsey shuffled through her meager possessions, her scent shifting to anxiety. "Where's my mother's photo?"

I'd forgotten. A sense of frustration clenched my jaw. "Here." I pulled a locket and necklace out of my pocket and handed it to her. The idea to get it for her came to me when I was shoving her stuff into my pockets weeks before.

She barely looked at me and fingered the cool gold in her fingers. She flipped the little door open and stared at her mother's protected photo. When she did look to me, her eyes watered and she flung an arm around my neck. After a brief hesitation, I hugged her back as best I could until she took a deep breath and pulled away.

Kelsey padded into the bathroom and turned on the shower. She was recovered enough that I'd have to let her go again. I'd do what I could to ensure that she had a new home and foster parents who gave a damn.

The second time around, and I still couldn't save her. I still didn't know how. I'd been a bludgeon in her life, not a savior. A thing that had taken her immediate pain away, but did nothing to help heal the wounds or help her grow.

She disappeared shortly before turning eighteen, releasing herself early from the custody of her latest set of foster parents, hiding until they had no legal recourse.

I crossed her path a final time, in Idaho, during the late seventies. By then, she was into opiates and prostitution, as much a product of her times as I was of mine. It was the last time I'd seen her, my last entry in the notebook; she wanted nothing to do with me anymore, determined to accelerate her descent without my help.

I never should have sprung her, never should have intervened the way I had in the beginning. My methods had no subtlety or lasting, positive impact—none that I could see. My methods meant more to me than anyone else, but I couldn't reason my way around not leaving Kelsey as her father's plaything. I couldn't make sense of what I did and I couldn't make sense of *not* doing what I did to survive.

CHAPTER 2

Now.

I wasn't at all comfortable with the thought of walking into a police station, but Roberts had sounded especially anxious on the phone.

The desk sergeant's head snapped up when I crossed the threshold of the small lobby. He eyed me warily. Sitting behind a tall desk, he had several inches on anyone except the most freakishly large. The desk, a cheap, worn pine stained the color of mahogany on a once-upon-a-time-beige low-pile carpet, matched the trim running around the entryway. The sharp smell of burnt coffee—the bitter fuel of far too many law enforcement agencies—floated in the air, and scuff marks the height of a vacuum cleaner marked the bottom of the desk. I couldn't see much of the officer but his shoulders and head.

There are no clear indicators when a human being would react poorly to my presence. Some kind of psychic, static field surrounds us monsters and can interfere with the composure of normal people. I didn't relish that happening in a building full of armed men and women.

I kept my hands in plain sight and wasted no time letting him know who I was there to see. Then I stepped a respectful distance back while he called upstairs. He continued to fiddle with his paperwork but occasionally glanced at me over his glasses. I was making him nervous and he didn't know why, so the sooner I was out of there, the better.

I smiled to myself, pleased that I could take note of such behavior and adjust my own without undue influence. In times past, awareness of such a thing typically led to a breakdown in control and short-term memory loss. A deep-rooted goading would cause me to play more to the downward slide than to controlling the situation.

I hadn't felt the coarse sway of my power for months. Not since the Queen of Dragons had put me back together after my apparent suicide. As often as I seemed to try it, self-sacrifice didn't suit me; it never took. I owed the interdimensional entity and that still bothered me. It had been my second death—counting the resurrection that brought me back as a shapeshifter nearly two hundred years before. Letting go of any control over the monster inside me had been the only option I could come up with to combat a horde of vampires. At the time, I hadn't been sure what would happen, and instinct alone had prevented me from doing it until that moment. The Queen inverted the entire process and packed the thing back into my dying body, keeping me alive. That particular trick wasn't something I could count on, however. That she had plans for me wasn't a good thought I dwelled on day to day or at all.

Passing the curse was out of my reach as well—a surefire way to put an end to oneself. It involves a blood relative, slow death, and a return to life with an implausible hunger. Ravenous enough to consume your attacker and complete the cycle. My creator had been a great-grandfather far enough removed that I'd never met him, had only heard rumors. Some things I'd learned in the harrowing months following his assault on me. Like the stories that he could shed his skin and don a new one that he kept hidden in a carved pipe. Since then, I'd purposely lost track of my siblings and any successive lineage.

Hundreds of scent trails marked the glassed-in area, a great number of minerals tracked in on people's shoes, their personal odors danced in the recycled air. When I took a deep breath, I could detect the myriad subtleties of human emotions on the oils that skin secreted. Stress mostly. And guns. Hundreds of them.

The telltale pop of flip-flops came to my ears and a young woman bustled into the foyer accompanied by an older woman I could only guess was her mother. The girl was slim with long, blond hair streaked through with purple and red. Sickly sweet perfume enveloped her and assaulted the area. It did little to mask the musk of recent sex on her. She wore tight black cropped pants and a low-cut tank top with "Pirate Tom" on the front that gave most attention to her full, perky breasts. She had a ring through her bottom lip, dark-as-night eye shadow, and a flaming hot chip on her shoulder. Everything about her was closed: shoulders hunched, eyes locked in a perpetual roll, arms crossed tightly. It was clear that the boys positively adored her. Likely the penultimate reason for her mother dragging her down there.

The girl's mother was just the opposite: a conservatively dressed woman, thick and middle-aged with a helmet of hair and sparse makeup. I doubted she'd done much of anything to earn her child's ire, but it never took much. She had to tell her daughter to sit three times before she approached the desk sergeant to conduct whatever business brought them there. More scents of tension were added to the suffering carpet.

I didn't want to listen to their problems, but I was thankful for the distraction—something for the desk sergeant to focus on other than me. I never wanted much attention from the police. They were an absolute necessity for a law-abiding society, and yet wholly incapable of dealing with the kind of monsters that humanity itself produced. Those were the cracks I tried to exist in, something to keep me going. In truth, it was subterfuge. I was starting to doubt this course. Without the echoes of mayhem in my brain, I could think more clearly and longer about my existence.

I was relieved when Roberts turned up. The sergeant buzzed me through the gate. When I'd last seen the detective, he'd been more muscular and well groomed, smooth of face and manner. Now his appearance was noticeably bedraggled. He wore a haggard expression under his worry and he needed a shave. He still had dark, smooth skin, but now it was marred slightly by stubble and deeper lines in his face.

Roberts came across my nose as the closest a black man in America could to his African lineage. Despite the cold appearance of his resting face, he had a professional acumen that could smooth out any situation. Today, an extra line of worry ran straight between his brown eyes nearly to the bridge of his wide nose. His scent—still the same, of course—was marred only by a slight sour edge. The stink of worry or aggravation, the same tinge that the lobby carpet carried.

"Thanks for comin' down. C'mon, lemme grab something from my desk and we'll head to the media room."

I nodded and stayed close in Roberts's wake lest someone mistake me for a problem without a chaperone. The police station was a dreary affair with the standard, city-funded color palette of dull, neutral tones. I followed him down a wide and sparse hall. The occasional uniformed officer passed by and gave us an odd look. Once or twice, Roberts actually spoke to them in a friendly tone rather than the cold shoulder he seemed to have defaulted to.

I took the time in the hallway to probe a bit. The weight loss was most troubling to me. "Have you been sleeping?" I asked quietly.

Roberts stopped and asked, "What?" He was blinking rapidly, a bit nervous.

I looked evenly at his eyes. At a solid six feet, we're about the same height. My shoulders were broader than his, but Roberts's frame carried more muscle when he worked at it. His dark skin looked sallow—which is saying something of a man with his complexion. His hair was longer than I recalled, though still relatively close to his scalp.

Mine remained the same short length as when we had last met. Swept back and curly, it was a glossy indicator of my mixed background. Some people have said I look like a tall Miles Davis with a better hairline.

"You're having nightmares." It was a statement, a plain fact that I suspected based on the tension around his eyes. It was apparent that he wasn't sleeping well. What I knew for sure was that his scent was off; it indicated months of stress.

Roberts's eyelid twitched once and he spat through clenched teeth, "Don't poke around my head. C'mon."

I held up my hands to demonstrate calm while he stewed. Then he turned and stalked through a doorway into a room with multiple desks and low cubicles. When he snatched a bag from a desk drawer and slammed it shut, heads turned and more eyes than I was comfortable with followed us. I accompanied the detective through the room and down a hallway deeper into the law's bowels.

Mind reading isn't even close to any talents I have, but I could tell there'd be no explaining that to Roberts. Better to view this recording he'd called me about and think on how to handle him later. Eventually, I thought I might be obligated to help him ease the nightmares, since I was the one who'd most likely been involved in giving them to him. All I knew about this sort of effect was that it got worse as the days dragged on. In the meantime, with no solutions to offer, all I could give him was space.

I thought I'd given him enough space, to date. It had taken me over seven months to decide to entrust my new phone number to Roberts. He'd forced me to dump the previous one along with my last apartment. I'd taken some time over the last few months to send my new information out and update various contacts across the country. A slow process, it was going to take years to sort it all out—and that was only if the information I had on record remained up to date.

It had taken Roberts an additional four months to call me since receiving the new contact information. We hadn't spoken for over a year—not that I'd consider his last screaming fit "speaking" under any circumstances. Understandable, since I'd nearly gotten him and his partner killed. He had most likely decided to hold me accountable for the death of his supervisor as well.

I believed he'd have come to terms with this new reality by then, but he was obviously still out of sorts with the idea that monsters like me—and the ones who'd killed Lieutenant Brown—existed. I was willing to bet that Roberts was suffering from paranoia and seeing monsters everywhere, suspecting even his comrades. Still, he was my only law enforcement source in Boston since Albert Brown had been murdered. *How now, Brown cop?* The late Lieutenant Brown had been an acquaintance of mine since he was ten years old. Before he died, he thought it'd be a good idea for his protégé to have my phone number.

We entered a small windowless room with media equipment stacked on grey shelves along the walls. The smell of ozone and electric motors enveloped us. No fewer than three televisions stared back from the mounts. There was room enough for three people to sit amongst a motley set of cracked leather chairs to review various media. Roberts closed the door behind us, locked it, and popped in a recording. Before queuing it up, he referred to his pocket notepad.

The image of two nude bodies filled the screen. The man was strapping, bald, and dark-skinned with a cock the size of his forearm. He was currently plunging his full length into a petite blonde on all fours in front of him on the floor. She wore the remnants of the uniform of a cheerleader and she had the iconic look: puckish nose, blond hair, full lips, and a curvaceous, athletic body. I felt a ping in my memory.

Currently, her eyes were squeezed shut and she was growling through clenched teeth for her coupling partner to redouble his efforts. Roberts reached over and ticked the volume down. They were filming on a set that looked like a crappy home gym. Sweat poured off of the man as he huffed, snarled, and continued to drill into her with both hands firmly clutching her round hips as she pushed back at him. She squealed with pleasure and I wondered how she could possibly feel anything other than pain in that position.

I also wondered at the sudden sense of familiarity. I've never watched pornography with any consistency or interest. The awkward feeling of being in a small room watching this with another man managed to break my comfort zone. Ironic. Especially considering some of the things I'd done in the past. Sexual freedom hadn't been a central belief within the culture I was raised, but violence certainly was. The blonde must have reminded me of someone, but I couldn't remember who. I tried to focus on her face, but the scene kept cutting to close-ups of the couple's genitalia.

"Five people were murdered last week and there're some...unusual aspects to the situation." He breathed deeply once and continued, straining to say what he had to say. "The scene was soaked in blood—it wasn't clear if any of it had been taken—the shit was spattered everywhere. All the victims had been beaten: nasty bruises, broken bones. It looked like ten men—or one very powerful perp—got in there and beat the hell out of 'em before tearing their throats out. And it must've been fast, too, since there's no indication that anyone had even managed to cross the room attempting to escape."

Roberts had proven himself trustworthy enough to keep his mouth shut about the monsters entrenched in modern society. He wasn't the only human aware, for sure, but it was always a crapshoot to see which ones could handle it. The benefit of keeping that information close was that he got to keep his job and his life. If he were identified as a source of concern, I wouldn't necessarily be the one to deal with him, but it would be on me if someone else had to. Clearly, the knowledge hadn't been sitting well with him; he boiled like a raw ulcer.

There was a polite knock on the door and Roberts's face twisted with annoyance. He held one finger up to me and spoke at the door. "Give us a minute!" When he turned back to me, he took a cleansing breath and told me, "The guy's Anthony Block, went by the name 'Duke DaCocksman,' and she has several screen aliases, but no real name has turned up yet. The most common alias for her has been 'Alexa Vexa.' Judging by interviews and other recordings I've seen, she's...enthusiastic and has gamely participated in several extreme gangbangs— nothing's too harsh for this girl when it comes to sex. She's been a regular in this campus sex series. They were in town getting some B roll at local schools, doing some promotion before the shoot. Here." He scribbled in his notebook and handed me the torn-out sheet. It had an address I assumed was the location of the murder scene on it.

"This is a bit far out of your jurisdiction. Isn't it?"

"What, you think I can't handle a murder outside of the ghetto?"

I just stared at Roberts in response. I didn't know what he was thinking, but I don't normally ask questions that require reading between the lines. The man was a ball of tension and I wasn't interested in seeing if he'd bounce.

There was another knock, this time more insistent. Roberts clenched his jaw and shouted, "Just a sec!" After several beats, he tried speaking to me again. "Due to the nature of the murders and our...shared experience last year, I got dragged into this one. Watch now; here it comes."

I continued to watch the screen. The camera operator began a slow zoom on Alexa's pleasure-contorted face as it jerked with each impact to her rear. Struggling to remember who she reminded me of, her countenance filled the screen and my eyes. Then it happened. I reached out, stopped the recording, and jogged it back. There it was again. Her canines extended briefly, snapped out and in as she opened her eyes and looked directly into the camera through a clenched smile. Alexa was absolutely a vampire, missing, and seemingly the sole survivor of an on-the-set massacre.

My, my, my, who might the killer be?

CHAPTER 3

"What the fuck do you mean, 'I'll pass it on'?"

Roberts was pissed and I didn't blame him, but it wasn't going to take much more of his pissy attitude to change my mind about helping out in any regard. I was the only contact he had for this kind of madness, and he seemed to have been hoping I'd simply take care of it. But I wasn't interested in hunting down Alexa Vexa and I told him as much. I don't go chasing down vampires unless they cross my line. What Alexa had—or may have—done is what was done all over the world more often by humans. That she might be on the verge of a rampage that would signal the need to end her life was the only reason I was willing to carry the information to someone who cared. Let the vampires deal with their own. When we monsters have gone on long enough, most of us lose control and need to be put down. It's the sort of behavior that had created a number of myths about us.

"You know this isn't what I do. The most I can do for you now is get the information to someone who *is willing* to deal with her. They take care of their own when needed."

Roberts was a bulldog of an officer, a man who sank his teeth into a case and gnawed until he'd gutted it and knew the situation from the inside out. It's why I gave him a way to contact me again if needed. He knew what I was but should have known better than to contact me until he bit into an odd case of murder or mayhem involving children, following no discernible pattern.

"I do not fuckin' believe this. Where were 'they' when that shit went down last year?"

He had a point. It had gotten bad enough that it was unclear who could be trusted. Still, that was a unique situation and the dangling carrot of immunity to the sun was irresistible to many.

"Listen, I know it's not a satisfying answer, but keep in mind that last year was something entirely different."

"What the hell am I supposed to do in the meantime? This bitch could be anywhere between here and Los Angeles; I can't chase her down on my own."

"Work with the LAPD, then; contact authorities in the Midwest; you're a cop, do your job as best you can. I don't think you'll be able to find her, anyway. Let me know if you locate her, and in the meantime, I'll pass it on. It's the best any of us can hope for."

"'Us'? Really? It's the best we can hope for?"

There came from the door a bang, more insistent and louder than before.

The arrogance and rancor coming from Roberts was the last bit of crap I was willing to put up with today. "I'm leaving. Fuck this, fuck you, I'll do what I said and no more. Don't call me about this again." I opened the door to the viewing room, startling two plainclothes cops, and headed down the empty hallway. Not how I wanted that meeting to end.

Roberts came close behind, shoving his colleagues aside and coming dangerously close to grabbing my arm. "Oh, no. No, you are not; you are going to deal with this and you are going to assure me of such fact when you are *done* dealing with it."

I kept walking and turned a corner. Roberts' scent had bled into pure anger. The bitterness flooded my nostrils, triggering nothing but sheer defiance. I heard two things after my exit: Roberts's footfalls and the door to the AV room close. Cop shit is beyond my last straw. That kind of *you bes' listen up, boy* line of authoritative bull has never gone down easy with me. Not when I was a young man fending off drunken racists in a Saskatchewan trading post, or right goddamned now.

I turned to face Roberts and recklessly let as much otherworldly heat bleed into my words as I could manage. "I do not work for you. I do as I wish and if you live long enough to be my age—and that's a great big fucking if— then maybe you'll understand, but until you get your goddamn head straight, *do not* speak to me again."

Then my stomach dropped out and I felt more hunger than I had in a very long time. My mouth watered and Roberts smelled like a big pile of fresh meat. When I met his eyes, he was frozen, horrified. I took a step in his direction and he wobbled backward. There was a disorienting blur as I sprang forward to catch him and I was shocked when I stopped myself halfway to his throat.

All of my muscles ached as a lightning strike of pain lanced my clenched jaw. I twisted back on myself hard, ignoring Roberts for the moment, listening inwardly. And there it was. The bastard was back; the manipulative force that allowed me to be a shapeshifter had waited for this heated moment to make a play. *Son of a bitch.*

Roberts trembled. He was good at resisting my aura, but he wasn't immune. He'd just been forced to feel a wash of primal, uncontrollable fear and he was doing everything he could to hold it together. Regardless, the tenderizing blast had left him primed for a takedown: it had flipped the switch changing his identifier from friend to prey. Somewhere in the moment, he'd tottered backward into the wall and watched me from a half-crouch. I stalked away as Roberts leaned there, looking nowhere.

Inside my head, I had the sense of lights flickering off in a random pattern around me. Where I had been spending most of my time in the clear, I was now being

pulled backward into the murky twilight I remembered
and hated.

42

CHAPTER 4

Outside, I took several deep breaths and considered what had just happened. The first lightning strikes of a bad headache flashed. My body swam with a brief wave of disorientation and nausea. I wasn't looking forward to getting back to the process of losing my mind again. Instead, I tried to focus on external problems, ignoring the immediate issue, falling into old coping habits.

I remembered my parents: stalwart, pillars of love, strong, indestructible. False, hopeful memories; the recollections of a child. They were human; they'd died of human problems—my mother of old age, my father with blackened lungs. Still, I strove to remember them as I had when I was a boy. I believed that my mother died of a broken heart after the world finally ground my father down to something fragile enough to break.

Two pair, always there, Netty and Claire. My sisters, I remembered them. They'd married back into the tribe, much to my mother's satisfaction. I knew they'd had children, but I'd never met them. It was a time shortly after I'd become what I am today, and I made it a point to loose myself from them, from what was left of my family. I didn't want the temptation of passing the curse on to one of their children or children's children or any other damned relative. As far as I was concerned, the life I'd lived until that point was right and properly buried. Since then, I'd been living a mess for nearly a century—the highest point being Ana. Everything else had the miasma of selfishness all over it, one flawed choice after another just to keep rambling on. Constantina I regretted more than others. Tina had been forbidden fruit, the leader's woman, off-limits. I didn't care and we had both paid for it—she more than I. After I'd killed her boyfriend, Curry, everything changed. It didn't matter that Curry had gone mad; the relationship was colored with that particular palette of aggressiveness and poor decision-making.

Decades later, I'd had an opportunity to find her in Seth. He'd known us both, had been Curry's right-hand monster. Seth died before he could tell me where she was. Seth, Mark, Terrell. Dead, dead, dead. Other people whose names I never learned or couldn't remember. All dead. Victims of other humans or monsters. Victims of mine, all around me. Still, I marched on.

If I wasn't careful, I would begin to wonder, "What for, why live?" because I seemed to be causing more trouble for anyone near me than ever before—though I had certainly found plenty of time in the past to blacken lives or take them entirely.

Roberts was coming unraveled, being whittled away by the truth he carried. I'd thought he would be more than capable of handling it, but that had been foolish of me. Wading into a melee with vampires who were hell-bent on sacrificing the last of several children, and then the situation literally bursting into flames, couldn't possibly have sat well under any conditions. Vampires can be bad enough, but when they upended reality, did the impossible, and practiced arcane magic, they outdid themselves.

In the year since, I sometimes wondered just how far he'd fallen. Where was his partner, Pepperman, on the situation and how did he figure into this mess? Pepperman had no idea that monsters like me existed. How could he reasonably support Roberts?

There is a biking and walking path that stretches from Jamaica Plain to the Back Bay and it runs directly past the station. I started heading north on that path, barely aware as I put one foot in front of the other. It was calming, there were few people out, and I was surrounded by as much nature as this city could manage. The path crosses several busy streets as it closes on downtown Boston. At the first corner, I fumbled my weathered Moleskine from its nesting place inside my jacket and flipped through the pages.

The thing was held together by electrical tape and double-wrapped in resealable bags. Under a scribbled heading of "Boston," I came across a scratched-out name I couldn't forget because my worst memories tended to remain intact. Brown had been my primary contact in the area since he'd grown up and decided to join the police force. In his childhood, he had been the victim of an uncle, taken for a harrowing week on what was supposed to have been an overnight fishing trip. His immediate family had unraveled around the event, which led to the uncle's incarceration.

Contrary to police reports, I had been the straw to break Uncle Roni's back. The uncle went to prison with a fresh and permanent disability. (I don't kill *everyone* I meet.) As he matured, Brown developed the steely personality of a protector, someone who would step into the line of fire without hesitation. He never married, never had children—perhaps Roberts had served in that role to some extent.

Several years after becoming Detective Roberts's supervisor, Brown was murdered at the clawed hands of a crazed vampire. A monster who, for the usual reasons, chose to stalk children. A wild revenant, but not wild enough to be noticed too soon. He did it randomly, without seeming connection or purpose other than to feed. There was nothing for law enforcement to latch on to, only a trail of mutilated bodies with none of the interpersonal connections or evidence that typically broke violent serial cases. The case didn't have the appropriate amount of blood, money, or blond hair for national attention, but it was on the cusp when Brown had called me. No one had been looking for a creature who went to ground during the day in the most inhuman manner until I came along. In a matter of days, we determined a few places where the creature had to have been hiding. When we did uncover the bastard, Brown hadn't demonstrated the proper amount of caution when dealing with a revenant vampire—a monster with little cognizance or restraint.

His death had made my connection to this area tenuous. He'd told me I could trust Roberts, somewhere along the way, but my recent history with Roberts seemed to be destroying the heir apparent.

Roberts's name was freshly scribbled in below Brown's. I scanned my writing to see if there was anyone else in neighboring states who might be of some assistance to the detective. According to my notes, the nearest kids I'd had a hand in keeping alive were in New Hampshire and Maine. And neither of their damaged souls were in any way suited to supporting Roberts—professionally or otherwise. There just weren't many people in my acquaintance who'd been introduced to the supernatural world and survived.

Farther out, there were others who owed me their flawed lives, of course, up and down the east coast: upstate New York, South Carolina, Florida, and more. A string of shattered children become broken adults. Their resiliency was amazing and their ability to channel their personal horror into enviable professional talents was even more so: encyclopedic knowledge of obscure subjects, influence in offbeat circles, art, and other creative pursuits. And a handful who secretly harbored the dark fantasy of becoming superheroes and rescuing the helpless. Finally, there were some who trained their minds to fit reality rather than fantasy: public service professionals. The whole formed a tenuous network of brains to substitute where mine fell short in my long age.

I had yet to come across someone who could help me.

So, why was I in Boston? It was a question I'd been unable to answer since I'd returned over a year before, one nagging question that I hadn't been able to untangle. I still didn't know why I'd come there, why I had stopped in this city. Roberts's call, at the time, had dragged me back from an impending insanity and I was grateful for the contact—not that I'd ever told him. Still, there were no clear answers on how I'd gotten to this town, only why I had stayed until now. My mental stability coaxed me into staying and now my mind itself was in danger of being stolen from me. Again.

"Alexander! Hey, Smith!"

Think of the devil and he obliges. Detective Pepperman jogged in my direction, waving one hand. He had what I was now going to assume was his usual look: dark suit, long coat, and five o'clock shadow on a square jaw that ended in a cleft. His dirty blond hair remained perfectly combed with some product to keep it in place, and his arrival was presaged by a cloud of cologne that did little to mask the smells of spent tobacco, sweat, and saliva. Pepperman had a neat appearance, but his hygiene was no mystery to me. The man was lax in that arena, to say the least, but meticulous in appearance.

I watched his ice-blue eyes twitch over me. A cop habit, taking in as many details as possible in one evaluative glance, gauging threat level. That I could break his neck before he could reach his weapon was something I didn't want him to know. That I had no particular grudge with him, I'd made sure he knew during our first meeting.

"What is it, Detective?"

"You just saw Roberts?"

What are you up to, Pepperman? "Yes."

"I need to talk to you."

"Mmmm. No, thanks."

I made to walk away when Pepperman stepped in front of me. His hands were up in the most non-threatening manner he could manage. He knew from experience how I reacted to presumed authority. "Okay, hold on. Please? Okay? Just…let me have a few minutes of your time. I'll buy you a drink. Okay?"

I ground my teeth together hard enough to squeak, feeling the push to say or do something damaging. This was going to lead to problems, I was sure, but maybe I could glean some insights on Roberts or help Pepperman help his partner. "Fine."

We headed up the street a few blocks to a hole in the wall. Judging by the sparse clientele, an unusually clean venue, and the scent of gun oil and ammo, it was frequented by cops. *Perfect.* I was glad it was early and there were few patrons. It looked like mostly older cops, probably retired and keeping some tenuous contact with the department. Thick men with grey hair and conservative dress.

"Hey, Bill." Pepperman greeted the bartender with a familiar ease.

The fellow behind the bar was built like a weightlifter who'd swallowed a medicine ball. Sure, he had a wide middle, but his arms didn't appear to be flabby and what I could see of his forearms looked like cable wrapped tightly around steel.

"Pep. What'll it be?"

Pepperman looked at me.

"Whatever top-shelf bourbon you've got. Neat."

"Chrissakes, that's the fuckin' expensive stuff."

Pepperman griped. "Boilermaker, Bill, please and thank you."

Despite his size, the barkeep's hands moved swift and sure. I had no doubts he was a retired cop and most of his clientele were from the BPD. He had a full head of hair and not a lock of it remained its original color, clean-shaven with the pale skin of a man who rarely spent time in the sun. He gave me the same look most cops did and an overconfident nonchalance leaked off of him as he poured our drinks. Not a drop sloshed as he set them in front of us. I took a sip and waited while Pepperman slammed the shot, grimaced, and chased it with a swig of beer.

"Fuckin' only thing that makes sense most times. Y'know?" He hefted his pint in salute.

I stared at him, still waiting.

"Jesus fucking Christ, you're a stick in the mud."

"What do you want, Detective?"

Pepperman sighed and removed his coat. After he'd draped it on the back of his chair, he spoke. "Fine. Look, ever since that cockup in PO, there's been something off with Roberts. Any thoughts on what that might be?" He took another gulp of his beer, followed by a wet belch.

More cop shit. Ask an open-ended question with an airy, uncaring attitude and wait for your target to fill in the blanks. He was being vague in reference to our penultimate fight with the coven at the Peter O'Neil projects. A fight that Pepperman had been present for but mercifully unconscious. "Be more specific, Detective; I'm almost done with my whiskey."

Another sigh, another gulp, and Pepperman screwed his face up, looking at the mirror behind the bar. "All right, all right. He's been irritated and distant. Working with him makes me feel like Charlie Brown on Halloween. 'I got a rock.' Know what I mean? What the hell is going on? I may have gotten knocked the fuck out, but I know something happened that night. Something…weird. And now this meeting between you and him. It's my case, too. Y'know? So…what?"

I took another sip, collecting my thoughts. "What do *you* remember from that night?"

"Pffft." He drained his glass and motioned for another while he swallowed. "I remember going into the building. What about you?"

I had to give it to him: he was cop through and through. He'd probably never have a stable relationship—unless it was with another officer. *Even then…* "Listen, Detective, I'm not going to start shitting at the mouth about anything. My arrangement is with Roberts and I hold his confidence." I covered up my wince with a sip of whiskey. I'd inadvertently let something slip for Pepperman to pick up. That I "held Roberts's confidence" meant I knew something. The little dick wasn't going to let it go at all now.

Pepperman hardly gestured when another boilermaker hit the bar in front of him. He sipped the top off the beer and dumped the whiskey into the brew before he started slurping again. "Oh, you're one bad motherfucker, ain't you? I remember how you snatched my weapon out of my hands. How the fuck did you do that, huh? Right. Out. Of my hands." He slammed the pint glass on the bar, held his hands out as if he were holding a pistol, then stage-mimed empty palms, magician-style.

"Practice. Want to see it again?"

Pepperman's eyes pinched the barest amount while the muscles in his jaw locked. I'd just made another bid for suicide by sarcasm and now I was wondering if I might have to snatch his weapon away from him again. Maybe I could smooth this out. *Maybe.*

"Listen, you were standing too close and I was able to follow your rhythm: breathing, blinking. I had my hands up like this. Right?" I held my hands up to about chest height. "Right at the height of your barrel. This close, no one's fast enough to react." I gestured to indicate space between us. "Just keep your distance."

He chewed on that for a moment, then washed his flash of anger away with a long pull on the boilermaker. Then he nodded and said, "You make me nervous, Alexander. I don't know why. Whenever you're around, I get the fuckin' willies, shit don't seem right. And I been around some gigantic assholes, guys'd as soon stick their thumbs in your eyes and lick the jelly off than say 'good morning.' Clear and present, dangerous motherfuckers. You? Kind of unassuming, quiet, but intense, and a goddamned smartass when you do open your mouth, but not the kind of big-ass bogey with a rap sheet makes a cop want to shoot first—"

"Or wait for backup?"

"Yeah, smartass. You got no record on you, nothing out there that I could find, anyway. You're a hole in my world, a fucking drain. And I don't like it."

What could I say to that? The least smartass thing I could come up with was a shrug. It was clear to me that Pepperman was sensitive to the "psychic field of annoyance" I had hovering around me, but he was capable and brave enough to resist. He didn't show much hesitance, just pushed through. It was something I could appreciate in his character—I needed to find something to appreciate. Or maybe it was the alcohol pushing him forward.

Pepperman rolled his eyes and moved on. "I remember going in and a couple of white males came at me from the back hallway. Then a door opened right next to me. An old black dude with half a head of kinky fro popped out and ducked back in. Startled the shit out of me. Next thing I know, I'm out."

"Curly."

"What?"

"Curly. They're tight curls, not kinks. 'Kinky' implies flaws or sexual deviation. I wear my hair short so I only have to deal with half of you people's labels and insecurities."

Shit. I knew where the sentiment came from but not the words. I didn't want to antagonize Pepperman, but I couldn't help it. I needed to exert more control before something really bad happened. I couldn't deny my history or my thoughts, but my actions had to be my own.

"Just listen to yourself, asshole. 'You people.' If I'd said that, you'd be over the fuckin' moon right now. You're playing at the same damn game and you expect everyone else to play by a different set of rules."

I met his eyes without blinking. "This isn't a game."

"Right, right, right. Micks, spics, guineas, niggers, chinks, whatever. Everyone's the same to me; you're either on the right side of the law or the wrong. And you—you are trying to play some imagined crack between the two."

"I'm not playing."

Pepperman leaned forward for emphasis and squinted at me. "You are never gonna learn. Are you?"

A jolt passed through my body and I felt a deep urge to grant Pepperman's intestines the freedom they so deserved and watch him die slow. "I already learned from the best assholes in the business. And by assholes, I mean 'you white people.' You think people spring whole from the womb with all these bullshit ideas about imagined races? I'll tell you the difference between 'you people' and my people. We get warned by our parents, you get taught. Then you validate the warnings somewhere along the way."

Either my poor attitude was bringing the monster from the depths or it was already up. Regardless, I needed to double down on controlling matters.

Pepperman motioned for another boilermaker. He kept his mouth shut while he steamed. I had information he wanted, so I knew he'd keep his inner asshole at a low boil with the lid on. For now. When the drink arrived, he downed the shot and stared at me.

"'Half.' Huh. 'Half.' Yeah, I see it now. Native American. Right? You're half Indian. Aren't you? Well, that explains your constantly shitty attitude. You done been double-wronged. I get it." He took a long pull on the beer. "It's no excuse, though. Is it? What the fuck does your cocky attitude do to make anything right? A dick's a dick, no matter what color, and all a dick wants to do is fuck whatever it can."

Pepperman was not entirely in error and I noted that he was more observant than I'd previously thought. The prick was listening. Closely. Yes, the chip on my shoulder was big enough to serve as a perch for the monkey-monster living on my back. The biggest problem was that I was barely half human these days, and the most recent episodes of malice and hunger had me even further on edge. Pepperman didn't need to know that, however. I slipped off the barstool and drank the last of my bourbon. Then I placed the glass carefully on the counter. Pepperman glanced at my glass and motioned the bartender for a refill.

"Tell me about the fire." He looked me in the eyes and added, "Please."

I took a deep breath and stalled while watching Billy pour out a fresh dram. With great mental effort, I put as tight a lid on my slippery attitude as I could. A sip to warm my heart and a deep breath before speaking. "We were upstairs. One of the murderers had a weapon, a firebomb—I don't know what it was—and another held a child hostage. Roberts put a bullet through the hostage-taker's brain and the other one set off the weapon. They'd been expecting us to try and stop them; it was a trap as much as it was the final step in their mad plan."

"Roberts's report stated something similar. Only when

Rob describes it in person, it's clear there's something more to it. You know he got a commendation for saving that kid *and* my ass?"

I shook my head no.

"He looked like they were serving him up a platter of hot, buttered shit when they gave the damn thing to him at the ceremony. Why is that?"

Vulgarity is no substitute for cleverness. I couldn't remember from where I'd heard the quote. Pepperman used vulgarity to distract, lull people into thinking they could pull one over on him; he hid behind the appearance of a misanthrope. I didn't have any concrete answers for his question, so I ignored it and moved to another subject of that past evening. "We had to jump from the window with the surviving child. An associate of mine dragged you out of the building. Two people with me died that night."

The detective's demeanor shifted a bit at that news. "Roberts never told me nothin' about that."

"He doesn't know." I hoped being aware of something Roberts didn't know would placate Pepperman a little. Which was stupid of me.

Pepperman swallowed another large gulp of beer before speaking. "Roberts is a good man, a good cop. Straight arrow, knows his shit. Tough, fair, all that good stuff. Only thing I can figure is you done somethin' to throw him off his game. *You.*"

I leaned back a bit, sensing the inevitable conclusion of the detective's thoughts on this matter.

While staring at the mirror behind the bar again, Pepperman took a final mouthful of beer and swished it around thoughtfully before swallowing with a loud gulp. He made a quarter turn in my direction before letting loose. "You're actin' jus' like him. Y'know? So full o' shit. Jus' fuckin' lyin' and vague. Tha's wrong for Roberts, but you... What'd he find? Huh? What won't you tell me? Huh? What are you two hiding? You tell me!" He lunged off the stool and took a handful of my lapel with his left hand and cocked his right to take my head off.

I clamped one hand over his on my jacket, pulled down and slid back, dragging him off balance. He squeaked when his wrist twisted. Sticking my forearm into the crook of his right arm, I was able to contain the wild punch and settle Pepperman back into his seat. He was drunk, slow, and off balance.

I closed half the distance to the door backward with my hands in the air, noting that Billy had his eyes on me and one hand beneath the bar. Then I turned and left as quickly as I could without running, the detective shouting at my back. "You're gonna tell me!"

Not if I see you coming.

Irrevocably irritated, I headed for the Sweaty Magus. Skirting Chinatown, I walked toward the side street on the edge of the Back Bay where the club existed. Majispin's club was a nexus of supernatural activity in Boston and one of the informal coalition of safe houses established to keep conflict among the monsters to a minimum. The supernatural understanding was one of the precious few traditions we all shared, and it was tenuous. The only thing, most often, preventing greater conflicts between monsters. I'd find what I was looking for there. It would be a long walk and I was damn hungry. I had no love for this all-too-familiar depth of gnawing hunger or the mental background crackle that accompanied it.

A delicious scent in the air captured my attention; there was a roti restaurant in my path about two blocks up. The massive Caribbean wraps would serve me well. I ordered two of the scorching hot meals and hailed a cab instead of walking.

On the ride, my mind wandered to my feeling of recognition regarding Alexa. Where could I have possibly known her from? It wasn't impossible, but I didn't think I'd met her casually, so again it must be that she resembled someone I'd helped along the way. Or perhaps a victim. Still, it would be foolish to rule out that I might have known her. Especially considering the holes in my memory.

After wolfing down one of the burning-hot roti, I dug into my jacket for the battered Moleskine notebook again. Despite the low odds of "Alexa Vexa" being her real name, I flipped through the pages and found the expected nothing. None of the entries revived my memory in any helpful way.

When I looked up, I had no idea where the cab I was in was headed. I watched streets whip by, hoping for something to come to me, but all I was rewarded with was the distant rumble of a chuckle in my mind.

"Sir? Where you wanna be let out?"

"Hm?"

"You tol' me to head downtown, now we here. What address you goin' to?"

The odd smells of a cab played against the membranes in my nose. Fake leather, car cleaner, plastic, and the scents of hundreds of humans. I had no idea how to answer the question. I couldn't recall my destination.

Anger lanced the back of my head, tightening the skin there. All the usual tricks that I'd developed as my memory deteriorated wouldn't suit in this situation. It wasn't much longer before I decided to simply bail on the entire affair, just as it didn't take long for me to gobble the second roti.

"Right here. Just stop." I sighed, paid the hack, and got moving out of the vehicle.

He roared off and I had nowhere to go that I could recall. What had I been doing before I got there? I needed to think, this was happening too fast, everything was wrong in a way that I had never before experienced. I started walking. Fast. Before I knew it, I was on the edge of the Public Garden. It consisted of winding paths around statuary, manicured beds of flowers and small bridges over the shallow pond that wound through the center. In between all of that, there were benches and grassy knolls. I avoided the benches in the failing sunlight and instead focused on following the grass to the slim footpath that edged the pond. My heart thundered in my chest and I had a wild feeling pushing at my thoughts.

There was a tight space beneath the bridge, I stopped at the center of it, put my back against the brick, and slid down on my haunches to bury my face in my knees and put my hands over the back of my head. I needed quiet and I tried to force as much of it as I could to calm the wildfire inside.

I did not want what was happening and I would not accept it. Not before and not now.

I began by *listening* to my breathing, imagining how it looked, feeling the air as it passed through my nostrils and down into my lungs as they inflated. Oxygen permeated the membranes there, being absorbed into my body, flowing from my nose, down my throat into my lungs, throughout my body. Into my heart, being pushed down my arms and legs, making patient progress to my fingers and toes. Once there, it looped back, making its way to my heart and lungs again.

Exhale.

Again.

I sidestepped the feeling of my anxiety and turmoil. The worry didn't go away, but its enveloping shape became manageable, malleable. I folded it over, made it smaller. With it no longer a formless threat, I packed it down into something I could regard with patience and objectivity. I compacted it and set it to the side. It was my worry, I had earned it and I would deal with it. But it was not a priority.

What was the priority? The present. I ran back through my memories and began unspooling them from this morning, starting with when I had woken up. What I had eaten, where I had gone. Who had I gone to see today? Detective Roberts. He'd called and wanted my help for something he felt was urgent. *Alexa Vexa.* We disagreed on the matter. Roberts himself needed help. I owed him. Pepperman was concerned for Roberts, as well. *Alexa is the vampires' problem.* I could speak to one of them at the Sweaty Magus.

That's where I was going.

The background static that had been a hallmark of my life for so many years, that I had not missed for the past year, surged to fill my ears. I allowed it to flow and slide past like a rushing river, giving it a channel and shores to follow. The annoyance subsided and faded into the background again. I'd won, for the moment, and had recollected my faculties. The power slid and rasped, uncomfortable with its loss after having been put on unfamiliar footing.

Maybe I had learned *something* in the past year.

The inside of the club remained unchanged. The foyer still had a deep blue, sea-themed lounge with what must have been a ridiculously expensive aquarium set under the bar. A light glow emanated from a few undulating, wrist-thick sea worms living in the tank. At least I thought they were sea worms—I had no idea what they were. I'd never seen the lounge full and today was no different. Patrons sat scattered about the area, keeping a discreet distance from one another. As always, there was a barkeep staffing the station and this one was my favorite.

"Hello, Benjamin."

The bartender hadn't changed over the intervening year. He still wore his thick, dark hair long to cover the tattoo. It was beautiful, in fact—his hair, that is. Straight and wiry, glossy black—it was strong testimony to what I could only assume was Japanese lineage. Or, at least, his last name "Hamayama" sounded Japanese to me. I never asked him about it and he'd never offered freely, so I had no real sense of his personal or family life. Benjamin himself was slim and usually gregarious, and where black clothing wasn't covering his pale skin, he appeared blue in the reflected light of the lounge.

"Alexander! Good to see you. Can I line you up?" He clinked an empty rocks glass onto the bar top and in return, I unholstered and unloaded the two Browning Hi-Power .45s I carried and slid them across to him. Benjamin secured the weapons and handed me a numbered tag. *Old hat nowadays,* I felt more than remembered.

Despite my longtime affair with bourbon, my primary interest was to speak with Majispin and get out to solve my own difficulties. There was much more attractive company I could be spending time with, anyway. I rubbed my temples, attempting to wish the headache away. The way this felt was different. Things had changed since the Queen of Dragons had stuffed my rampaging monster back into me. Now its disruptive ways were back and doing more damage than swiping memories. Some of the meditative techniques I'd learned that year had saved me. I wondered how far that could get me. Upon reflection, I'd learned something new about this affliction and how it worked. I found it hard to believe that I was the only one doing that; there had to be others. But I'd never met nor heard about them. Maybe I was just getting lonely. Maybe that explained Maria. Maybe she didn't need explaining and I was making something simple into something complicated.

Back to matters at hand, I answered Benjamin's very important question. "That all depends on whether or not Majispin is available." I knew better than to ask after the magician's specific whereabouts. None of his employees would answer that question satisfactorily.

"He's not, and I'm fairly certain the amount of time he's indisposed is undefined. Care to wait or I can pass a word along?"

I slid onto the nearest stool, nodded at the empty glass, and attempted a smile which I could see in the bar's mirrored wall was more of a scowl with a patina of grimace. "I'll wait. May as well make the best of it."

The bourbon warmed the back of my throat and spread the closest thing I knew to joy throughout my chest. I was reminded of its uncanny ability to clear the taste of blood from my mouth. When I wished it. Benjamin returned from making his phone call.

"You haven't been in very often. Keeping busy?"

"Not the kind of busy you've seen me in the past, but that's not necessarily a bad thing."

"Settling down?"

"Impossible. Say, where's Barros? I haven't seen that thug for a few weeks now."

"He took a...sabbatical, I guess. Had to head down to Arizona to straighten something out. I have no idea whether he's okay or not."

Barros had been clear about not wanting to return home. Whatever was going on must be serious to drag him back. I reckoned I could ask Maria more later, if I wished. "Listen, let me ask you about this; I might not need to see Majispin after all." The barkeep gave me his full attention. "Do you know of a well-respected vampire or some such? I've just learned of a female vamp who may be on a rampage. I want to pass it on."

The last time I'd asked for Benjamin's advice, I'd ended up being sexually assaulted by the extradimensional entity known as the Queen of Dragons. And I was in too deep with a favor she'd extracted from me during that particular incident. I still wasn't sure how that situation was going to end. The favor had yet to be called in. I didn't blame Benjamin, because he'd had no idea what was going to happen, but it reminded me just how dangerous seeking guidance could be in this world. The answers might be entirely unpredictable. I was fortunate, however, that I could more often get information from him that didn't involve assault of any sort.

Benjamin thought about it for a moment; he knew that it was in the respective monsters' best interests to end any shapeshifter or vampire going berserk. "You might try Deanndrea. She's in the number four private room with her favorite. I *think* she'd be willing to get involved. Tall; waist-length, dark hair; aquiline face; weird green eyes."

I nodded and commented, "Where the hell was she when the coven tore its way through here, where were any of them?" It was a rhetorical question. I'd never met Deanndrea, and she certainly hadn't turned up to help deal with the vampire conspiracy to gain immunity to the sun. Unless she had been a part of it. I knew that even though the four conspirators had been killed, there were still scores of followers loose. Just because I hadn't heard from any of them didn't mean they weren't still out there.

I decided to wait for either Majispin to turn up or Deanndrea to finish. The club employed several Faithful, people who fetishized giving blood to vampires. They exposed their necks willingly to predators and I didn't have much respect for any of them. It shouldn't take long for Deanndrea to get what she needed.

After sipping my way through three more bourbons and making idle chat with Benjamin in between customers, I realized it had been far too long a wait for Deanndrea. "Are you sure she's back there?" Benjamin made a positive sound in response, pursing his lips. I finished the finger of bourbon in front of me, dropped some bills on the bar, and made for the back of the club.

"You shouldn't—"

"Don't bother, Benjamin; I'm going to do this."

"At least knock first!"

The first time I'd come to the club, I had taken the red passage from the blue lounge. It had led me into a ritualistic dance floor scene that had to have been choreographed in hell. The energies swirling in that room had nearly gotten me killed. A crowd of mixed-breeds engaged in a dance so primal and raw, it brought a tidal wave of wild energy into the room. The fact that they existed and that their gathering to simply have fun had led to such a loss of control still bothered me.

I could hear music thumping down the hall, so I wisely took the alternate route. A velvet rope had been set up with private hanging from it at the entrance. With Barros on leave, the club was shorthanded in the muscle department, so no one manned the door. Not that he'd stopped me the first time. The lot of Majispin's shapeshifting employees were undisciplined at the time of my first visit, to say the least, and Barros had left his post unattended for reasons I'd never learned. I had a flash of difficulty recalling why they had become a tighter crew. As the memory unspooled, I was reminded that the eater of my memories lost its mojo when I was in the midst of recalling something. Lucky me.

Majispin's four shapeshifter employees had become a true pack in one day thanks to me, and in the same day, they suffered devastating losses while helping me. By sharing blood with their erstwhile leader, Mark, we became brothers in spirit and my power helped tie the four of them together. For all the good it did. The cost came high in two lives. Seth was killed, followed closely by Mark. I still remembered the unfamiliar feeling of knowing his life was in the balance. Being connected as we were, an odd line of power strung between us, and feeling him near death, I'd managed to hold him in place for a few moments by pulling on that connection. It was both exhilarating and disturbing and I doubted I'd forget that particular incident.

People tended to die around me. It's not something I expected or invited. Hell, I tried to avoid people in general. But I'd needed their help and someone other than me had paid the price. Another problem that occurred too often. I had debts that would never be repaid, and at least one of them had resulted in literal haunting.

Information from my past had died with Seth and I wondered if I'd ever recover that piece of my life. He'd known me many years before and he'd known Constantina, a woman I needed to find again, one day, and set our relationship straight, if I could. Seth had admitted that he knew where she was, but he had died before I could negotiate it out of him. I didn't have an inkling of what Tina had been up to since we'd parted ways. That I remembered her at all was recent, a reclaimed memory Seth had taunted me with. He'd loved her too, but from afar.

I smelled the first signs of death on the air. Maybe this was why Majispin employed shapeshifters: they could keep a nose on things people couldn't see. Well, he was shorthanded now and as much as I hated to even appear to be acting as one of Majispin's proxies, it seemed to be something I couldn't avoid.

There were five private rooms at the back of the club. Reserved mostly for well-heeled vampires who wished to do exactly what Deanndrea was doing now. I found the door with an elegant number four on it and knocked on the wood with as much politeness as I could muster. There was a soft rustle inside and a slow intake of breath. She hadn't been breathing, which meant she'd either been asleep or deep in contemplation.

"Come in; it's unlocked."

As I opened the door with caution and kept myself out of direct line of sight, my nerves jangled. Something was wrong. I could see long, pale legs ending in toes painted a pearlescent sea green extending onto the plush, plum-colored rug. A pair of shiny black stiletto heels rested in the corner. On the couch, Deanndrea reclined. She wore a simple dress colored to complement her eyes and cradled her dead partner gently, both hands visible, and regarded me.

"Please, sit down; close the door."

I slipped into the room, decorated floor to ceiling in shades of plum, closed the door with as little sound as possible, and eased myself onto the opposite end of the rounded couch that took up half the space. "My name's Alexander."

"Mmmm, the shapeshifter." Her eyes were downturned toward the Faithful; she turned his head into her breast and gently stroked the dead man's hair. "Did Benjamin tell you I was here?" She raised her eyes to me. They were a brilliant green. Straight black hair shifted and shimmered as it fell across her bare, pale shoulders.

I nodded.

"Then I'm ready."

I was confused and said so, not at all understanding why she'd said that. Her eyes regarded me anew; I could see shimmers of silver within the multifaceted emeralds set below her soft, arching eyebrows. I felt threatened and it must have shown on my face. I had no idea what this vampire was capable of in close quarters.

"One of Majispin's chief enforcers comes to visit, and I jump to conclusions." She smiled, showing her fangs briefly. "I'm sorry, why are you here?"

If I were looking for a new reason to be annoyed with Alivara Majispin, then I'd just found it. I'd be sure to tweak the magician later. "I've recently become aware of a vampire who has likely killed several people at once, spilled quite a bit of blood."

The smell of the freshly dead body continued to fill the room. It lay upon every surface, tainting wood and textile alike. There was no scent from Deanndrea, just the clothes on her back and the buried smell of cologne from the Faithful's beatific corpse. I noticed that her responses were coming more slowly.

"Ah." She sighed and settled back, continuing to stroke her former suitor's hair. "Do you know this vampire's name?"

"Alexa, but that's likely an alias. To the best of my knowledge, she's a pornographic actress."

"Oh, *that* one. I know of her. She's with the church."

CHAPTER 5

I wasn't sure I'd heard her correctly. It's not that holy ground, crosses, or blessed water would hurt a vampire, but the whole idea of God, Jesus, and the rest tended to go out the window with the rest of your humanity when you became a monster. Doubly so for a vampire. Their faith was found entirely in blood; their reality shifted to accommodate their weaknesses and their needs—just like us and our need to hunt and eat. Vampires and shapeshifters who placed their lives in the hands of unseen, unheard beings tended to die young—maybe we weren't so different from humanity, after all.

"I can see by your expression that you're…unfamiliar." She sighed and adjusted the corpse in her arms to snuggle closer; I could see the remnants of a serene smile on the dead man's face. I began to suspect what Deanndrea's personal talents might be. "Our Lady of Perpetual Death was inevitable, I guess, since our bid for the sun failed. You may as well contact them about your errant little whore of a vampire.

"You *were* wondering if I'd been a part of *that*, weren't you? Of course I supported the effort. Can you imagine living your life trapped in half the time everyone else exists in?"

"I suppose you'd live twice as long."

She snorted. "I've lived long enough; this will be my last 'mistake.'"

The events that had passed in the room now made more

sense to me. She'd effectively committed suicide by killing the Faithful under Majispin's roof.

"Where is this church?" She'd gone still, frozen in the inhuman way vampires could wait. "Deanndrea?" She drew no air—needing none to breathe—she was done talking. I abandoned the idea of shaking her and left the room interested only in leaving Majispin to his problems and doubly irritated that simply passing on this information had become so complicated.

Majispin was sitting at the bar when I made my way back to the front lounge. He had his back to me, and the familiar jumble of signals wafted off him. He used some kind of magic to scramble his scent profile, but he seemed to have underestimated how unique that made him to my olfactory senses. And I wasn't going to tell him.

I watched the club owner for a moment, counting the seconds and noting the crisp white suit which served as a brilliant counterpoint to his dark, bronze skin. Majispin was from somewhere in southeast Asia—no one knew where in particular. At the count of twenty-two, he turned in the seat to stare at me. His right hand remained on the bar, tapping out a steady rhythm, the only indication of his irritation. He'd known I was there and now he knew I'd known that he knew. Childish, certainly. And worth it.

I took the occasional opportunity to tweak the erudite magician because he was an asshole. We each knew where the other walked and neither of us was accommodating enough to move. There was a friction between us as well as an understanding. Majispin owed me his life. The incident that had left him with a limp was directly related to breaking the vampire conspiracy a year before. Without me, he would have drowned in his own basement, poisoned into paralysis.

I slid onto the stool next to Majispin and he watched me as impassively as he could manage.

"I hear you're looking for me?" Majispin's haughty

British accent grated on me and I took pleasure in the fact that he tended to drop the affectation when he was angry.

"Sort of. I started with you and ended up looking for Deanndrea, but she's quite finished being helpful to anyone."

"What the hell are you on about?"

"I've been made aware of a vampire who's likely reached the end of her sanity. It looks like she killed several people at once. Messy."

"Hmph. That doesn't sound like a happy blood-drinker to me. Benjamin was right; that seems to be something Deanndrea should help you with."

"I don't need any help. I just wanted to pass the message on to someone who'll do something about it."

"Wait. What did you mean by 'she's quite finished'?"

"It looks like she murdered whoever was in that room with her."

"Demon of a bitch! Benjamin, call cleanup to meet me at…"

"Room four," Benjamin filled in.

"…Room four." Majispin slid off the tool and scooped up his cane. The length of the stick was inscribed with runes that meant I-don't-know-what. Whatever it was, I was sure the damn thing was dangerous, so I never touched it. I had one more question for Majispin.

"Tell me where the Church of Our Lady of Perpetual Death can be found."

"What? Never heard of it. I have work to do, Alexander; excuse me. Or go to Hell. Whichever." He hustled toward the back of the club as quickly as he could.

Bye-bye, Deanndrea.

I sat at the bar for a while longer, thinking of everything that I'd learned so far today, the events following my meeting with the deteriorating Detective Roberts and his partner, Pepperman. Alexa, the malevolence I carried within, the murders, Deanndrea's teasing information, Majispin's purported ignorance—all of it. The one final fact that had not escaped my notice, a reaction that was too important for me to ignore: my headache was gone, the static receded.

I was onto something new and intriguing. I needed to find the church.

CHAPTER 6

The awareness that the sun had dropped below the horizon tingled at the back of my brain. Many years spent on the day/night cycle had me attuned to the daystar's comings and goings. As I made my way to the club's exit, it crossed my mind that nighttime might not be the right time to kick the vampire hornets' nest. Some of my investigation was going to have to wait until morning, most likely. Besides, I was supposed to be at Maria's apartment by now. She, like my adopted daughter Ana, regularly lamented that I didn't have a mobile phone. It probably had something to do with my dislike of tethers and restrictions, or the plain fact that I didn't wish to answer to anyone. My deal with the Dragon had firmly broken that streak, however, so maybe it was time to reconsider fully joining the modern age.

Benjamin had the phone pressed between his shoulder and ear when I collected my pistols and made for the exit. As I snapped the magazines back into them, it occurred to me that I'd been doing this for a while without thought or consideration. As near as I could tell, no one in the room watched me, but it was impossible to know who around you was paying attention to what. Plenty of club patrons checked weapons and other dangerous artifacts at the bar. None of them were me, however, and I was starting to wonder if staying put for so long after so many years was going to work against me in a manner that I couldn't compensate for.

Outside the club, three figures huddled near the

entrance. I knew without trying that they were vampires and they, I'm sure, realized what I was. I didn't know that they knew who I was until one of them spoke up.

"Back on your path to futility, cousin?"

The tone of the remark coupled with its oddity forced me to take better stock of the three. Paranoia sparked at the back of my head where it was merely a dull warmth a few minutes before. The speaker had the round face and blond hair of a typical college student. The other two were alternately taller and shorter, with darker hair. The bloodsucker on the left had heavy brows and a full shadow of stubble, while the other wore his dark brown hair long, past his cleanly shaven jaw. They all sported dark clothing—most vampires I'd known adopted the trend eventually—and stood nearly shoulder to shoulder in a unified front, unhesitant.

One opponent I could handle, two were difficult, but three would be a problem—especially if they were determined. A vampire's bite contained a paralytic venom that wouldn't kill me outright but would slow me down long enough for a killing blow. Three upped the odds of getting bitten. I'd already done that sort of dance before, so I wasn't going to dwell on the odds. Instead, I faced them as unhesitatingly as they did me. Blondie kept one hand in his jacket pocket, so he got my full attention.

"Excuse me?" I placed my hands casually on my hips, the better to quickly draw one or both of the pistols at the small of my back. Monsters like us weren't easily killed with small-caliber weapons, but it still hurt like hell and .45 rounds would damn sure slow them down.

"Are you still keeping your appointment with oblivion? That's what working for Majispin is going to get you and the rest of his wayward fools, you know."

That was the second time in as many hours that someone had mistaken me for an employee of Majispin's. I was going to have a serious talk with the magician the next time we met. Either he had spread this rumor or he'd allowed it to blossom. Regardless, it made me unhappy. Unhappier than usual, anyway. "Maybe you've wrapped your lips around one too many stupid people, because you're not making any sense, boy. *Try* to speak like an adult."

The blond started at that and took a step in my direction, only to be held back with a gentle hand to the shoulder by one of his compatriots. He made an ugly face in my direction the way only a vampire could: with a pliant bone structure and supremely flexible skin. Pure hate emanated from his features. "You disgust me. You and your arrogance and your accomplices in disgraceful, wandering ignorance!" His friends began to lead him away, but he wasn't finished. "Your day will soon be here; we will return to our rightful place in—"

He snatched his hand from his pocket and came up short against my pistol shoved in his face. I glanced at his hand, holding a dark, wooden crucifix.

"You can barely contain your murderous ways!" He tossed the crucifix at my chest and it clattered harmlessly to the sidewalk.

His assessment had not been incorrect. I struggled to not shoot him in the face. When they'd gone inside—the blond all the while proselytizing—I knelt and examined the crucifix before picking it up. It was a cross, of course, but the figure on it was not simply the familiar silhouette of Jesus. The dark piece of wood was delicately carved with a petite woman seductively curled around Christianity's savior in crucifixion. It was striking for the gender addition. I'd never seen a woman depicted on the cross in addition to Jesus—though surely religious maniacs full of love for their god had found cause to crucify scores of women in years past. Two figures. I looked closely and it was clear that the woman's mouth was clamped securely to the ersatz Jesus's neck.

I looked up and jumped. The boy stood inches from me, staring with dead eyes. My little blond ghost haunted me at awkward times and never portended anything good. He appeared to be mostly intact this time, missing only one hand and a single eye. Dry, not bleeding; I was unsure how to feel about his appearance, as it was far less distressing than what usually disturbed me. Thinking about it, I realized that he hadn't made his presence known for some time. I was pressed to remember the last time he'd bothered to haunt me. I was dead wrong about one thing, however: he wasn't staring at me. Instead, he stared over my shoulder in a direction I couldn't make sense of. Several people walked around us and I got the usual odd looks when something like this happened, because I was staring at a point in space. A point where no one could see the spectral form of my first and last child victim.

I stood and dropped the cross into my jacket pocket. When I headed for Copley Square and my beloved set of pay phones, the flashing lights of an emergency vehicle rumbled past. A dreadful feeling tingled in my chest. I glanced around for the boy, but he was gone. The vehicles, however, where moving in the direction he'd been staring.

Roberts picked up on the second ring and was less than enthusiastic that it was me.

"What is it now, something else you're not willing to help with?"

"There's a complication involving Alexa."

"No shit, we've got a second slaughter, a wealthy *family* in the Back Bay, the patriarch was torn to pieces, some of the missing are children. Interested now?" The line snapped dead. Another set of blinding lights painted the surrounding buildings, closely followed by a news van. I had a clear idea of where the latest crime scene was located.

I hadn't expected Roberts to hang up on me, but there it was. A second murder scene. I had no proof that it was at all related to Alexa Vexa, but morbid slaughters in Boston don't come often and, when they do, not in pairs. A family missing. A thick sense of frustration clogged my thinking, I had turned away from Roberts when he'd asked for help. Now this and there would certainly be more. Clearly this wasn't an aberration and I had been let it on the ground floor only to get right off like selfish idiot.

Now the situation was more complicated than Roberts even knew. Complicated, indeed. The first set of murders was lurid and certainly a PR problem, but a wealthy family in the Back Bay was next-level shit.

Why several murders at the first location and only one at the second? Why take the other family members? Snacks for later? It wasn't impossible that someone else was picking up the ball for a spell granting vampiric immunity to the sun. It was unlikely, however, as the information and experience to do so had died with the four vampires in the coven. I'd personally destroyed their imprisoned vampire treasure from the Mayan age; a starving monster so ancient and insane, it had babbled incessantly about magical techniques that had been lost long ago.

I stared in the direction the vehicles had gone, knowing that there was no way I'd be allowed access to the crime scene. Roberts wouldn't be in charge of something this large and I surely couldn't go unnoticed even if he invited me onto the scene.

My hand brushed against a freshly crumpled paper in my pocket. The note from Roberts with the address of the porn massacre; I'd forgotten I had it. A darkness crept across my brain, a need for carnage and fresh blood lit up my saliva glands. Without awareness, I'd taken steps in the direction of the newly minted abattoir. Furious at my weakness, I turned and headed for the address that Roberts had given me. A familiar chuckle echoed in the distance of my mind, its contempt tickling the hairs at the back of my neck. The bastard and I were still tied at the soul, but we were headed to the first crime scene according to my will.

CHAPTER 7

The first slaughter was located northwest across the Charles River in a decaying loft. I kept the note with the address crumpled in my fist like a child incapable of remembering something as complex as a street address. The old brick building sat amongst the remnants of Boston's industrial past. A strength the entire United States seemed to be losing. The bridge across the river, like most incidental pedestrian ways in this town, provided an exposed and straight path. Easy enough for cars to navigate, but anyone on foot suffered the wrath of mechanical exhaust and nature's unsubtle hand. High winds and leftover sand from the winter peppered my skin as I crossed. The scent of a dump below stabbed at my nose every time the harsh winds shifted. This was the very worst a city had to offer me regarding an olfactory profile: engine exhaust and garbage.

After a stroll through what seemed to be abandoned buildings and streets, the location appeared before me. Active mailboxes here and there let me know that people still lived in these buildings. The properties had the look of sorrowful heads jutting from the concrete, incensed ghosts stewing for whatever came next in their now-aimless existence. Wedged between crooked barbed wire fences and other dull, red buildings, several pieces of crime scene tape across the door marked the entrance I sought. Dark windows covered with rusting iron grates caught the scant light. Deep shadows and the detritus of industry littered the spaces between the buildings.

I navigated my way to the back and set to climbing the rear of the structure until I was on the roof. The access door's knob and apparatus were rusty and weak. Even a normal man could've broken the passage open. At the bottom of the stairs, in the hallway, more yellow tape marked off the loft in question. I slipped in between the plastic strips, not wanting to leave any more obvious evidence of my visit, taking care where I stepped. Even though we monsters leave no biological traces, we can leave footprints.

In one corner of the loft, what was left of the set took up one quarter of the space. Three small dots showed clean in the blood splashes. The points formed a triangle—they were likely the feet of a tripod. On the carpet, two matching depressions on either side of the bed and clean spots like two giant letter Xs, where the lights had been. The vestiges of burning blood hung in the air, so the lights must've been hot when they'd been spattered. In the corner, a paltry representation of weightlifting equipment sat just behind the bare twin bed, all a match to the video. Roberts's description of the crime scene had been accurate. Everything was streaked in evidentiary trails of dried blood. Congealed trails led all the way to the front door, ending in a single splotch against the doorjamb. Even parts of the exposed pitched ceiling featured splashes and drops. One unfortunately large gob hung down an inch or so, dried in place. The smell of sour, wet iron remained spread over the burnt stench and mix of leather gun-belt-wearing men and women.

The room was warm despite the cool air brought by the beginnings of spring. I took a deep breath, sorting through the death hanging in the air. There were far too many human smells to make much sense of other than that there'd been people, but I hadn't smelled what I feared. My last misadventure in Boston had started while tracking a killer who'd been more dead than alive, a puppet for a cabal of vampires intent on making themselves and their followers immune to the sun. The almost-dead thing was called a Thrall, and its scent had reminded me of stagnant water. I imagined the empty husk of a soul, remembering what Majispin had told me about the process of creating such horrors. To my relief, I sensed none of that.

I had been concerned that the remaining vampires participating in the conspiracy might have reconnected somehow and started anew. Instead, I now assumed this church Deanndrea had mentioned had filled the void.

The sense of a shape invading the room tickled the back of my neck with a slight shifting of atmosphere. What was not present before made itself known as I felt a prickle of energy that put me into a state of nervous awareness. I turned, needing to rely on my eyes—there had been no change of scent or sounds to pinpoint. The entire room felt menacing and I wasted no time checking the ceiling as well.

In plain view, between the lousy movie set and the front door, the blond boy stood. My shame: an enemy's child slain for misguided vengeance more than a century ago. I had never learned his name, my little ghost, but he always found me when my fate was about to turn for the worse. This time he stood, eyes blank, looking just past me, one hand missing, the other pointing at a place just to my right. The child had never raised this kind of alarm in me before—nothing but normal dread and guilt upon realizing he was there. Blood pooled at his feet and was smeared across his pointing hand and accusing face.

I wasn't alone in the room, my ghost notwithstanding.

A sigh of a voice, creaky and low-pitched, spilled into the air like an oil slick on water. "Ah, I wondered how long it would take you to notice me here." The vampire melted from the shadows with precise steps. He was bald and pale, face interrupted by blood-pools for eyes with little islands of pupils. Sharp cheekbones and pouty lips punctuated the mess of an uneven face. Neat, nondescript clothes clung to his slim frame—all of them black but for his bone-white collared shirt. The hem of a black three-quarter-length coat hovered above his knees. He grinned lopsided, showing no teeth, one eye nearly winking. "It took you long enough to get here. I was beginning to wonder how many cattle would need to be slaughtered before you woke up."

The monster was about my height and our eyes met across the room. "You killed these people."

"Tsk, 'people.' Really? That's how you see them, Alex? I thought you were older than that, smarter. Hmph, only immature fools play with their food. Waste not, want not." He looked disapprovingly about the crime scene. "No, I did not kill these 'people.' None of that matters now, anyway. Perhaps you'll be able to weep later for the ignorant."

He knew my name. I had no idea who he was. If he was to be believed, he was not the monster responsible for these murders but clearly trying to draw me out. His sense of familiarity with me disturbed my core where the black pool of ill will that served as my battery bubbled.

"All right, now, enough chit-chat. Where is she? I would have her in my company."

Confusion spread across my thoughts. There's weren't many women associated with me. The few that were was a recent occurrence. It didn't take long to shorten the list further, in a cold realization, I had no doubt he was asking after Ana. My adopted daughter, the only "she" in my life who would be difficult to locate. The cold power coming off this vampire kept me at an uncomfortable level of alertness. Agitated, I wouldn't give him an easy death if he begged me and I certainly would not give him Ana. Regardless, I had no idea where she was—not that he needed to know that. Tossing away any sarcastic remarks, I opted to go all in with defiance. "You'll have to do better than that."

He looked sincerely amused, seeming to involuntarily smile, and knitted his brows in condescending humor. "Last chance, boy."

After four heartbeats, I couldn't contain my laugh. "Really, is that supposed to hurt my feelings? 'Boy'? You'd better have an army in your pocket if you want to get me worried."

He went to stone, unearthly still as only they can. When he spoke, only his mouth moved. "Oh, we'll get to that; in the meantime…"

I expected his attack—was prepared for it, in fact, but his was a speed I'd never faced before. There was barely time to react before he'd crossed the room and was inches from my face. I stepped back, swatting his arms to my right, pivoting for an advantage that never came. He twisted like a snake in a hurricane, blasting my arms down and slapping his cold palms to either side of my head.

There was a disconnect, like someone had tripped over my power cord and pulled the plug. A sudden shift in perception and I felt ice water pouring over my brain. The beast at my core howled, maddened beyond comprehension. Threatened in its dark hole, it thrashed. My body seized, unable to move, chilling tendrils laced my muscles, and my assailant's blood-tinged eyes invaded my mind. My thoughts stretched out of me, creating a sickening pull at my forehead, and the world tumbled.

For the briefest of moments, I saw the tunnel from me to him, a blurry passage filled with errant thoughts and memories. The incomplete recollections slid in all directions—the beast within me having stolen the bulk of the set over the years. My adversary dove deeper, leaving an undefended path, a passage I chose to see as an opening instead of a trap in his black maelstrom of a mind. Rather than continue to struggle, I did what I always do when cornered without options: move forward.

I dove into his mind, scraping and pulling to squeeze my bulk into his. There was an electrified current of pain the deeper I went, a molecular torture that threatened to destroy us both. Images flashed between my grasping mental fingers. Viscous thoughts streamed around me, congealing into a gelatinous grip. Images played between us: a little girl, puckish nose, staring straight ahead. Her father in the driver's seat, angry—always angry—until the evenings when he was hungry for something he thought his daughter could sate. A distorted face, dislocated jaw, protruding canines, dead eyes. Hissing, the sound of hunger, of desperation. That face morphing from normal to vile, the bloodied lips of my current adversary. A slaughter, overturned furniture, an empty bassinet. Two bodies: my neighbors, friends.

He screamed with me, matching my pitch and volume, and we both raged to disconnect. I sat down hard in dried blood and he stumbled away, holding his head as if it might explode.

Simmering with anger and pain, he staggered from the loft, holding his screams in the back of his throat, fading away until I could hear him no more. When I managed to pick my head up, the blond boy stood in my line of sight, shaking his head slowly. The world spun once and I slipped under the darkness creeping in at the edges of my vision.

There was a muffled sound in my ears, a repeated barking. The same cadence, over and over until with a strike like fire, I felt a sharp pain across my face. Pulling from the fathomless mud of unconsciousness, I awoke with a grunt, sitting up, flailing my arms, and immediately regretting it. Wincing, I ran my hands along my head, fully expecting to find a fresh hole somewhere. My mouth was dryer than I'd ever felt before, as if I'd been gnawing on crackers and trying to wash them down with sand. My heart fought to escape my chest while I tried to steady myself. Sweat spread across the back of my neck, a prickly invader in all the crevices of my body. When I looked up, there was a repeating light splashing across the ceiling and muffled voices came to my ears. I was still alone, despite the experience.

Hauling myself to my feet, I lurched to the window to see the bright blue and red lights of a police cruiser and a glimpse of dark uniforms entering the building. Someone had called the police. I needed to be gone, so I stumbled to my feet.

The door, I found the door. Went through the tape, up the stairs, onto the roof. With a stumbling start, jumped to the next building. Flew. Fell, flailed, caught the ledge. Loosened mortar, bricks slipped through my grasp. A desperate scramble, legs pumped, feet dug for purchase. Up and over the edge, I lay still, hidden by the knee-high barrier encircling the tar roofs. Breathed. I just breathed and processed. I wasn't sure what the vampire had been able to see in my mind, but he'd dislodged at least one memory from my tattered recollections. I remembered who Alexa Vexa was, why she was familiar, where I knew that face from. A long life with spastic memories means getting bitten in that ass over and over, it seemed.

There was something more that I'd gained, however, as I'd been in his mind. The disturbing trip had not been a loss, but the memories were.

CHAPTER 8

I lay in the gravel on the tar roof, listening to the cops talk as they played their lights around the opposing rooftop.

"Looks like someone was in there, though."

"Sure, but where'd they go? Nothin' here, nothin' out back."

"You think they jumped?"

I watched the light splash on the exhaust pipes and chimney of my roof.

"Hell, no. You think you could make that jump?"

"Fine. C'mon, we'll check the rest of the building. Let's finish up with the caller and wrap this up."

Even though they'd left, I remained prone, feeling the gravel dig into the back of my head. I needed to sort through my thoughts. *Nikolaus Graamvater.* His name meant nothing to me. I'd seen the image of another vampire in his mind, a feral thing, the murderer of Ana's parents—her sire. I'd dispatched him shortly after he'd bitten her. She was just a baby and I'd never expected her to survive, to thrive. It was unheard of, in my wanderings, for a baby to survive a vampire bite and grow to maturity. I hadn't had the heart to finish her. A time before, yes, I would have, but not then, and not anymore. I felt I owed it to her parents, who were my nearest neighbors. She lived in her own way and I raised her, this undead child. She's never seen the sun, at least not directly. Never felt its warmth or been exposed to its banal and deadly nature.

Why was this bastard looking for her; what did he want? Was he connected to the feral vamp who'd bitten Ana? Was he its sire? Ana was safe for now, her location unknown, but I'd have to warn her when I could, if possible. If I could find her.

Precious few stars could be seen in the night sky. Mottled black was smeared across the world as I knew it, fading to a lighter hue at the edges. Having seen the stars outside of cities—before they were fully realized—I knew the small feeling it could engender if you weren't careful with your thoughts. I remembered the first time I looked up while standing in a city proper and realizing that the light from the ground was beginning to outshine the lights in the sky. The advent of electricity had allowed humanity enough power to rival the gods, it seemed. They threw light with abandon into the sky, into the gods' faces. In the cities, Man's light blotted out the illumination of the universe, creating a world of false light. The kind of world where people like Alexa Vexa were created.

Alexa. Vexa. Stupid, made-up porn name. Kelsey was her real name, Kelsey Thomas. I'd saved her from her own father once upon a time. That rescue had ensured that she lived long enough to become an addict, to allow herself to be filmed having sex, and to become a vampire.

Listening close, focusing inward, I searched for the hum of my power's personality. I found the barest traces of a shudder; it was still there but cowed by the invasion. The closest thing to sanity I could hope for. If I were lucky, it would stay there. Maybe. Considering what passed for luck in my life, I fully expected it to come raging back when I least expected it.

The crunch of footsteps on the gravel snatched my attention. No scent to speak of preceded his arrival, but his face was all too familiar. The little man bowed to me, grinning ear to ear, with far more teeth than he should have had in his head. He still held the umbrella, but it was folded and hooked in the crook of one arm, bent perfectly horizontal to the roof.

He gestured with the other hand, a theatric flourish, as he reached for the doorknob on the rooftop's door. I could see the bolt keeping the door locked in the gap between door and jamb, but when he turned the knob, it slid back with a metallic creak. A light dusting of rust fell and parted as a cloud mixed with gold and silver flecks rolled in, bearing the Queen of Dragons.

I swallowed hard, attempting to digest a knot of fear and desire. She smiled, sultry and knowing, eyes squeezing to comical slits while her crookedly smiling lips parted to reveal one wicked canine. Her hair cascaded around her shoulders in a display that looked like night had been liquefied, stars and all, before being poured over her head and shoulders.

The fog she slid in on settled to the rooftop and began to spread. I cringed, shimmying back as far as the lip of the roof would allow. I wanted nothing to do with that gentle and glittering touch. I knew without being told that there was more influence in that atmospheric disturbance than I was willing to cope with. Here was a being which it had only taken me one meeting to understand that I could neither resist nor disobey outright, only ride out her influence as one does a storm.

"Alexander." She drew the soft vowels of my name out, and the obscene purr of her voice made it feel as if my individual cells vibrated. She stood, wrapped from wrist to ankle in shining silk. I couldn't see her feet as she seemingly glided in on her own storm front, wisps of the cloud clinging to her and mimicking every gesture.

I was nervous enough that I didn't want to use my voice, uncertain as to how much influence she had over me while I was in her presence. My words seemed inadequate. "I…didn't think you could be here. Like this."

She inhaled deeply, an amused smile playing around

her mouth. She glanced at her little man, enveloped to his knees in the fog, he grinned adoringly at her and they shared a private joke at my expense. "I begin to fear you're always going to be this close to understanding, but..." She unclasped her hands and held her thumb and forefinger a hair's breadth apart. "No matter, I have faith in you."

Not one sarcastic remark or gesture left my body. I barely had a coherent thought. "What do you want?"

She tittered at the back of her throat before answering, "So much more than you can give. Don't worry; I'm not here to collect. Yet."

My relief was not palpable because there was none. An inter-dimensional entity powerful enough to subdue me with a terrifying nonchalance stood before me. She winked and I had no idea how to interpret the gesture.

"Oh, relax, Alexander. I'm just here to be sure my...asset will still be in play when I need him. You've met someone troubling this evening. Yes?"

I nodded, probably the safest gesture I could come up with.

"I can tell. He leaves...traces." She wiggled her fingers in my general direction. "Graamvater's very existence is something of a problem. The pieces of the game are not supposed to move on their own—I'm sure you take my meaning." She shrugged in gentle dismissal.

I did not take her meaning and I also did not say so. I wasn't sure I wanted to understand.

"Regardless, I want some assurance that you won't let this rogue kill you."

"I'm not sure I can provide that."

"Well." The Queen stretched out one elegant arm, examining the back of her long hand. She rubbed the back of it with her fingers, gently touching the tiny scales that appeared to extend from beneath her silks and end near her knuckles. "You *could* ask a favor of me. With your...cooperation, I could perhaps deal with him directly." One eyebrow arched even further as she directed a sly glance in my direction.

There was no way in any number of hells that I would offer her another bargain. In response, I wanted to say something as colorful, but what I came up with was "No, thank you." My loins, however, begged to differ. Parts of my body remembered the circumstances of our last pact and tightened with intent.

She made a small sound of acknowledgment that was neither encouraging nor damning. Then she fixed me with her stare. "So, what then, Alexander? If you die, I'll be quite vexed. How can I be sure?" She inclined her head in my direction as if she were speaking to a child.

Remembering how I'd been able to hold Mark together when he was near death made me reconsider whether my own death would allow me to escape the Queen. She had stitched me back together once before.

"Faith?"

She pinned me with her stare, diamond-like eyes the only sense of motion from her as they glittered in my direction. Then she laughed, full-throated. I am not ashamed to admit that I flinched when she did.

"Touché, my wayward beast. Very well, I suppose if anyone here can deal with Graamvater, it'd be you. I have your word, then?"

The gears tumbled so hard in my head, I could hear them grinding. Or maybe that was my teeth? "I think not."

She laughed again, sweeping her arms wide as she turned for the doorway. When she spoke, it was to her little man. "You see? I told you he could learn."

He bowed deeply in return, the smile never leaving his face, and held the door for her.

She paused at the entrance and looked up. "Such a waste. Hm? Blotting out the sky. Maybe things would have been different if humans hadn't turned out so…insulting. What do you think?"

That last was directed at me. I thought with care and answered in the same spirit. "I think a lot of things could have been different."

She stared at me for a moment and then said, "Ah, your ancestors. On both sides. An unfortunate bit of history. Odd how it all turned out and here you are. Hm? Good night, Alexander. Remember that we have an arrangement."

She passed through the doorway and all the mechanisms slid back into place as before when the door closed. Then the attendant bowed to me and strode across the roof until he was out of my line of sight. They were gone and I unclenched everything I'd had the muscle control to clench in the first place.

With no interest in moving just yet, I sifted through my thoughts about Kelsey. The memories dislodged by my conflict with Graamvater were banging around in my head. A hot ball of molten mistakes come back for more.

CHAPTER 9

My joints ached and my skin burned where Graamvater had touched me. My brain was still not firing cleanly as I hauled my sorry ass off the gravel-and-tar roof, so I did what any man would do, given the opportunity: I went to see a beautiful woman.

When I arrived at Maria's apartment in the South End, I was even more haggard. She was hardly the stereotypical Latina popular media preferred to portray, but Maria was forward, most often. It was a flinty quality I liked about her. Not typically a smartass, no, but certainly not a pushover. When I'd arrived, she wasted no time in making an observation of my condition.

"You smell like death. Go wash that stink off."

Nothing had changed in her apartment since my first unfortunate visit. Situated in the grey area between Roxbury and the South End, it was one-sixth of a three-story brownstone that had been carved into apartments. She had well-worn, studded furniture—a few pieces upholstered with a hideous flower pattern to match the wallpaper—and a beautifully detailed ceiling. Well, it would have been more attractive if decades and layers of paint hadn't reduced the details to the appearance of a melting butter sculpture.

The younger shapeshifter rarely wore much makeup, her bronze skin and copper-red hair providing all the color she truly needed. Full brown lips matched the rest of her full brown body. I lied to myself about why I continued to see Maria after the death of her boyfriend, Mark, but I didn't lie to her. I simply kept my mouth shut.

Before Mark had died, I'd made him my brother in blood, healing wounds that I had dealt him, ending our most serious disagreement. We waged war together as tuka, war partners. Mark had been irritating and irritated; we were openly in conflict about everything—planning, leadership, Maria. After all the turmoil between us and within himself, he'd died an honorable death shortly after our conciliatory phase. My sharing blood with him had opened us both up to possibilities we'd never experienced. Maria had felt something similar as well.

There was a magnetic tug between us, an inevitable force that wanted us to cast off our skins and mingle. At times like this, when one of us was hurt, the attraction was even harder to control. Which was why, after shoving me into a hot shower, we fucked desperately somewhere between the bathroom floor and the hallway.

Our strength and nature gave sex the potential to be a violent event. If we weren't of like mind and species, then we'd likely kill each other. The power we held made it possible to not only have sexual stamina beyond that of a normal human being, but also in positions that would make Vātsyāyana sick with envy. After our desperate start on the floor, we leaned upright against the hallway wall. I held Maria's leg tight over the crook of my right elbow, her other leg wrapped around my waist. Arms and hands interlocked, our mouths alternately gnawed, nipped, and kissed. We were equal participants in thrusting and grinding. I worked hard to forget the Queen of Dragons, focusing on Maria, supplanting the agonizing sexual need the Queen engendered in me for the barreling train of lust I felt for Maria.

Maria was confident enough to take what she wanted. I'd come out of the shower wet, but now I was sure that had been replaced by a sheen of sweat. Maria's enthusiasm, energy, and raw sexiness always ended me sooner than I expected. She'd already been around the bend and was now devilishly focusing on me. A renewed aggression rose like heat between us; a near-palpable energy enveloped our struggling bodies. More than sexual fluids mingled when we orgasmed together. The bright, hot, shapeshifter power boiled in unison, buckling my knees and bowing my spine as we sank straight to the floor, all of her supple weight on my thighs.

Gulping for air, she found her voice first. "You know, that's the second bathrobe of mine you've shredded."

"It was in the way." My eyes never left the bite I'd delivered to her shoulder, watching the skin struggle to close up, the dents slowly filling back in. I could feel my own skin swimming, blending like warm wax. "I'll bring you another." I'd snapped the robe's belt in my haste and separated the collar from the main cloth.

"I hope it's made of steel threads this time." She put her hand on my chin and traced a long, three-nailed scratch that started there and led down my chest and across my ribs. Her fingers came away with traces of sizzling blood as the vital fluid burned away, leaving no trace. "Damn, you still heal faster than me."

"Well, when you get to be my age, it takes a lot more to keep this human shell going."

"I bet that's right, cradle-robber."

Maria was younger than I in shapeshifter years, but she'd never age beyond when she'd been turned. In human years, she was somewhere in her late thirties, just right, in my opinion.

She leaned in and kissed me, I kissed her back, and then we shared that familiar awkward moment where we both realized that this wasn't a complete relationship, that we were going nowhere, that Maria wanted something from me that she was afraid to ask for and I was too withdrawn to coax her into talking about it.

We clambered to our feet and did a little dance over who would go into the bathroom first. I relented and squeezed her hand when she passed. Maria squeezed back, slid out of my palm, and gently closed the door, our relationship stopping in the same worn space as ever before.

While she bathed, I raided her refrigerator, planning out a meal and digging pans from the cabinets. As before, when the Queen of Dragons had driven my power into a tight coil and unburdened me with its needling, my insatiable hunger had subsided. Relatively normal portions of food would be fine. I focused on preparing a simple meal, determined to erase the cumbersome end to our lovemaking.

The kitchen was small but serviceable. A slim white stove was packed into the single granite counter along the wall, almost abutting the dishwasher. As much cabinetry as the space could stand hung mounted above the counter, and the white fridge served as a buttress for the whole affair. It was perfect for one person but handled cooking for two just as well.

Maria sauntered into the kitchen just as I was pulling plates out of the oven. "Your ingenuity in the kitchen never ceases to amaze."

"One of many distractions along the way. Learning how to cook is a memory that has stuck over the years." She took a deep breath, eyes closed. I allowed myself the distraction of watching her bosom rise and fall, disappointed at my lack of discipline in the matter of lusting after Maria. She wore a loose, purple scoop-neck and formfitting, black athletic pants.

Without opening her eyes, she said, "Eyes up."

"Well played."

"You're not that complicated. So, what is this good-smellin' plate? I recognize the chicken."

I shrugged on the way to the bathroom. "Improvisation.

Consider it a Latin-influenced saltimbocca. I had to work with whatever you had in the fridge; I'm glad you buy fresh ingredients." When I returned, Maria's enthusiasm for the meal made me feel better for coming over in the sloppy way that I had.

After a few moments of chewing and simply enjoying the food, I knew Maria was waiting patiently for me to share something of what had brought me to her apartment late and disheveled. She tended to have the functionality of a straight razor, slicing through to whatever it was she wanted to know or do, which made whatever remained unasked even more acute. With me, she'd learned more subtlety in how she cut—but not by much.

"I had many unusual things happen today."

She met my eyes but continued to work on the meal, speaking around a mouthful. "Tell me; couldn't be any crazier than last year." Damn, I appreciated her forthrightness; it helped me to know where I stood.

Maria didn't know about my situation with the Queen of Dragons and I was going to keep it that way. I'd tell her the rest, however. "Detective Roberts called me."

"The cop...from the projects?"

"Yes." *The place where you saw your boyfriend impaled on a dead tree.* "He asked me to come to the station this morning and watch a recording. Turns out he's got a vampire on video. A woman calling herself Alexa Vexa. Everyone involved in the film shoot was murdered, blood everywhere."

"Mm-hmm." Maria slid out of her chair to get some bread off the counter, turning her back to me.

I watched her hips, the curve between her lower back and—

"Focus."

"That's twice now."

"I said you weren't that complicated."

"Mm-hmm."

"So, you're looking into Alexa Vexa?"

"I wasn't. I'm not a vampire hunter unless they mess with kids. Anyhow, I told him I'd pass it on for someone else to deal with."

She made a dismissive sound. "I'm sure he didn't take that well. Didn't sound like no vampire, anyway. Blood everywhere, you said?" She sat back down and began sopping up what was left on her plate. "Ever since that fiasco last year, the bloodsuckers have been disorganized. I bet you didn't get nowhere."

"Yeah. I spoke to Deanndrea—"

"Weird green eyes? She got her ticket canceled today."

"I know. She told me the vampire in the video was affiliated with a church. Our Lady of Perpetual Death?"

"Never heard of it."

I nodded, expecting as much, and dug into the pocket of my jacket on the back of the chair. "A proselytizing vamp threw this at me when I left the club at sunset." The clack of the crucifix on the table seemed unusually loud.

"*Dios*... That's a vampire wrapped around Jesus. Isn't it?"

"Looks like to me."

She eyed the little crucifix a moment longer and slid it back across the table. "Vampires finding religion. That doesn't sound good. The day I was turned, I stopped believing. All of this was the tipping point. A benevolent being, the unfathomable wisdom; my ass. Bad enough I was pushed to the limit when my...my—ah..."

There it was. The roadblock between us, what lay unasked. Her words stumbled to a halt. I plunged on before the atmosphere became uncomfortable.

"The whole situation was getting stickier by the minute. When I called Roberts again, he told me there was another murder. This was one person, the rest of the family—including children—are missing, same MO for the killing itself."

"So, you're in now?"

I gathered up the self-loathing to kick myself for not getting involved sooner before answering. "Yeah, but it got stranger, of course."

Maria smirked and swiped the plates off the table, rinsing them in the sink before placing them in the dishwasher. Then she moved the pans to the sink for washing. This time, I didn't admire her backside but rather appraised the situation. She'd gone cold for a moment and was distracting herself. I thought I had some idea what it might be.

"I went to the first murder scene. While I was there, I was ambushed by a vampire—a very powerful vampire. He was some kind of tactile telepath. He got into my mind."

Maria turned from the sink, her hands soapy and arms tense. "Is this a warning?"

"No."

"Do you need my help?"

"I don't think so. Maybe."

"Gonna have your little vamp girlfriend help you out?"

I considered what Maria had just asked me. The question smacked of jealousy on many levels. She'd known Ana before we met, and the two of them had never gotten along. In fact, the feeling was mutual and I've never truly understood why. Whenever they were together, they cut each other with belittling comments like catty high-schoolers. Now she was trying to push my buttons, but I didn't have the patience for that sort of thing. "You know she's not my girlfriend, but yes, I can always use her help."

"What she could use is a suntan."

Right. I didn't know how long I'd be with Maria, but this was something I could fix. It was time—she needed to understand my relationship with Ana. "She's never seen the sun, Maria. She's always been a vampire."

"What? Bullshit."

"Since she was a baby, the entire time *I raised her.*"

"She—*Jesus*. What? That's…different."

"To say the least."

Maria stared into space. "I don't think I've ever put my foot so far into my mouth. I'm sorry. That…explains a lot." She relaxed, but only the barest amount. I could see the gears tumbling in her head. Maria understood that anything I said to her was privileged information.

"This vamp who attacked me? He was looking for her."

She chewed on that for a moment, struggling to understand before she blurted out, "Why?"

"I'm not sure. He's somehow related to the vampire who created her. Maybe, functionally, he's her grandsire."

Maria shook her head in that futile way, to unscramble thoughts. "After the last time, Alexander, y'know—you get into some crazy shit. This right here sounds like some extra-crazy shit."

"I know. It gets better."

"No, it gets worse." She turned back to the sink and started scrubbing the last pan.

She was not wrong. "Turns out that I know the woman from the video. I rescued her from her own father in the late sixties."

Maria hung her head, dried her hands, and faced me with crossed arms, waiting.

"I got her away from him, got her out of that, and lost track of her."

"Now here she is. A whole new bag of problems."

"Yeah, one of mine."

"She's not *your* problem."

Yes, she was my problem. And I told Maria what I remembered from my time with Kelsey.

CHAPTER 10

Maria stared at me, probably as incredulous as I that there was a time I'd considered myself in good spirits. There were so many shortsighted choices in my past that I wished I could correct. Considering how long my life was and was potentially going to be, it was humbling to wallow in what had been. Part of the reason I avoided doing it.

"Alexander, she made her choices; you can't be responsible for that."

Also true, but I heard something more in Maria's tone. She didn't sound sure of herself to me. What I believed I'd picked up on was that the sentiment shared had something to do with her own personal experience; it hinted at something I didn't know about her past. Her statement was an absolute truth, but she didn't quite believe it herself.

"What is it, Maria? What's eating at you?"

"Nothing." She moved back to the kitchen sink and squirted some lotion into her hands.

"Listen, I know it seems like I haven't been forthcoming—"

Maria snorted loudly.

"There are things in my past that I truly wish would remain there." I glanced around the room, wondering if my little boy ghost was going to appear. "I've made plenty of mistakes, just like everyone else, but I've had more than a hundred years to make an inordinate amount."

"I've borne witness to some." She stood leaning against

the counter with her arms crossed.

"You have," I admitted. "And there's more to come. I hate to say this, but when I was your age—"

Maria snorted again. Loudly.

"When I was relatively young with this power, I was wrong to a degree that can't be set right. You, however..." I hoped Maria would read what I'd said correctly. I wasn't at all sure how to explain what I wanted her to share with me. There was a hole in our relationship, but I couldn't make out the shape of it; I couldn't even guess, because she'd been so cagey about it.

"I don't..."

I waited, resolved to patience.

I didn't want to push, and long, bitter experience told me that women don't necessarily want a man to *fix* problems for them. If she wanted my help, she'd ask. I just wanted her to know that I was here if she needed.

When her effort to decide whether to speak or not became visible, I spoke instead. "Is it something I can help with? Because if it's not, I want to know anyway, I want to...understand you; I want to be here for you."

A pause. The kind of pause that wasn't pregnant yet but definitely rounding second base. Her brow creased and she looked at me like it was the first time I'd ever sat in her kitchen. "I have a son. The situation involves my only child."

My stomach felt cold. I knew the kind of pain and passion a loved one like that could raise. "Does he know you're still alive?"

"No. My son's an addict, a bad one, and he's destroying himself. They keep him for their amusement, as a servant, a pet." She spat her words at the last. "He thinks I'm dead and I can't help him." Maria began to shake. "He's my only boy and *I can't help him.*"

The sharp scent of anger slipped over her. It dissipated a moment later to be replaced by sorrow. All of her signals were tweaking all of my senses. I wondered if she were picking up on any of mine. It took a long time to learn how to read those minute changes.

"Why not? Why can't he know you're alive?"

"His father was a super-mule for the cartel, arranging transport and storage. He was brilliant at it and I got wrapped up in his mess for years before he was killed in a power shift." She made a sharp gesture, clearly upset at the father of her child. How much of her anger and regret was self-directed?

"It was stupid—I was stupid. I let our son be exposed to this mess. Like any young boy, he was fascinated with how his father spent the day."

I remembered wanting to follow my father into the mines on more than one occasion. After his death, I had. And I would've have died of the same affliction but for being saved by my own distant relative.

"Mario would have made it through okay, but he was greedy and skimming, setting up his own network under their noses. When his bosses were taken down, the new ones discovered his schemes and killed him. They took my son. I was nearly killed and I fled, hoping they'd think I was dead, too, waiting for an opportunity to get my son back."

"Why would they have thought you were dead?"

She lifted her shirt and showed me the small scars scattered across her lower torso. I'd nibbled on the marks many times but had never thought twice about them. They didn't look like anything I was familiar with and I knew they'd occurred prior to her being brought over.

"This was shrapnel from the assault on our home. I was dying when I escaped, bleeding to death. I'm not certain they were entirely convinced, and now my boy is bait for me. I hid with distant relatives until...this thing happened." She indicated herself and I knew she meant the transformation. "I freaked after that and ran again.

Even the new me can't go up against a cartel."

I knew the folly of snatching kids back from those who've taken them.

"Those bastards manipulated him, raised him, created a little inner-circle pet. And it's not just him now. He has a wife, kids—my grandkids. Children of my children that I've never been able to meet, whose lives I can't be a part of, can't protect. They're all in danger."

I wondered how much of Maria's past Ana was aware of. She'd alluded to something when I'd asked her about Maria, but she wouldn't share. Could she have known all this or even suspected it? "Where did all this happen?"

"I came up here from El Paso and Majispin recruited me, fixed my identity for me. They'll kill us both if I show up. I stay away and the result is he kills himself slowly with their junk, with their bullshit. My family dies, strangled by drugs and neglect. I show up, he dies quick. There's only so much I can do from here without drawing attention; I don't know how much longer he'll live."

I knew gangs could hold a grudge, but this was decades. They weren't known for their moralistic thinking. Even though I was slightly incredulous, I kept it to myself. Rather than go with my first thought—that she abandon her son and steal her daughter-in-law and grandchildren away—I instead I held my tongue and watched Maria repack her emotions down tight. She clenched her jaw, refusing to blink, and ran the heel of her hand roughly across her eyes.

The same gesture she'd used after we'd been magically gassed by a fleeing vampire sorcerer. I wished I hadn't opened the gates for this conversation and that—of all things—we could go back to that time when Mark was still alive and vampires weren't out to put humans in corrals. Then I could just be the asshole passing through Boston. Now I cared about Maria. It wasn't love, no, I wouldn't call it that, not yet, but I moved to hug her anyway and she used a stiff arm to keep me at a distance.

"I'm sorry, no. Not now, not now..."

I hugged her anyway. And then I ruined everything by being myself.

I needed a few hours of sleep and decided to have them at my place. I had my reasons and that didn't sit well with Maria, but she had the stony grace not to ask why. I needed to find Ana and I wasn't sure how to go about it. Typically, she found me when I wanted or needed to see her most. She always claimed the ability to locate me and I'd seen no evidence to doubt it. As much as I denied it, I was going to need a mobile phone soon.

My latest apartment was located in the Fenway, near one of the green tracts within Boston that make up the so-called Emerald Necklace. Excepting baseball season, I enjoyed the location, the ebb and flow of college kids notwithstanding. At least I wasn't surrounded by teenagers and toddlers as I had been in Dorchester. The vibe here was definitely less harrowing for my tendencies. Given the reappearance of my more homicidal side, I was glad for the scenery change. Thinking of which: I still only felt the barest whisper of my power's malevolence. The vampire's attack had definitely done something I couldn't fathom.

Inside, my apartment was empty. My expectations of simply running into Ana were dashed and I was exhausted. My current home was as simple as others I'd maintained. Only the barest amenities in the one-bedroom affair. I had two couches in the main room and one table and chair in the bedroom that were littered with junk mail and missing-persons flyers. It didn't take long for me to collapse into a demanding sleep.

We don't dream, that I'm aware of, us monsters. I've spoken with others about this and we all wake up clear of any dream memories—if we have them at all. When I sleep, there is nothing until I awake. More often than not, it's a light sleep, a sort of predatory rest; some part of me is still alert.

Tonight was different, for the first time in nearly two centuries. My first sense was an awareness of drifting. I was moving, floating in darkness, and a syrupy thrum of sound caressed my bare skin. I tried to focus on it, make sense of the muddled emanations. There was a staccato rhythm to it, some sounds repeated, others not. Over and over, each time with more urgency. I determined that they were words, some kind of communication. I tried desperately to make them out and listened with increasing awareness until I could feel my entire body tightening with effort. The muffled words were urgent, directed at me, struggling to be clear. The environment shifted the tiniest amount and the murk began to lighten, the sounds to recede. I felt suffocated. Swimming in place, struggling to breathe, there was a snap and an overwhelming sense of concern and dread flowed over me.

When I passed through the membrane of the nightmare, I was surrounded by flora. A deep blue pall painted the forested lands around me. A clear night and a bright moon, larger than I've ever seen, lit the landscape of dormant trees. A latticework of shadows that looked like rotten blood in dead veins spread across the ground. I felt the discordant prickle and softness of pine needles on my face and I smelled nothing. That was the beginning of my short understanding of what was happening. My skin, bared to the elements, seemingly more sensitive than ever, puckered at the low temperature.

Raising myself to a crouch, I ignored the needles sticking to my body. Instead, I lamented that I could not smell such a lush forest with bare trees and floor thick with pine needles. It was as if one of my limbs had been removed. I was blind. That was the last of my understanding.

A sense of air shifting warned me of the ambush, but it was too late. A blur from the dark broadsided me, rattling my teeth and bowling me over. The aggressor melted back into the shadows of the forest as quickly and quietly as it had come. Was it another shapeshifter? I came back to my feet, rolling with the impact, the familiar metallic flavor of my own blood in my mouth. I couldn't smell or hear my adversary. Only the delicate displacement of air and the soft crush of dirt beneath my feet let me know where to give chase.

In a shocking moment, the forest floor gave way to a solid concourse as my feet slapped on concrete. Trees bled out of my vision as the forest blended into the city, seemingly locked in combat. I was struggling to see my target—like trying to watch a water droplet slide across your eye. I realized that it was faster than me even though, in all likelihood, I'm one of the oldest living shapeshifters on the planet. Nothing on Earth should be able to easily outrun me.

The hazy, dark shape continued to move silently ahead as my feet continued to smack the pavement with a noise like meaty firecrackers. There were no people on the streets—the city was an empty shell, devoid of life. A grey despair hung over the city and *I knew* that more of the country had suffered a similar fate. A calamity was fast claiming the world.

In the air, a peal of sound, a repetitive, metallic striking. Slow at first, it became more insistent and faster, one sharp tone after another until the sound blended into a long, irritating ring. I stopped short, chasing nothing as my ears began to throb with each salvo.

I was awake and confused, but not alone. I remembered the dream—if that's what it was. Had I been awake? There were no pine needles and I wore the shorts and tee shirt I'd put on last night. The last prickles of sweat worried my skin as I imagined I was losing my mind in an entirely new way.

Sunlight tinted the room orange, splashing across the back of the other couch. It had been reversed in the night. The angle of the sun meant it was late morning. Ensconced under a blanket, my vampire daughter lay still as only her kind could. She'd be unconscious until the sun set; she'd be like stone. She's stealthy, but no one can overturn a couch that quietly. Her arrival hadn't disturbed me at all. I fluttered between concern and relief that she was there. I couldn't recall the last time I'd slept late, and not because my memories had been stolen. I just don't sleep for very long.

With some indecision, I considered waiting at home until Ana awoke, but bitter experience reminded me that investigating anything to do with vampires is best done during the day. I still needed to learn more about this church and there was someone I definitely wanted to ask about it.

Thinking of Pat, I pulled the book he'd given me out from underneath some miscellaneous junk mail. I hadn't read the thing yet and I was certain the misshapen, androgynous shopkeeper was going to be upset about that. There wasn't much Pat wasn't upset about, but he'd given—sold—this book to me with a wink and a nod. It had something to do with the supposed origins of shapeshifters and vampires, but I hadn't yet had the patience to crack the spine since my power had cooled down. It was foolish of me and I resolved to read the book at my earliest opportunity. Pat wouldn't appreciate any of that, of course.

At the bottom of the stairs, before I could pull the door open that led to the stoop, I felt a familiar tingle. Maria sat on the edge of the stoop at the bottom of the steps. Droplets of the sun sprayed through the edges of her curly hair, enhancing the reddish-copper tint that came naturally to her locks. It sparkled and blended with the sheen of the gold hoops she wore. No makeup, no fingernail polish, just the simple jewelry to offer a modicum of enhancement to her full-lipped beauty.

She spoke first as I walked down the steps, "You're an asshole."

Truer words and all that. "I know."

"And you're not sorry."

"Not in the way you mean it."

She stood up, facing me on the sidewalk. The punch came without the typical shifting of weight or shoulder twitch. Maria knew how to fight—another quality I enjoyed in her. The blow struck my arm hard enough to turn me sideways and caused a muscle spasm to bloom. She'd nearly dislocated my shoulder.

I spoke through gritted teeth. "Feel better now?"

"A little bit. Where are we going?"

"Pat's bookstore." I huffed and massaged my sore shoulder back into place.

She gave a discontented grunt and fell into step with me as we headed for Pat's shop. "I hate that guy. Total pain-in-the-ass loudmouth."

"True. But, uh, he knows plenty about what happens in this city. So, you have no idea what he or…she is?"

"What do you mean?"

"Troll, dwarf, elf, what?"

"Eh, you know elves can't exist here for long."

I did know that and I'd had the unfortunate experience of being around one for the short moments she was here. Not something that should be forgotten. If the race could be judged by just the one, then they were nasty pieces of work.

Maria glanced sideways at me. "The little bastard is a boggan."

"Never heard of it."

"They're, uh... You'll have to ask Majispin. He mentioned it once; I didn't pay much attention."

So much for that. Damn, I didn't want to ask Majispin and I certainly didn't want to ask Pat. Regardless, it wasn't a problem worth digging into, merely a curiosity. Maria and I passed the rest of the walk in silence.

We didn't hold hands.

At the shop, the first thing I noticed was that the air in the place had a taste of feline in it. That was different. A number of independent book stores have cats, but Pat's had been pristine the last couple of times I'd been in. Now this. And more than one cat, as well. The rest remained the same. The scents of old paper and wood mingled with a slight mold. The storefront's windows were cemented glass blocks that allowed little more than light to show through. The high front counter served as a barrier to anyone wishing to wander into the stacks behind it. Several long rows of bookcases stretched to the rear of the store, and a spiral staircase to the left of the desk disappeared into both the ceiling and floor. The place was bigger than I knew, but Pat had never invited me behind the counter for our chats, which weren't much more than the creature being annoyed with my very presence.

Pat wasn't pleased that I hadn't read the book. It was the first thing he'd asked about when I walked into his shop and his tirade in response didn't seem to be letting up. I'd never heard such a steady stream of invective come from a single person. It was impressive. And long-winded. A glance at Maria confirmed that she was gobsmacked as well. I was going to have to figure out how to derail the..."boggan," was it?

I still had no solid ideas about Pat. The little bastard

seemed sore about everything. Just thinking about him…her…was confusing. Considering the ways in which I had fouled up relationships in the past, I settled on "he" for Pat's pronoun. I started to wonder why he was here in the States. Wouldn't he be happier with his own folk? He spoke in a kind of pidgin reminiscent of several European cultures and looked like a flesh-colored marshmallow with arms and legs. He dressed quite well, however, and knew far more than he ever let on.

"An' that's just yer face! Since ye seem to be wastin' so much time, I can give yer brain a once-over for the next few hours! In fact—"

"Pat! Damn it, you know I wouldn't just wander in here for your sunny disposition; this is important."

"Aach! 'Important,' eh? Ye've got somethin' important on yer mind, eh? Oooh, what's brought the native dog to me doorstep this time? End o' the world comin' again, 'nother conspiracy involvin' vampires?"

"Uh, maybe."

Pat stared at me for several beats and rolled his eyes dramatically. "For the love of—what, ye bloody—what is it now, what did you do?!?"

"Hold on, it's not anything I did."

"Bull! Word's all over Boston: you're a thorn what needs a pull!" Pat turned his attention to Maria and his voice dripped with saccharine-laced sarcasm, "Is that why she's here, one o' Majispin's pets?"

Maria shifted her weight, prepared to respond, and I held up a hand while trying to rub the ache in my forehead away before responding. "It's concerning some kind of church called Our Lady of—"

"Of Perpetual Death, yeah, yeah. Here!" He rummaged in the trash behind the counter and slammed a crumpled pamphlet down in front of me. "There were some sorry blood-lovers come in here a fortnight ago, proselytizin' 'n' carryin' on. I gave 'em the double-barrel and the bird when one of 'em found the courage to drop that afore they scurried out."

I remembered the cannon Pat kept behind the counter, and being mostly acquainted with the business end of the thing, I knew it could be an effective conversation stopper. The pamphlet was a crude, excessively photocopied affair on cheap paper, folded in half. The cover featured a lousy photograph of the crucifix that had been thrown at me. Below it, a poorly typeset benediction:

> For we received from the former Lord what I also delivered to you, that Jesus on the night when he was brought took bread, and when he had given thanks, he broke it, said, 'This is my body which is for you. Take this in remembrance of me.'

And inside, another:

> The cup of blessing which we bless, is it not the communion of the blood of Christ? The bread which we break, is it not the communion of the body of Christ? Christ was the savior, the shepherd of our lambs; he was of the sun, the light, the way of Man; he was the first of the lambs and we supped of him; the savior's blood is our savior, the blood of Christ; we feast of his flesh, the flesh of Christ, the flesh of Man. –Ah'na

The sign-off was unusual but reminiscent of a dozen different ways of saying "amen, or it could've been a typo. The rest of the pamphlet was a grammatically treacherous treatise relegating the human race to food status and imploring other supernatural half-breeds to repent. The church's position on humanity was clear: they wanted no part of the status quo.

I handed it to Maria.

A tiny meow sounded from behind the counter and Pat bent over, muttering platitudes. He sounded almost...kind. When he stood up, he placed a scrawny orange tabby on the counter. The cat looked me in the eye, hunched up, and hissed.

"Oooh, there's a good girl, Magdalene." Pat stroked the cat's rump and smiled at me.

I clenched my teeth and tried to finish gathering my thoughts. It was déjà vu all over again and I had no idea what this particular group might have up their collective sleeve. Which reminded me of the vampire I'd fought at the movie set. The timing of our conflict combined with this situation coming to light—I could only hope that there weren't any more like him.

At the thought of the vampire, I felt a disconcerting tremble at my core, the power driving my long life bubbling and contracting, leaving me with my hand over what was left of my heart.

Another cat hopped onto the counter, this one jet-black with bright green eyes. It hunkered down like an evil little tea cozy and growled in my direction. Pat started stroking that one as well.

"An' there's my pretty lady, Magdalene."

"You named both your cats 'Magdalene'?" Maria asked.

"As if they give a rat's ass what I name 'em, hah? Little bastards don't listen nohow, anyways." Pat turned his attention back to the cats. "Ain't that right, darlings?" And just as quick to turn vitriol back on us: "Hey! Tha's all I got here, fuzzy wuzzy; move along now, eh? Take yer bitch with ya." The boggan's caustic retort brought me back to the present. This time, I had to put a restraining hand on Maria.

Pat suddenly switched to a more saccharine delivery. "Or are ye and the lass interested in bein' payin' customers, lookin' fer books, are ye?"

"No, I—"

"Then get out, damn it, and read the bloody book I done sold ya already, imbecile! Go!"

I left the shop, pushing Maria ahead of me. It was fast becoming clear that this was how I was always going to part ways with the shopkeeper. It made me want to remember to ask Majispin about boggans one of these days. The thought reminded me of how comfortable I'd become in the last several months. Complacent. *Civilized.* It was becoming more obvious by the minute that my time had not been well spent.

Maria boiled. "That little shit. I hate coming here. He treats everyone like that. If he didn't have so much information at hand, I don't think anyone would speak to him."

"Still, I was surprised to get as much as we did."

She sighed and looked at the pamphlet again. "This is a bad thing."

I nodded in response and we walked aimlessly for a few minutes, deep in thought. My mind—likely due to proximity—kept coming back to Maria and the clearly defined hole in our relationship. The respective thing we never spoke of to each other.

"Maria."

She stopped short and stared at me with an eyebrow cocked. "That was a serious tone, Alexander. You're using the serious voice."

I grinned. A little. "The things we don't talk about between us. Things in our past. I... There's no way you can help me with mine. It was too long ago and..."

She stepped forward and touched me, put a hand on my arm. "Alexander, it's not always direct assistance that we need."

I sighed and then snorted. "There are things that I've done in the past that are not worth dredging up."

"They are worth it if they hang around your neck like a dead weight. It puts a drag on whatever you do."

"Is it that obvious?"

She just grinned and turned her head to the side.

"As obvious as what you'd been keeping from me?" I said.

That got her attention. She poked me in the chest. "You changed the subject. We were talking about *you*."

After a deep breath, I looked away, into the sky, searching for the words, if not answers. Picking over the past had never been my idea of moving forward.

"There are some pieces of information that do irreparable damage sometimes, that we would do best to keep to ourselves. Do you agree?"

"Yeah, that's life. What's your point?"

"At this point, I give some, you give some, we end up going down in flames together. Not everything needs to be known between two people."

She rocked back on her heels and crossed her arms, eyes sparkling beneath a flinty brow. "Bullshit. You're cherry-picking possibilities."

Direct. I still liked it. "What I don't want to talk about took place more than a hundred years ago. It's haunting enough and I don't particularly want to rehash it."

She chewed her lip before responding. "So, that's it?"

"What do you mean?"

"You tell me this." She uncrossed her arms and shoved her hands into her coat pockets. "You tell me just enough to piss me off. Not a day after I trusted you—"

I sighed and held my hands up. "When I lived in Saskatchewan—"

"What?"

"Canada. The province where I lived in Canada, where I grew up. There was a particularly nasty mining company owner. He tortured and murdered several of my people— the people I would prefer to be remembered as being a part of. His violence included children. The man had an acutely racist attitude—are you sure you want me to keep going?"

Maria stared at me, running the question over in her head. At least I hoped she was seriously considering not going down this road; I had no desire to rehash any of my mortifying past. "I have a son. You know the situation my only child is in."

She had a living problem, I had a dead one. "Okay. This man thought he owned everything in sight and he treated everyone as his property. He had a wife and one son at the time." I licked my lips, mouth going dry, and nodded to Maria, begging for patience with my eyes because I couldn't do it with words.

I twitched, unsure if I really could just tell Maria what it was that was eating me. The truth was one of my deepest shames and I couldn't call it an accident or a simple lapse in judgment. My actions, over a hundred years before, still rode my conscience like a vicious dog. This thing not only hung around my neck, it bit into it, bled me every day, tainted everything I did. The worst part is that it made me question every decision I'd made since then, every relationship. Ana, Tina, Maria. The kids I'd known, like Kelsey. Could I have sincere compassion anywhere in me when I'd participated in such a horrific act? Was the first step truly admitting it to yourself and everyone around you?

"I killed that man's son. I murdered that boy by inches, saw him only as a tool to teach the robber baron a lesson. And I enjoyed it. This monster, this…thing that we carry, is more than a burden on us. It's a scourge on humanity if we're not careful. Our own humanity and everyone around us. I made the wrong choice, I let it happen, and I enjoyed it."

She sobered up a bit and looked hard at me. "Jesus, you're fucked up."

Right.

CHAPTER 11

We walked in an aimless way through downtown, each of us digesting the other's history. My thoughts, however, drifted to the current problem and leaving the past behind, where it belonged. Business as usual for me, but Maria seemed on the edge of bursting. I think I was the only person to whom she'd entirely confided her story. I wondered if Majispin knew the whole thing and, if he did, why he hadn't helped. I could only assume that he didn't know; it'd be the only way I could avoid having yet another conflict with him.

I decided that maybe we could both use a time-worn distraction. "Want to get some steak? I know a place nearby."

Maria perked up a bit at the mention of beef. "That'd improve the day. A little bit."

She slipped her arm through mine and we walked to the restaurant. Midday crowds on the sidewalk parted before us on the invisible wedge our monstrous nature generated. We were able to make a beeline to the eatery without carving the zigzagging path that local pedestrians tended to adopt. The place I was thinking of had developed its own technology for searing steaks. They only used butter, parsley, and salt for seasonings—a definite plus. The large portions were right up our alley and the restaurant provided in aces.

We spent a solid two hours keeping each other

company, speaking about nothing at all. It was disturbingly normal for us. I think it was the first time we'd sat down in a restaurant and had a meal together. I believe it was when we found ourselves sharing a slice of toasted coconut pie that we began to feel uncomfortable again. *Much closer to normal.* The pie was not wasted, however, and we left the restaurant without further incident. Each of us, I'm sure, had thoughts of how we might pretend that our lives weren't the way they were, that we had a carefree future ahead of us. What it would be like if we pushed it all aside and just pretended it was all gone, that what flawed us never happened. Maria's personal problem could be fixed to a certain extent. It would require work, but some changes could be made. There was no changing my past.

Looking at being up to my neck in vampires again, my concern peaked. Nothing about this boded well and I had very limited options in the "available to assist" column. With Ana out cold for the day, I considered the short list: Majispin was lying low but needed to be informed. The club's pack was shorthanded, to say the least, with Barros out of town and the deaths of two members who'd yet to be replaced. Roberts seemed to be cracking up, and that left…Pepperman? There was no way I was going to call that asshole into this mess. I had no way of contacting the Queen of Dragons—the very thought of her brought a shiver to every cell in my body. My indebtedness to her was a terrifying backdrop, waiting for her to find me one day and call in the chip. Best not to even think of the possibility.

I considered calling Majispin when we passed a pay phone near a downtown train station. Then I resolved to inquire with Ana about getting a mobile phone. It'd be simpler overall if Maria could let Majispin know when she got to work. There was no need for the magician and me to antagonize each other right now.

"Majispin needs to know what's happening."

"Yeah, *we* need that. I'll tell him about this vampire church."

The warm afternoon air enveloped us in a cornucopia of greasy and rotting scents from society's unnatural garbage. I hadn't missed Maria's emphasis; there was nothing else for me to do but accept it. I grimaced and a glance told me that she remained unaffected by the stink in the air. I was sure that inside, she was a turmoil of emotion. It was a worry she'd had years of practice keeping under lock and key. I had some idea of what it meant to worry about your child's safety. And to keep your feelings buried.

"Tell him they have an agenda, that it's something to worry about, and this vampire, Graamvater... I don't know why he's looking for Ana and I can only assume he's associated with the church."

"Too much coincidence."

"It'll get your boss's attention."

"You got that right. I'll call him before I go in tonight."

Maria placed a strong hand on my rib cage, part caress, part suggestion, and leaned in. I didn't hesitate and bent to kiss her. Soft lips reminded me of what worked between us. She grinned and walked away. As she did, the guilt and doubts flowed in like a tide, washing away any lines that we'd drawn in the sand. I sighed and tried to move on. There was nowhere else to go but forward, the only direction I ever felt comfortable with.

"Maria, wait!"

She turned back, halfway across the street, and met me at the edge of the sidewalk with a quizzical look on her face.

"What's his name, your son?"

She smiled a bit, her face a mix of sorrow and relief. "Alejandro Juan Sandoval."

"If I can..."

She nodded and bustled off.

Before I forgot, I made a note in my book and made sure to highlight it.

I knew I needed a sympathetic vampire, and that was always going to be Ana. She seemed to have a strong understanding of what was going on socially within the loose-knit community. I hoped this would be no different. With this particular monster looking for her, she needed to be warned and I needed to be with her. On that thought, I headed home.

It was nearing sunset when I got to the Fenway. Less than an hour before we had to start worrying about the old vamp. By now, Maria would have told Majispin about the situation and his conscience would be stewing. It almost made me smile.

The familiar scents of death tickled the edges of my senses. As I entered the foyer of the building, a more predatory mode overtook me. The power surged, causing my skin to burn. The smell of blood was strong in the air.

Ana wouldn't spring up early and go on a rampage with the neighbors. I repeated that to myself and rolled any other possibilities over in my mind. There was death upstairs. And so was my daughter.

I charged up, following the scent, and found my apartment door ajar. Ana was gone. It was early, but not too early for her to have moved on her own. Which didn't explain the blood scent. Wet iron and copper wafted on the air, strongest on my floor. I stepped back into the hallway and listened closely, hearing nothing. Not the shift of garments, not the shuffle of feet, not a breath or any of the usual sounds people made at home. None of the doors were locked, all were damaged. I only had to glance in one to know that every apartment on the floor held the same grisly ruin of death: people sucked dry, throats rent.

A metallic scraping and a thump drew my attention to the basement. I scrambled downstairs, taking them two at a time, twirling around the landings. Slamming the door open, I plunged into the gloom of the basement. It had sounded heavy, whatever it was, thick and heavy. The dirt on one of several large drainage grates was disturbed in the floor. An opening far too small for me to pass through, but not so for a vampire. Even carrying another vampire.

Outside, I crashed into the failing sunlight. Ignoring any foot traffic, I popped the top on the nearest manhole, dropped in, and backtracked to the building. I found the drainage point and evidence of someone passing through, but no scents, nothing to trace. A chilling sense of déjà vu passed through me and I went on high alert. Around me, shadows melted from the walls. The last time I'd been in a sewer, I'd been attacked by multiple vampires. This time, I managed to surprise them. I turned and plowed through the nearest bloodsucker, leaving him on his back in the muck.

I made my way further down to another access point and exited through the manhole there. A vampire poked his head up, reaching for me, and got a taste of the last rays of Sol. I dropped the cover on his smoking head. The final tendrils of light were dissolving on the horizon and I had no idea what to do next. Panic leapt into my heart, thudding solidly in my ribcage. Fear gripped me. *This was my daughter and she was gone.* Somehow, she was gone, and I floundered in fear. I couldn't track her. I couldn't call the police, couldn't rely on anyone. I was alone in this; there was no one to call. *Maria.* I could call her; she would back me up. As I headed back toward my building, I heard the clunk and scrape of the cover. I hadn't expected them to chase me so readily in public.

I needed to get back into my apartment and use the

phone. I hoped Maria'd be home soon. If not, she'd be at the club. I kicked myself again for not having a mobile phone. Maria had one and I could have reached her at that number. There were more than a few people on the street as I raced down the block with pale men and women chasing me. Bystanders looked on in curiosity until I unholstered a pistol and fired it into the dirt of a small yard. People screamed and scattered, streaming away from me and my pursuers. It left me an opportunity to turn and take a knee, only to be surprised by a hot round zinging past my head and ricocheting off the pavement behind me. They were armed; the bastards were learning.

I squeezed off two rounds into the chest of the lead vampire. He spasmed and flopped onto his back. I knew it wouldn't kill him, but .45 rounds weren't called "man-stoppers" for nothing. More bullets flew in my direction as they attempted to scatter for cover. I made every shot count, knocking vampires off their feet with bullets hitting them at center mass. I reloaded, popped off two more shots to keep them occupied, and sped off to my building.

The little blond boy sat on the curb, watching me as I passed. He shook his head slowly as blood from his wounds puddled at his feet and slithered through the gutter. Guilt and sorrow clogged the back of my throat. I nearly let go at that moment, loosing my power in a flare which would help no one. The distinct clatter of my old phone drifted to my ears. Without thinking, I raced back up the stairs and snatched the receiver from the cradle.

"Alexander!" Maria's panicked voice came over the line; there was a crash in the background. "I need your help! There's—" Another crash, thumps of footsteps, furniture scraping, and the grunts of fighting. Hissing, scrabbling of claws.

Disconnect.

Footsteps pounded up the stairs to my apartment. This was all happening too fast and I needed to adapt before I was put down. Our lives were crumbling before us and it was never more obvious that someone had planned for our demise. I made a wild choice and plunged into the hallway, moving low to the top of the stairs before they could mount the landing. A bullet slashed across my neck, leaving a searing trail, and another pinged into the plaster near my head sending a spray into my face. Amateurs. They wanted a head shot so bad, they were throwing bullets high.

I slammed into the first vampire, pushing the barrel of his weapon up and jamming my pistol into his mouth. As we toppled on the undisciplined lot behind him, I kept pulling the trigger. Round after round exited the back of his head, thudding into the others as we all tumbled down the stairs in a heap. Hot brass pinged off my forehead and one or two settled in my shirt. I rode their pliable bodies to the bottom, where they cushioned my fall, some bursting into oily puddles. Unholstering my second pistol, I pumped the full magazine into them and bolted out the door.

The first time I had visited Maria's apartment, I was unconscious, and only later did I learn the address. Since then, I'd come often under my own power and learned repeatedly that she was a passionate lover and equal to me in being incapable of sharing what held us back. I thought that might have evolved now, but there were still some things I needed to share with her—with someone I cared about. Foolish decisions from my past that still haunted me, still brought a deep shame to the pit of my stomach. The insanity of a nameless ghost flitting in and out of my life was still too strange to share despite our odd lives, but I could try. The dread of never having the opportunity to find out otherwise drove my legs as I ran.

Somewhere on the journey to her apartment, with the blood of vampires dissolving from my hands and face, I felt a familiar flare of hot energy between us. Familiar because I'd felt it when Mark was impaled on a dying tree in the courtyard of a dying community. As then, I instinctively grasped at the tendril of power, only this time it slid through my metaphysical hands like a thin rope, cutting heat across my palms, leaving a disorienting sensation in my body and an ache in my heart.

As I rounded the corner of her block, I could see someone sitting on her stoop. Pale, smallish, a mop of blond hair on his head. My ghost. I hurried forward, moving quickly down the empty street. He was in one of the worst states of decay I'd yet seen, cradling the stump of his arm, blue and black bruises blossomed all over his skin, and the puncture wounds in his torso leaked down the steps to pool with the ghostly ichor which flowed from his arm. One eye had collapsed, but the other rolled toward me and remained frozen, fixed on my person. I walked up the stairs, knowing what I'd find, and his eye followed me until his neck craned and continued its turn so that his face hovered over his spine. He crumbled in degradation down the stairs and out of sight. I entered the building, already knowing the truth.

At this proximity, I could typically sense Maria. Her energy tended to spark against mine, an unusual attraction. No more. *Nothing.* The door to her apartment was closed, but the jamb was cracked. It drifted open at my barest touch, the bolt having torn the catch from the wall where it had been forced. The apartment wasn't in ruins as I'd expected.

There was a tear in the divan I'd awoken on during my first visit. The coverlet I'd been under, jumbled on the floor next to it. Other furniture had been moved, but none overturned. They were fast; she'd been overwhelmed after they broke in. There was one long and moist stain near the slightly charred spot where she'd died. Maria had taken one of them with her.

I placed my palm in the last place she'd existed and spread my fingers in the remnants, feeling the inert ash beneath my fingertips. A human wetness dropped from my eyes and soaked into the spots between my fingers—an unexpected and honest experience. I felt like a rudderless thing, floating without a course through what passed for my life nowadays.

Her phone rang. It had an old-fashioned clapper, insistent and overbearing, reminding me of my own phone and the odd little congruence between us that I always enjoyed. I stared at the thing, incredulous at the coincidence, nowhere close to believing it could be for me. Then I snatched it from the cradle and held it to my ear, listening.

"Alexander?"

Kelsey.

"You need to stop this foolishness." Her harsh whisper crackled across the line and her last word rolled off her tongue awkwardly. It was not a part of her usual vocabulary, I could tell.

"Where are you, Kelsey? What have you done?"

"I ain't your concern; leave me alone."

"Whose concern are you? The church? The people profiteering while you have sex on camera? Who?"

The rustle of the phone being switched from one ear to the other. "You have to stop this, stop interfering in my life."

"This isn't a life, Kelsey; you're buying into something that can't possibly succeed."

"Oh, really? And what you do is a successful life?"

Point for her. It wasn't. But that wasn't the only outcome of what I did to survive this long. "You've been given a second chance and a third. I don't know how many more you're going to get. Give this up; tell me where the church is."

"You're going to Hell. You know that? The real one. You resist what you really are, you deny it, and it's going to be your end."

"You don't have to be a part of this cycle over and over; you can break it. I'll help you, if you want."

"There's no 'help,' only salvation. I am saved, I'm with those who truly love me. Your...path is unjust."

"I know you're different now. Life is different for you now. There's a whole new future for you that does not need to be defined by other people."

"People like you?"

Inwardly, I sighed, this was going to be tricky and I was desperate. I wanted her to think for herself—needed her to. I needed her to help me find Ana. "Not like me, not like anyone. I want you to make your own decisions. Whatever you hear is for your consideration; it's not something you have to do."

"So, you're not telling me what to do?" She said it with such contempt that I began to wonder how much I'd been on her mind in the intervening years.

"No, I'm not. But I don't want you to make a mistake that's going to cost someone else a person they love." Stress had my heart pounding. This woman held the key to my daughter's life in her hands and seemed unwilling to acknowledge that. Even if she likely didn't know, I believed it unlikely that she had no idea what the church was up to.

"Futility." Again, another word that stumbled off her tongue. "That's what you embody."

"Those aren't your words, Kelsey; it's not who you are."

"You don't know me; you don't care about me! Where were you the last time?" She chewed out her last words and choked off a sob.

The last time? Her last crisis. Oh, gods, when she was

turned. "I don't know where I was, Kelsey. I couldn't find you after the last time. You fled; I didn't think you wanted me to find you again." *Great spirits, what had I set in motion when I saved this girl from her father?*

"I thought I'd finally found something I could do well. I wasn't on drugs anymore, but I could still *fuck* like no one's business. I could do that and I was going to make it in the business, I was determined, I earned good money. Then that bastard—said he was a fan—found me... He found me and he..." She began humming, a warbling, toneless sound, a sadness world-weary enough to weigh my flawed heart down.

So much had happened to her at such a young age. She'd lived more than one lifetime in the space it took others to reach legal voting age. Now she was looking into an abyss and making diving motions. How many more were there like her in my wake? How many kids grew up to be monsters? *What could I do about it?* My mind stumbled over itself trying to imagine the possibilities. All the children I hadn't kept track of, the ones that didn't seem like they'd be useful in the future. I'd thought of them as nothing but tools, stepping-stones for me to stave off my madness and get to my future. It needed to end, that much was clear, but there was no cleaning this up; I doubted I could backtrack and fix any of them even if I wanted to.

"I'm...sorry. I didn't want any of this to happen to you." It was all I had and it was worth shit, as usual, because I got the usual contemptuous response.

"It doesn't matter; you're all going to die. I'm going to be protected. I'll be safe now. The Rapture is coming and it's going to be your end."

"I don't believe that. *Help me,* Kelsey; help me find my daughter."

"Just like it ended your girlfriend, just like it's going to end your daughter—another denier. She'll be someone new, soon, a better vampire. Like me."

What the hell did that mean? The mention of Ana set my head on fire. Kelsey did know. A pure rage bubbled up my throat which I barely checked. Blasting Kelsey with angry words wouldn't get my little girl back. I knew this, but I did it anyway. "You damn well better listen to me, Kelsey—"

"Stop calling me that! I'm Alexa now; it's what I choose—not you, not my daddy, not that fucker who made me this, no one *controls* me—"

"Stop being a child, and tell me where my daughter is!"

Kelsey's voice wavered. "No, you—"

"You can't possibly believe they're trying to help you! This church is a one-way ticket to the end of your existence; you have to help me fix this. Let me help you; tell me where you are."

"I... I am a *vampire.* This is where I belong. Not with you. You can't *help* me; I've already been saved." The sounds of fumbling came from her end of the phone and silence followed.

"Kelsey, wait. Goddammit. Kelsey!" I slammed the phone down hard enough to crack its plastic casing. It was enough to make me remember where I was and what had just happened. I felt regret for causing the damage and struggled to calm myself. I used Maria's phone to make one call and left a message.

Swallow the guilt. Swallow it and stuff it away with the rest, I could take it, it wouldn't kill me. Not yet, no, but someday it might. Until then, forward at all costs. *Always goddamn forward.*

I took several deep breaths inside Maria's apartment, absorbing the scent, recollecting the last pleasant memory I had there. And with the sun below the horizon, its light struggling to maintain the barest of appearances, I made for my next destination. I started running toward the safe house. I needed insight and answers, I needed to save someone, I needed *help*. There were precious few people I cared about and they were dropping away in a manner and at a pace that I couldn't bear. Ignoring any startled looks, I ran as fast as I could, weaving through traffic, cutting down greenways and across the Common through downtown.

I burst into the club at a speed that brought eyes up in wary glances. Benjamin stared at me with his eyebrows slammed firmly together above his nose.

"What happened to y—"

"Where's Majispin?"

"You know I can't—"

"Damn it!" I slammed my hand on the bar, bringing even more attention.

"Alexander, you've got to calm down."

"Where's Majispin?"

"You know I can't—"

"*Benjamin. Maria's been murdered.*" The gravity clinging to the utterance of his name and the news that followed stiffened the barkeep. I sloshed power across the room, at least two people jumped, and the gigantic worms in the tank curled into themselves. I was again in danger of cutting loose. The light behind my eyes flickered in what threatened to be a violent blackout until I wrested control back.

Getting angry here would do nothing to help Ana or avenge Maria. I needed answers, not blood. *Answers first, blood later.* I held my hands up to Benjamin, palms forward, imploring him to wait a moment. The hunger, an urge to kill, bubbled in a pool of menace. My fear and anger were an opportunity for the monster, a weak spot that could be wedged open and allow it to run loose again. No more innocent victims, never again.

The bartender stuttered and managed to squeak out a few words. "I... When? How?"

"There but for the grace of Our Lady is our wildly

ignorant cousin, brothers."

Every stretch of nerve from the top of my head to my feet electrified in a maddening arc ending in my closed fists. This interruption I welcomed. The three bloodsucking numbskulls—one of whom had tossed a crucifix at me—now stood not three feet away. At the moment, I couldn't think of a better way of finding the church that didn't involve physically extracting the information from their brains.

"Charlie, knock it off; let's go."

"David, just a moment; I need to enlighten—"

Benjamin knew I still had my pistols, but it wasn't clear to everyone else in the room until I drew them on the three vampires. Blondie—Charlie—was going to die first; I was sure of it. His more sensible friends were going to follow shortly after, when I had the information I needed. My back had been to them and they hadn't seen the motion to pull them as I turned. The barrel of one pistol pressed firmly into Charlie's mouth through broken teeth and the other pointed square at David's chest. The third vampire froze in place, unsure of what to do. Young vamps, unused to violence. My exact opposite on the spectrum. Too bad for them.

The pistols felt wrong and I realized the weight was off. The one in my left hand was empty and the one in my right only had one or two bullets in it. I hadn't counted my shots earlier or reloaded. Stupid. They didn't need to know that, however. One or two bullets would be enough.

"Now we know what the next thing into your mouth was, Charlie, let me tell you what's going to be coming out the back of your head."

The club patrons behind the trio vacated their seats posthaste.

"Don't do this, Alexander," Benjamin reasonably said. "There are too many consequences if you do this. And they're dire; you know it."

I ignored my friend's advice and continued. "My day hasn't been so great, Charlie." The vampires took my appearance in, their eyes betraying their thoughts. They were in too deep, faster than they'd ever expected. "Tell me the church's exact location, David, if only because I've been itching to kill someone for the last half hour. It doesn't have to be you."

Charlie shook his head furiously, casting warning glances at his friend. My finger tightened on the trigger with deliberate drama; I wanted Charlie to see the hammer going back.

"Alexander!" Majispin's voice cut across the room.

I didn't take my eyes off of my three victims; there was vital information to be had. I could see Majispin peripherally, standing stiff and angry, leaning on his cane—a necessary aid since the vampire attack the last year. I wanted to tell him to mind his business, to leave me before he suffered further injury, but Majispin was the ultimate authority here. We were standing on his premises, under his jurisdiction. It was only a matter of time before he was forced to react.

"Where. Is. The church?" Ana's plight and Maria's final destiny hovered in my mind.

"Damn it, Alexander, you know the only reason you're not dead right now, you know it. Put those weapons down. Now."

I heard the telltale clack of Majispin's cane on the floor as he limped in my direction. The rage took me unexpectedly, an eruption born from frustration that had been capped for too long. I felt like I was going to explode and it manifested as a roar.

"WHERE IS MY DAUGHTER?"

"*Praestringo!*" With a gesture, Majispin threw power.

My right hand took on a few extra pounds. A two-inch thick layer of ice encased my hand, the cold crackling up to Charlie's mouth, leaving a fine powder of ice crystals on his face. The sudden use of magic in such proximity brought an accompanying pain. I couldn't pull the trigger; my hand was numb, frozen. My other hand, however, was free but packing an empty weapon.

"Stop this now!" Majispin had the temerity to grab my arm. "*Please.*"

The vampire howled from the back of his throat and jerked away, his companions catching his arms. He shook his head and pawed at his freezing face. "You ignorant— You can't kill a cause! We are more than you'll ever be! You will never find us, never be a part of the truth that mills the faithful right under your murdering eyes! We rise in solidarity!"

Majispin stepped around me, a smoldering heat gathering in his palms, and a ripple of utter contempt crossed his features. "Get out of my house. *Now.* You're *banned*, all of you. Never return!"

There was a flash of light and warmth I could feel through my clothes. The crowd around us gasped and fell back anew. The three vamps scrambled for the exit while Majispin held me in place with a palm to my chest, energy crackling against my aura, keeping my feet in place with a tingling not unlike electric current zipping up and down my spine. I watched the only place I thought I could find answers fade away.

"Mr. Majispin." Benjamin's voice sounded distant to me, as if my hearing it were an afterthought.

"Hold that thought, Benjamin. Alexander..."

I holstered the pistol in my left hand, feeling the tingle of healing spreading through the fingertips on my right. "Damn it, Majispin!" I brought my hand down hard on the bar, shattering the ice and releasing the freeze; bits of ice scattered. "They were the only lead I had for finding Ana!" Massaging my hand as life came back to the frostbitten skin, I slumped back against the bar.

Benjamin's voice again, a more insistent tone: "Mr.

Majispin."

"Benjamin, just a minute."

The magician looked at me long and hard, as if he were trying to peer into my past. Before I could say any more, he spoke. "This…explains much, if I heard you correctly. I'm sorry, but regardless of our past, I couldn't allow you to do what you were planning."

The only answer I had for him was a glare.

"Alivara!"

"Damn it, what is it, Benjamin? What's so important *right now?*"

"Maria's dead."

Majispin absorbed that information while staring at me. No one spoke as the room cleared in earnest. When we were the only ones remaining, he twitched and asked me, "What did you do?" Frost tinged every word.

Why the hell did everyone think I'd set this off? *"It's not what I did,* Majispin; it's the fucking vampires around here. Do you think I allowed this to happen, that I wanted it? These bastards can't simply exist anymore; they need to measure their self-worth against how hard they can step on someone else's neck! The damned church is fallout from the coven."

Or was it? I was angry at Majispin but couldn't justify directing this particular malice toward him. My emotions spent, I needed a different straw to grasp. That the church was the direct result of our last caper was an easy explanation. Too easy. Graamvater complicated matters. It was rare to find a church that sprang, simple and pure, from the goodness of any community and rose to popularity with such speed. Graamvater had to be at the root of this somewhere, the evil bastard.

"Then its fortunate that Barros isn't here for you to somehow get him killed, too!"

"That's bullshit and you know it; I am not responsible for their deaths." Even as I said it, I didn't feel like it was true. I hadn't brought the situation to Boston, but I'd stumbled upon it first. If I hadn't needed their help or if they had refused... Could they have? While working for Majispin, could they have chosen *not* to get involved? Wouldn't the situation have spilled over into the safe-house system eventually? We'd never know. "Their sacrifices hadn't been for nothing, Majispin. You have to recognize that."

Majispin slid onto a barstool and rubbed his temples before looking up at me. "She was good."

"She was." I agreed and the awkward moment became disconcerting for me. Not for the usual reasons, but because it reminded me of Maria. What we shared, more than anything, were significant personal problems. This was the second relationship with a woman that I'd left incomplete or in tatters. I marveled at the fact that there were only two in my lifetime.

Majispin sighed and adjusted his suit jacket before shutting down his attitude. "How are they even cooperating again? I wouldn't think a church would be enough to pull them together, but... Am I to believe that this church has stolen Ana somehow? Is that even possible?"

Once again, Majispin doubted information he'd not uncovered himself. It was a flaw in the magician's makeup, along with his poisonous dabbling. I unclenched my teeth and tried to use my brain for a moment. My daughter wasn't a vampire to be trifled with. It would need to have been someone formidable to have taken her. And just before sunset at that. "Not the church, not exactly. I think this old one—"

"The tactile telepath...that Maria told me about?"

"Yes. I think he may have taken her. With a touch he can—I don't know—invade your mind, attack from the inside out. I'm sure he's attached to the church somehow."

"You have proof of the connection?"

"No. Not since you let my only options run out the door. Ana's gone and all the while, you've been holed up, hiding."

"The local vampires have been agitated enough; there was no reason for me to be out here riling them up any more than necessary. We have you for that, and clearly you don't need my help doing it. Why couldn't she have left of her own volition?"

"Because my daughter does not come to me one day and disappear before the next."

Majispin rocked back in his seat, considered what I'd said, and licked his lips. I realized then that he'd not suspected my true relationship with Ana and what I'd just said was final confirmation of words uttered during my tantrum earlier. "Why would he have taken her?"

I finally gave voice to what I'd been thinking since I'd met the monster. True or not, Graamvater believed what I didn't want to believe. After tumbling around in his memories, however, I had to accept it. "He's her grandsire, I think. Ana is the product of a revenant vampire that this bastard created. I have no idea why he took her." I couldn't remember the last time my voice sounded so deflated, undeniably broken.

We stewed in silence for a few moments. I wondered if Majispin could keep himself on track after the juicy news about Ana. I kept reviewing my run-ins with the three stooges over the past couple of days, and something about this last confrontation nagged at me. What had Charlie said as his friends dragged him away?

Majispin said, "All right, look. I have contacts outside of Massachusetts. Let's head to my office and I'll give them a call. Maybe I can find out—"

"No. Wait." *What had he said?* "That idiot blond, what were his last words? 'Milled right under your nose,' right? That's an odd choice of words for anyone to use. These conspiracy zealots seem to enjoy rubbing noses in allusions to whatever secret plan they've got going."

Benjamin stepped back into the conversation. "You think that's a literal reference? To what, a factory?"

"It makes some sense." Majispin fingered the handle of his cane thoughtfully. "But I can't imagine where in this small city that'd be possible without people stumbling over it."

"'Right under your noses,' he said. 'Milled.' I know there are plenty of old mill towns here, but how much of that was in Boston?" I needed to see old maps of the city. "I have to go to the library." The topography of Boston had changed significantly when the Back Bay was filled in.

"Alexander, wait."

"I'm through waiting, Majispin; I don't have time to—"

"Stop being so damned headstrong! The information you're seeking is online; you can use the computer in my office. Right here, right now. Or you can run along downtown and break into the Copley Library."

I still wasn't accustomed to having people around me; it had been too long. Especially people who might be useful. This was the worst I'd felt in years and I knew better than to behave like this, given my history in Boston. Still, when the opportunity presented itself, I'd backpedaled to old habits and it wasn't helping.

"Okay. Okay, yes, that'd be best."

Majispin rolled his eyes at what was likely the closest thing he'd ever get from me resembling an expression of thanks. When he turned and limped ahead, I followed.

We made our way up the private staircase nearest the loading dock at the back of the building. It led to Majispin's offices and laboratory. Inside, we were greeted by the same austere wood paneling and exotic rugs. The wingback chairs were in the same place and we passed straight through to the lab. Inside, on the same steel table, where one of the club's naive employees had been violently drained of her blood, a brass contraption…floated. It hung a few centimeters above the table, a chaotic mess of pipes and joints leading up to a concave platform. The whole thing was about the footprint of an old television; a man's arms could barely get around it.

"What is that?"

"It's a device that Dr. Bismark and I tinkered up when we were sharing projects. He could send things to me and vice versa. Now that he's dead, however, I'm disposing of it. It's going to take a while to deconstruct the device."

I knew Bismark had somehow survived the vampire coven's attack after I'd last seen him. He'd been coerced by the conspirators into giving me misleading information, but the crafty alchemist had managed to slip the noose and enabled me to find the coven. Shortly after that had been resolved, I'd received a clay-smudged letter from the good doctor. I had never told Majispin and, it seems, neither did Bismark.

In a small study off the lab, Majispin had a nook of an office. Keeping with the decor of his anteroom, the office was appointed in warm and dark colors. On a small desk of smooth walnut, intricately carved with writhing figures scrambling up the sides from an inferno, a screen and keyboard waited.

"Before we get into this, I don't suppose there's any chance that you've swallowed anything that might be helpful?"

I gave Majispin a nasty look. "No."

He was referring to a spell he'd used to track the coven. Its central component had been a hand I'd managed to bite off. It had tasted bad going down and even worse coming up. Not this time, however.

He shrugged. "Eh. Just checking. I'd be willing to bet this telepath left an imprint in your mind, however."

That gave me pause. "What do you mean?"

"It means he was walking all over your brain and you were all over his. There's probably a shadow in there." He tapped his own head. "Something connecting you two, however tenuously."

I thought hard about that while Majispin continued speculating.

"In fact, I'd wager the more often he does it, the stronger the connection, the deeper the imprint."

Now I started to worry. Graamvater had only been inside my mind once, but he had Ana. The longer he had her, the more damage he was going to be able to do.

"You think you can pull something out of my head to track him?"

Majispin grinned, a wicked curve of his lips and narrowing of his eyes. It only accentuated my agitation. "Maybe. Let me grab a few things."

I sat down to stew while Majispin puttered around in another room. This was a long shot; I could feel it. I was open to a Hail Mary, but this seemed sketchier than usual. I didn't particularly want Majispin in my mind. After Graamvater, he was probably second on the list of people I knew who were better kept at a distance when it came to personal matters.

Majispin returned with a few items wrapped in burlap. He unrolled the bundle on the desk. A pungent odor lit up my nose. Sulphur. Some kind of pine oil, and chalk. Of everything in the roll, the most concerning was the dagger.

"What the hell's the knife for?"

His hand moved swiftly over the items, rearranging the burlap so that it was flat and everything else was to the side.

"Penetration." He grabbed the chalk and drew a rough circle and began filling in the margins with symbols I didn't recognize.

"Stabbing. Yeah, I know that. Why do you need it here now?"

He paused, regarding his work, and never looked at me when he replied, "You don't want to know."

I looked at the dagger again. It was a slim, shiny blade

mounted on a stone handle wrapped in rope. "Majispin!"

"All right, fine! The dagger will be enchanted to penetrate your mind. When it's withdrawn, I should be able to use the psychic residue to—"

"You are not going to stab me in the head."

"You're being dramatic."

"Am I?"

Majispin pursed his lips and ran his tongue around his mouth when he met my eyes. Then he cut away and said, "Not really, no."

I stood up, ready to leave. "That dagger is not going into my brain, Majispin."

"Listen, it will be enchanted, shifted to the psychic plane. I won't even be able to hold it without this." He pulled a glove out of his pocket. "You probably won't even notice."

"That's complete bullshit."

He twitched in response. "You can go on your hunch or we can try this. I think this is the better option."

"Of course you do! With this option, you get to stick a magic blade in my head."

"I won't deny some...interest in the procedure."

"Oh, fuck this." I made for the door and was halfway through when Majispin's voice stopped me.

"What wouldn't you do for your daughter?"

I wanted to say, "Get stabbed in the head," but it wouldn't be true. I closed the door and slunk back to the chair. Majispin didn't even try to contain his glee.

"Excellent!"

After using the chalk on the burlap, he next rubbed oil and sulphur on the knife blade. What I thought was the bastard humming to himself became a murmur. I could feel the magic in the room build; the hairs on my body stood up and my skin began the run from becoming uncomfortable to unbearable. He never made it to a full shout, but his voice was loud when he finished and a jolt of energy bowed my spine.

Majispin smiled at me. "Sorry. All done. Here, look."

I massaged my temples and stretched my back. The knife lay in the chalk circle on the burlap. Majispin reached for it with his bare hand and his fingers met the desk. The dagger remained untouched. He pulled the glove on and picked it up effortlessly.

"Just try to relax."

I barely resisted giving him the finger. When he plunged the damned thing into my head, I regretted the restraint.

It felt like a piece of ice had been slipped between my ears. The room went black and pain shot down my arms and legs. I wondered if my fingertips and toes had exploded. When I came to, I was breathing raggedly, slumped in the chair, a fine sweat dampening my armpits.

Majispin hummed to himself while examining the blade. He saw me staring hatred at him and said, "What? Was it so bad?"

"Want to trade places?" My voice was raw.

"Point taken." He cleared his throat. "There isn't as much here as I'd hoped."

Swell.

He wiped the blade on the burlap and crumbled the chalk into the center before tying the whole thing off with twine. Then he held the improvised sack in his palm and weighed it with his eyes closed for a few moments. When he opened them, he looked disappointed.

"No. No, this won't work." He dropped the sack into the garbage.

I gripped the sides of the chair, counting the ways I could kill him, and said, "Log me in to the computer. Now." I tried to make it sound as much like *when this is over, I'm going to kill you slowly.*

Majispin ambled over to the rolling chair. "You'll want to look at the Norman B. Leventhal Map Center collection. They've digitized the entire series of maps in the archive. It's all available online through the BPL's website." He logged in to the machine and within a few keystrokes, the Map Center's website came up. He rose and waved for me to have a seat. "Show me what you're thinking."

I wanted to show him the insides of his chest, but that would be counterproductive. Instead, I ran over what I could remember. I needed to find mills in Boston. I selected a collection titled "Growth and Development of Boston During the Nineteenth Century."

To Majispin, I said, "It's just a hunch. A safe place for a group of vampires to congregate could be underground, out of sight of both prying eyes and the sun. Maybe there were nineteenth-century mill projects buried when the bay was filled in."

The magician made a noncommittal noise over my right shoulder, acknowledging my spoken thought. He didn't sound convinced. Looking at the collection, it was clearer than ever that the Back Bay had been a massive landfill project; it had changed the shape of this city forever. The ocean used to fetch up quite a bit farther into the city's limits than any non-supernatural person could remember.

I filtered the maps by location and then by subject: "City Planning." There was one detailing the reconstruction of the shoreline, and there was one mill on that map, a gigantic tidal mill that stretched for hundreds of feet along what was now Beacon Street. Flipping forward in time, the one significant structure on the project was somewhere near the Harvard Bridge.

"There." I pointed. I stood up, removed my pistols and

popped the empty magazines out. Majispin seemed taken aback and I realized that I was inside his club, fully armed. I slammed in two full magazines and re-holstered the weapons.

Majispin made a skeptical face, shaking off his earlier surprise at the lapse in security. "Maybe. Wait—you're going now?"

I had a target, an area to search, and for only the second time in over a century, I was concerned for my daughter's safety.

Damn right I'm going now.

CHAPTER 12

Where Massachusetts Avenue met the Charles River via the Harvard Bridge, I hustled down the walkway to the riverbank. A bike path wound its way along the bank and the occasional rider or jogger whizzed past. All of this seemed too open, but I scoured the underside of the bridge where it met the embankment anyway. Cars whipped by on the river way, their mechanical hum amplified by the steel underside of the bridge overhead. In the gloom, I could make out a space where the bridge became an overpass on the other side. Silhouettes huddled in the murk.

Rather than possibly cause some kind of incident where a driver spotted me on the roadway and called the cops, I shimmied up a girder and scooted across overhead, all the way hoping a truck wouldn't come along and scrape me off. On the other side, I came down just where soil met concrete and crept into the darkness. At this proximity, I could smell discarded humanity above the oil and exhaust. The homeless huddled here. Some of them startled as I passed, and like a wave, one after the other turned wide eyes in my direction. None of them spoke, but they cringed and pulled their meager possessions closer. I moved on, disappointed that they weren't prey and saddened that they often were.

I knew I was in the area I'd targeted on the map, so I headed farther down the road to an overpass knot that served Kenmore Square and other destinations. In amongst the unkempt berms at the center, an entrance might be hidden. This time, I caught no scent of humanity. Instead, detritus from the traffic careening around me had gathered. No signs of any kind of recent activity, nothing disturbed by anything bipedal. The amount of overgrown weeds and such would betray anyone's recent passing. I kicked an old soda can hard and it zipped off the ground into the street where it was immediately crushed by a speeding vehicle.

This search only made sense as far as the BU Bridge; after that it was an entirely different Boston, unaffected by the shoreline changes. My heart began to tighten at the idea of finding nothing more than the underside of filthy old New England construction out here. Giving up any pretense of nonchalance, I ran farther west until I passed a boathouse and the path took a sharp turn to a wooden footbridge underneath what looked like an abandoned railway. The railway, in turn, ran beneath the bridge, bisecting it at an angle. Floorboards rattled as I moved too fast across it, scanning the cement and overgrowth where bridge met land. Frustrated, I turned back from the other end and took a deep breath, forcing some semblance of calm.

The rattle of the bridge warned me that someone was approaching on a bicycle. The hum at the back of my head warned me that my beast was becoming impatient. I reached out with my senses and waited for the cyclist to pass. The scent of sweat, oily rubber, and chain grease flashed in my nose, followed by the overpowering wetness of the Charles, rotting wood, and eternal plastic. I picked my way through it all looking for anything out of the ordinary. Nothing but plants, soil, grease, and garbage. Iron and concrete. Fiberglass, paint, Styrofoam. I listened for what seemed an interminable amount of time: traffic, lapping water, scratching. I focused on the scratching, following it back to the end of the footbridge I'd started upon. A rat scrambled out of a pipe near the base of the bridge, disappearing into the undergrowth. The pipe was wide. Wide enough for a person to squeeze through—easy enough for a vampire—but at least one-third submerged. No other sounds to indicate anything larger than a rat escaping the dark hole.

My head felt like it was going to burst. Ana had been raised during the height of the Industrial Revolution. She was comfortable with technology and city life in ways that I still had trouble grasping. I remember she'd once begged to have a photo portrait done. It was one of the precious few photographs that existed of us together, and I wondered if she still kept it somewhere. At the time, she'd been younger than her current teenage appearance. Truly a little girl, still wide-eyed and optimistic at a world she couldn't participate in with any true normalcy. Photography was still in its nascent phase along with so much else, and she loved the mechanics of it all. My chest tightened and I swallowed a knot that fluttered around in my belly.

I leaned over the railing, ready for defeat, crumpling emotionally, the slowest train wreck in existence. As I doubled over the rail, that barest closing of the distance between myself and the outlet brought a fresh sound to my ears, that of many voices in harmony. Chanting came to me as gently as a mist of rain.

My first impulse was to hop the rail and crawl through the pipe. But that couldn't be how anyone was getting in there with any regularity, however, and I resolved to check the surroundings more carefully. With more than a little desperation, I began combing the grounds, searching for any kind of regular disturbance or revealing scuffs. I thought there might be some kind of false wall or sliding stairs at the back of the boathouse, but that notion proved fruitless. I went back over to the pipe and listened again, this time from above, where the concrete block it passed through settled into the earth. Hearing nothing, I panicked a bit, clenching and unclenching, worrying at my inefficiency. When I looked up again, I began to notice the construction of the bridge's foot. Intersecting bricks laid in a standard pattern on top of concrete blocks, stacked right up to the curved girders supporting the roadway above them.

Stepping out on to the footbridge again, I continued to look upward, thinking of my daughter and one of her favorite insights: "No one looks up." Near the corner where so many parts of the bridge met, I swore I could make out seams darker than the rest of the brick's mortar. As much as I could see in the dark, shades of color were difficult to perceive. Everything tended to shift into a deep blue-black spectrum. From the bridge, I waited a moment before springing over the wobbling railing to the concrete base. I scrabbled up the wall a bit, grabbing a girder for support, and levered myself up to what I could now confirm was a seam. I pried at it with my fingers until pain told me to stop, but I'd felt some give.

The hatch looked as old and scarred as the rest of the stonework under the bridge. More than anything, it had the appearance of something useless that the city had sealed a long time ago. With closer examination, however, it was evident that the seams were too clean. There was no apparent hinge or handle as I ran my hands around the square of bricks.

My skin buzzed with anticipation and sweat prickled. I had a sharp undercurrent of concern burning through my brain as my thoughts kept turning to Ana, followed closely by regret for Maria. Ana had been my daughter for over one hundred years; we were connected in ways that were difficult to explain. She always claimed to be able to find me when she wanted. I never understood how, nor had I been able to share the cryptic ability. I wished I could. What father wouldn't? All I had was a burning sensation that my little girl needed me and I couldn't find her. And I just plain wanted to wrap my hands around the bastards' necks and squeeze for Ana and Maria, both.

After climbing a bit higher to face the section defined by the seam, I braced my back against the girders and tried pushing. With increasing strength, I pushed at the section until I felt it sink in. With enough force, it operated like a push plate. Once I had the slab moved back about an inch, it started to slide easily. I could hear the hiss of hydraulics behind the rasp of bricks scraping. When the slab slid out of the hole, it swung away and settled. I peered into the dark space, which appeared to be a small, forgotten hollow haphazardly filled with sand. It sharply tilted downward for a little way. At the end of the slope, there was a crude wooden door.

I resisted the urge to kick through the door. Instead, I inched forward and inhaled, relaxing myself, taking in as many scents as I could. Initially, I smelled nothing out of the ordinary. Wet concrete, soil, mold, bird droppings—everything one might expect to find under a bridge. There were traces of gun oil on the doorjamb—not much, but enough to know that opening the door could mean getting shot.

The faint sounds of a chant touched my ears again. I closed my eyes and listened to the monotonous sound muffled by the thick door. I had nothing to go on, no clue what lay on the other side of the portal, and no choices left. There was no play that I could think of that would ensure a win.

As quietly as I could, I opened the door.

CHAPTER 13

Warm, yellow light flooded my eyes and I saw a sweeping concrete room organized around a wide dais directly down an aisle to the left of me. Two rows of pews on the left and right formed a central path. The doorway I'd just come through was situated near a corner. Congregants sat in the pews, echoing the song of the pale pastor behind an ancient lectern. His hands were upraised to the wan light coming from the makeshift chandelier above the center of the room. The sides of the hall were lined with gigantic curtains the color of dried blood, from floor to ceiling. By the gloomy light near the top, I could see cracked stone, and the entire room appeared uneven while holding back tons of earth and rock. Rusted bolts and fractured beams of concrete and steel jutted from random places on the walls and floors. This was the remnants of an industrial room, it seemed, that had once held machinery. They'd set up church in the gutted carcass of Boston's past.

The sight of so many vampires in apparent collusion filled me with nervous emotion. I didn't want a repeat of what had happened only a scant year before. An acute sense of my vulnerability swept my brain like an unexpected wave. I knew it wouldn't be long before someone noticed me, so I began quickly scanning the space for other exits, a way farther in. To my right was nothing but the ragged corner. Ahead, there was little space between the pews and tapestries. I couldn't tell if there was more room beyond or nothing but concrete wall.

"You!" Charlie's now-familiar screech of indignation brought the service to a sloppy halt. "How in the savior's name did you find this sacred place?" He surged from his seat and strode toward me, his mouth agape and showing the teeth I'd cracked earlier to be fully healed.

In mid-stride, I straight-kicked him with my right foot. He skidded onto his ass, shutting his mouth.

Armed vampires appeared on either side of me, melting from behind the thick fabrics like an ill wind carrying the stink of death. I flinched, snatching one of my pistols from its holster at the small of my back and considered that my handguns wouldn't last long in a hail of automatic fire. They held the rifles firmly to their shoulders, aimed at me. Nothing in their bearing revealed unprofessionalism. I raised the Browning in surrender, not wanting to be filled with bullets when I was so close to my goal.

My eyes followed the barrels of two automatics now uncomfortably close to my face—the infinite maws of twin black deaths focused on my head. They were so close, it was a strain to see the faces of the vampires holding the weapons. As sure as I knew they were vamps, so it was that they were aware of my nature.

The pastor's deep voice boomed across the rising cacophony of agitated congregants. "You're not welcome here, cousin." He strode from the dais, moving confidently, completely unafraid, unhurried.

The ghost of my little blond victim stood in his way, eyebrows knit ferociously with steel in his eyes, accusing me—always accusing me. And with good cause. He was smooth-skinned this time, all of his limbs intact, no puncture wounds or tears in his body, resolute as the priest strode through his ghostly form.

The pastor had a thick brown coif, perfectly combed and trimmed on the sides. His features were dominated by a strong nose and glittering brown eyes so dark, they were nearly black. He smiled, canines retracted and nonthreatening. In fact, his teeth looked like a perfectly white picket fence. Or two rows of marble tombstones. "We have no immediate quarrel with you or your brethren. This is a peaceful congregation."

Anger fueled by loss drove my response. Sarcasm was probably going to get me killed one day, but I damn well had to respond somehow and perhaps buy a little time. For Maria, and especially for Ana. "All the automatic weapons threw me at first, but when you say it, the whole thing seems legitimate enough."

The pastor, with some amusement, reached out and plucked the pistol from my hand. "That kind of sarcasm never serves, cousin. What you see are the faithful willing to provide protection for their fellows less capable." He swept an arm in Charlie's direction. The vamp had clambered back to his feet and stood seething, watching the scene play out.

"From what? Who's coming after vampires that you'd need an armed force?"

The pastor's eyebrows rose comically and the corners of his mouth turned down as he raised his forearms, palms up, presenting me and my weapon as evidence. Several congregants laughed openly, but before it could spread, he turned his palms down and quelled them. The confidence in the room was palpable and I could feel mine weakening in the face of it. Now that we had everyone's full attention, I scanned faces for Graamvater's crooked features.

"I believe we got off on the wrong foot, Alexander."

He already knew my name. I was far too popular among the vampires in Boston. That needed to be dealt with and soon. The tension started to crawl across my back and shoulders. I saw no way out that didn't involve getting shot to pieces. I looked inward and found my core of power was still curled and bubbling—subdued, where it normally goaded.

"We could get off on a better foot if you tell me where you're holding Ana."

The preacher twitched a bit at her name but otherwise ignored what I'd said. "My name is Preston Cauldwell, but you may call me 'Father.' We seek nothing but a peaceful transition to our rightful place above our food source."

I locked eyes with Cauldwell and, for a heartbeat—mine, not his, the dead bastard—we were evenly matched: flint for flint. Then he said, "Cast him out."

"Wait. Let me talk to Graamvater—" I didn't see the first rifle butt come at me and it didn't matter whether I saw the second or the third. I was hopelessly disoriented, adrift in my own body. Blows rained down from all around. I protected myself as best as I could and rode the beating like flotsam in the surf. I tumbled, rolling on the ragged floor, swept by a current of fists, feet, and whatever else was at hand to hit me with. I tried to tap my power, but it just flashed and settled back down, inaccessible. Bastard.

Through the tangle of legs and arms, I caught a glimpse of Ana. My little girl, her face blank, being led by a figure whose face I couldn't see, but his warped silhouette was familiar enough. In the briefest of respites, I surged to my feet only to be thumped back down and further crushed. I'd failed her, my dangerous little girl. She was lost to me forever and there was nothing I could do but stumble further into failure.

I remember how soft she had felt when I first held her: barely four months old, a tiny pile of flesh. I'd just dispatched the wild revenant who'd first murdered her parents and taken Ana for dessert. She'd been discarded on the floor, mewling and forgotten during the fight. I could see the two puncture marks on the side of her belly and a trickle of blood. Her eyes had been clenched shut, her breathing shallow and rapid. When I'd scooped her up, determined to finish the job the demented vampire had started, and she'd opened her eyes. Eyes that swirled too large and black. Impossible and so fast. The very idea of a baby becoming a vampire broke every piece of logic in my brain. How in the bloody hell would a creature like this feed? Or be fed? And by who?

She'd been changed so young—it was unheard of. I couldn't kill her; I already had one child's death on what was left of my soul. A mix of guilt and respect for her parents, my then-neighbors, had flowed into my chest and I took her home. What need had I for a child? It would be years before I could answer that question with confidence. My love for Ana was a tether to my humanity, and I couldn't lose her now. Not like this, not with such...finality. I had been so close.

I lost consciousness. I had a sense of being dragged. Cool grass tickled my skin. I blinked, and there was a familiar face too close to mine. Alexa Vexa. *Kelsey*.

"Haven't you screwed up my life enough? The film crew, those humans—our *food*—got what they deserved: punishment for their...assumptive nature. Go away and leave us alone. You can't fight the...the natural order. It'll all be fixed soon. All fixed."

Father Cauldwell floated into my vision then, placing his hands in far too familiar a way on Kelsey. Gently, he stroked her shoulders and hip while he spoke. "I want to thank you for saving her so that she could be delivered to our grace." He smiled, sincere and smug, pulling her close. "Hand me the machete."

The vampires around Cauldwell looked from one to the other; some of them gave minimal shrugs in return for his trouble. The nearest said, "We don't have one, Father."

Cauldwell rolled his eyes, sighed, and said, "Then give me an axe." His hand hung, impatient in the air.

The vampire guard put his hands up. "Uh, we don't have one of those, either."

"Then what the hell am I going to cut his head off with? We don't have one inside?"

The guard grimaced.

"None of you have a knife?"

One of the guards pulled out a folder with a blade about the length of his palm.

"Are you serious? It would take all night to saw his head off with that thing."

Kelsey kneeled down near me and looked into my face.

I coughed, my lungs burned, and I could barely speak through the blood and phlegm from cracked ribs and a punctured lung. "Kelsey, I was the first to pick you up when you were broken. I was there the second time, too. And here we are again." A tiny glint floated in front of her cleavage, I reached out and weakly tapped the locket around her neck.

Her features softened briefly, the barest hint of a crack in the petulant facade. Cauldwell, in turn, stiffened, brown eyes blazing. I saw an opportunity to strike back, however futile and weak.

"Oh, Father, don't think I can't see that you want *Alexa Vexa,* not Kelsey. You preach about a new order, but you're no different from the *humans* who prey on their own children."

She glanced at him just before he kicked me in the side of my head. The world flopped and I rolled back slowly so I could face him and quell the nausea. Then I spit a tooth onto his shiny shoes, and he kicked me entirely out of the conversation for my trouble.

"Let him be purified." Cauldwell muttered through clenched teeth as he checked the chamber on my gun and flicked off the safety.

Before it began, I noted with mental distance that I'd never been hit by a .45 round, and especially not from my own weapon. The first slug felt like a sledgehammer to my chest. After the next six, I was sure I'd been pummeled into the earth, buried like a railroad spike.

More blows came that I heard rather than felt, he was

doing his best to punch a hole through my spine. Cauldwell jammed the spent pistol into my mouth, cracking teeth and burning my cheek with the hot barrel. When it wouldn't stay, he shoved it into my jacket.

"All set with that; you can keep it."

Cauldwell pulled with rough jerks at my pants' waist. Was the bastard going to sexually assault me now? A trill of panic caused me to convulse and I was rewarded with a rifle butt to the head, then a blast in my ear. My consciousness swam behind a purple cloud. The pastor removed my belt and said something I couldn't make out. I was turned on my side while he lashed my hands together behind me. Someone tied my ankles together with my own shoelaces. The thin rope bit into my skin.

More hands on me, a few muttered orders, and my clothing felt heavier. They were going into my pockets, shoving whatever rocks they could find on the shoreline in wherever they could.

I first felt the cold in my ears, as if it flooded my brain. Icy tendrils crept into my skin. When I opened my eyes, a cold murk enveloped my senses. I could feel a banging deep in the back of my brain, an insistent throbbing pushing against the membrane—the monster inside me trying to survive. Far below me, in the swirling darkness, I could see a dull light coalesce. My little boy ghost. He stood amongst hypnotic black tendrils, reaching up with them, encouraging me to come down. His blond hair waved in time with the leaves; a steady line of bright blood leaked from his body at the raw stump where his arm ended. I opened my mouth to apologize as always and cold entered my throat, my lungs. Gagging, I struggled to breathe and was rewarded with a terrifying realization. *Water*. I was in water, drowning, sinking. This would be a perpetual death. Weighed down, I would drown and revive in a torturous cycle, never conscious enough to swim, too heavy to float without air in my lungs.

Into darkness, again.

CHAPTER 14

Awake. Like a lightning strike across my brow. An insistent roar in my ears, the power did not want to die— *I did not want to die.* I flailed numbly, the cold stealing what was left of my warmth. Sinking. A grim hand of shadows enveloped me; my lungs were full of water. I tumbled with the slow current and the dull remembrance that they'd filled my pockets with rocks. I fumbled in a futile effort to free my hands.

Where was the Queen of Dragons? Didn't she want me now?

"I'm right here, Alexander."

I floated in a formless dark. There was light as if from a fire in the distance. A bellows of warm air gently wafted across my skin, leaving a sensual feeling. *Will you help me?*

"Will you keep our pact?" The warm air current shifted like a deep intake of breath.

I'm not dead yet.

"No, I suppose you're not." Another gust of warm air and I was back at the bottom of the river.

Alone.

CHAPTER 15

Awaken, struggle to breathe, fade away. I couldn't keep track of the cycle. One moment, I was desperate, pulling at my bonds, and the next, a chilly numbness overtook me. Sometimes, I tumbled with the weak current, and other times, my face was dragging across the muck and silt.

I heard more than felt a dull thump against the side of my head. My body rolled over and a rock, puckered and slimy, slid across my face. Another tumble and my head broke the surface of the water. I was close to shore and wedged in amongst the weeds and detritus of Boston's Charles River. Insects chittered all around and a cool breeze brought the shivering sound of tall grasses to my ears. Silence.

A rush of sound slapped my body. I must've dropped into unconsciousness again, but when my eyes snapped open and I tried to breathe, nothing happened. My lungs felt much heavier than normal, burdened with extra weight. Water. My diaphragm heaved and water gushed from my mouth and nostrils. Again, a violent contortion; more fluid dribbled over my lips. Another round before I heaved in a breath and settled on a coughing fit that caused my ribs to ache even more as they knitted. A final, violent cough brought two bullets up. I could feel the others sliding out of my skin like cold, dull knives. It was a torturous effort to roll over and get to my knees. I felt something hard and unyielding pushing into my ribs.

The leather of my belt around my wrists was

waterlogged, softened by my time in the river. I managed to wrestle my hands out while sitting in the mud. Then I fumbled my pistol out of my jacket and dropped it.

Everything hurt—moving, breathing, even my eyes and ears ached with effort. A full-body fire raged as healing power resurged with the intake of oxygen before hitting a wall of hunger. I needed to eat, needed energy of some sort to heal. Everything had been spent keeping me alive under the water. With numbed fingers, I struggled to loosen the laces around my ankles. Water had had the opposite effect on the synthetic rope than on the belt. The knots had tightened with my struggles, and being wet only made them hold faster. My fingers trembled as I fumbled with the knot, struggling to use my fingernail to gain purchase on one of the loops. I made attempt after attempt, exhaustion creeping in at the edges of my vision, and I sat awkwardly pawing at the string, suffering the burning sensation of the thin ropes cutting grooves into my ankles.

The damn knot was more like my life than anything else at the moment. If I had had a knife, I'd stupidly cut through it, ruining everything. As it was, I didn't have a tool and needed to muddle through until it was solved. After minutes that were starting to feel like hours, I managed to loosen one of the loops and unravel the knot. Too shaky to restring my boots and short on patience, I pocketed the laces.

Dragging myself to my feet, I stumbled in the direction of civilization, out of the river way. I paused and tottered back to the muddy bank and found my pistol. The slide, clogged with silt, ground back into place when I released the catch. With my old friend back in its holster, I felt some semblance of familiar balance, but no comfort at all.

Cauldwell had shot me with slugs designed to hit a body and stay. I wouldn't be alive if he'd thought to roll me over and fill my spine with bullets. I'd have to remember to thank him for this small oversight the next time we met.

My sense of time had a hole in it that was over a day in shape. It had been many hours since I'd been dumped into the slow-moving river. The streets were moist and cold air stole what little warmth I held in my wet clothes. The city of Boston was well into the time of night when everything was closed. Too weak to hunt—and nothing to hunt, regardless—I turned to my next best option. After a torturous block or so, I came to one of the many small eateries that dotted this college-heavy part of town. Working my way around the building, I made it to the rear corner before a coughing fit began to tear my insides up. After several minutes of this, I heaved up four more bullets that had made their way up and into my throat. The others are probably still rattling around somewhere in my torso. Pain lanced through my jaw as teeth that had been shattered began regenerating, trying to drop into place as if they'd never been broken, filling my mouth with the taste of my own blood again.

Slow healing made my entire body ache, a potent reminder of the trauma I'd suffered in the last twenty-four hours. It took several minutes of struggling with the door before I was able to enter directly into the kitchen stores. A living creature would have served better, but this would do for now. I put the Japanese hot-dog-eating champion to shame and headed back to the streets.

Hunger barely sated for the moment, I took stock. Deep inside, I could still feel my power, knew it still made me both more and less than human, knew that it had kept me alive until then. But its "benevolence" was spent, drained to keep a spark of life in my body. Everything about me still felt like it had been through a cement mixer and crushed into the sidewalk by a steamroller. It also continued to give me the oddest sensation of being coiled, hiding from…something. For the last several hours, it had been more tightly controlled than even when the Dragon had tamped it down. The way I felt then, it would be another day or two before I got back to what passed for normal again. It would not do.

Before dealing with that, however, I had to consider what I thought would've been an impossibility. Something I didn't want to believe or consider. Ana might be a part of the church, deeply involved, lost to me in a way that I could barely comprehend. She had been gentler of late, more caring and useful than I could last recall. I'd never known her to stay put for as long as she had in the past year.

A surge of guilt—an emotion I tried to ignore—flared in my stomach. It mixed with my fear and uncertainty, a weakening and toxic brew that stank of failure. The ghost of my child victim watched from the street, the occasional car passing through his willowy form. The boy bled and decayed in perpetuity. What I once considered my greatest failure moved into a distant second place after the loss of my daughter. He slowly shook his head, features shifting from tortured and distressed to an unnerving calm and back again as he began to walk slowly toward me. I felt a hot path trailing from my eyes as the boy reached toward me with his good hand.

When he brushed my face, a quiver of power swelled in my torso. The ghost disappeared with a chilling prickle and I glanced down to see that I had been crying blood. I wanted them all dead, the entire church, every damned vampire I could find in this city.

Yes, kill them all.

The echo came from inside me, a distant rasping support. The monster inside was willing to play along when I was willing to commit my all to carnage. I wiped the blood on my cheeks against my palms, realizing that I'd sworn an oath. When I took a deep breath, it felt like my lungs had nails in them. The blood on my palms sizzled, caught between being outside of my body and the proximity to my skin. Over a hundred years of fear inside me. So much time spent hiding from what I'd strongly suspected for so long and denied. I had to address what I was forced to believe was a completely different personality.

I whispered, "I'm going to need your help."

You'll need to give us something first. The being I drew my abilities from hissed and slithered, unspooling at my core, anxious for something other than freedom from me, its distorted voice difficult to make out inside my head.

"Whatever you want."

Give us a life.

"I've given plenty of that already."

Not the proper way; not like you did in the beginning. I need it. You need it. Us.

I struggled to remember, trying to recapture the feeling and failing. I had no idea what that meant and said as much.

Give in to the pleasure; wallow in your prey's fear. Let go.

I ground my teeth, suddenly struggling with the idea of entering into a pact with something I'd run roughshod over for more than a century. I owed it nothing and I owed it everything. Ana was gone; I needed help. I needed the power to cooperate rather than undermine. With that in mind, I set out to give it just what it wanted while my ghostly observer trailed me with cold, dead eyes before dissipating like a morning fog.

My ghost and I could settle accounts later. I needed to rest a moment and get my bearings before plunging backward, even further into monstrosity.

CHAPTER 16

At some deeper level, I've always been aware of what I carried. Unwilling to confront it and always so desperate to drive it deeper, and it, in return, repeatedly welled up, a living anchor clawing its way up the chain, strangling me whenever it could. I'd tamp it back down and we'd repeat the process, over and over. Just like I now denied that I knew where I was going and who I was hoping to see. Guilt isn't a bullet that can be dodged; it's black-and-white, hit-or-miss, and no accident.

I arrived at the Peter O'Neil projects an hour or so before dawn and began skirting the sides of familiar buildings. As I walked, I massaged my arms in vain, trying to rub away the pain. My joints screamed with every step, betraying the trauma that had brought me to that point. I was lying to myself if I was hoping for a crime to be committed in front of me—anything to reconcile the decision I'd made to be here, to seek out one scent. The full memory of our last meeting and every scent marker I'd picked up from that time came clearly to my mind.

A faint trail tickled my senses. The farther I went, the clearer it became, leading me into one of the bland brick buildings and on to the second floor. Before mounting the steps, I had a sense of awful anticipation at using my body to climb stairs.

Sweat, gunpowder, and a fried-grease smell hovered in front of the door I was looking for. Inside, I could hear the thump of hip-hop and the voices of three men. One familiar voice, rising in pitch and agitation: David.

They were arguing about profit and loss, whether David deserved anything at all, and how ineffective he'd been lately. Imagining his ineffectiveness, I remembered that I'd broken him last year. The man had been condemned the moment he made the mistake of coming at me, whether he deserved it or not. I had no idea what he'd been up to before we'd collided that day. I doubted he'd taken the lesson. So few of these wayward, casual criminals-turned-predators ever learned caution or societal respect.

I stood in the hallway listening, struggling with my own thoughts. There were no prompts from the monster inside, nothing to sway me one way or another. This was a decision I'd come to on my own. The only victim I thought would be easy on my conscience, a man overdue for death. The first time I had met David, he'd assaulted me in a stairwell, unprovoked, spouting gang shit, demanding to know who I was while he held a gun to my head. Then I had shown him. Dragged him back to his apartment and tortured him, stepped close to killing him before leaving him a whimpering mess. This time, there was no driving impetus, nothing to excuse what I was doing. There was no way for me to find out why the beast wanted a death, but I needed its cooperation, considering the last forty-eight hours. I needed allies, and more than that, I needed the power to flow with me.

I banged on the door hard enough to rattle the wall, ignoring any aches and pains, steeling myself for what came next.

"Who the fuck?"

"Five-oh, dog."

"Naw, man, those motherfuckers got to say it's them."

I held my hands up. The most nonthreatening posture I could come up with, knowing one of them would take a look through the peephole. Adrenaline and darker stuff began to flow freely and my joints loosened up; my muscles flared bright with manic energy.

"Who the fuck are you?"

I said nothing. Waited. Then banged on the door with the same ferocity. It swung open and a swaggering young man occupied the space. Barely out of his teenage years, he wore sagging, oversized jeans, black boots, and a dark blue tee shirt. He kept one hand slightly behind his leg. The hand that clasped the gun.

"I axed you a question, mutha—"

There was no need for subtlety. A snap kick to his groin distracted him long enough to grab him by the loose material around his shoulders and bounce him off the wall behind me. His body went limp and his weapon clattered on the floor. I kicked the gun back into the apartment and flung the punk in after it.

"Man, fuck you!" A second thug, taller, with diamonds in his ears and wispy facial hair that betrayed his youth, came at me. He snatched a gun off the coffee table in front of him and turned in my direction.

My palm smacked into the side of the weapon and my fingers locked over the slide. One overhand punch across my body to his neck stunned him while I reached underneath the gun and twisted, snapping his trigger finger. He choked in pain and I smacked him again with his own weapon, watching him drop to the ground like an empty set of clothing.

I faced David, unlocking the slide and splitting the handgun in two, letting the barrel assembly go one direction while the rest of the weapon dropped in the other. The fear coming off David was intoxicating. He stuttered and stumbled, words struggling to come out of his mouth. He seemed smaller, shoulders narrower. He'd lost weight since last we met.

"You!" He managed to squeak.

A deep hunger bubbled up, forcing a sigh of need from

me. It was followed quickly by a deeper sorrow. I knew what came next in the spiral from humanity: a rush to the top of the food chain and the bottom of human morality. I *remembered*. "Who am I, David?"

"Nuh, nuh, nobody, man, y-you a—ghost."

"Not anymore." I kicked the door shut and moved toward the fumbling gangster, transforming as I went, shedding jacket and shirt, pants and shoes. He stumbled away from me, a pile of panicked meat, scrambling for the back room.

I met him there and gave in to my basest instincts. His final breath, taken in for a scream, never released. I clamped down on his face and rendered his mortal shell to its most entertaining pieces. Chewing until there was nothing left, separating garments from the flesh, cracking bone and splitting tendons. His passing was like holding a dream, a fantasy come to life. There was a spark, like the flash of a bulb shattering, and his *life* flowed into me. Not memories or emotions, just the raw energy of whatever it was that had made him human surged down my throat and swirled in my belly to warm me anew. I felt refreshed and invigorated by David's death as I pulled the monster back inside, folding and shoving the mass uncomfortably into my center.

I felt fear.

Yes, that's it, Alexander. The truth of the matter. What we really are, the potential you've wasted all these years. Wasted and denied. YOU HAVE TRIED TO IGNORE ME.

"Are we done?" My voice trembled in my throat as I stood naked, fists clenched hard enough to crack all of my knuckles. I'd been working hard to get back in touch with my humanity. Now it felt like the effort had been washed away with one wanton act. I had what I wanted—what I needed—but was the cost worth it? I pulled my clothes on in angry jerks and strode from the bloody room and out of the apartment.

For Ana: everything was worth it. I would crack the planet for her, but none of it would help me. I would keep piling the misfortune on until I was erased from this world. Of this I was certain. And with that small flicker of certainty came forward motion.

At the corner market on the edge of PO, I used a battered pay phone to make a call before heading to Majispin's. I was certain that I'd only have one opportunity to contact Dr. Quentin Bismark. I'd thought the crafty alchemist dead after he'd been coerced into misleading me on my last case. Then he'd sent me a letter from the grave with an odd sequence of numbers that turned out to be a puzzle. I fumbled my battered notebook out of my jacket and found the numbers I was looking for. The answer for the puzzle was the number I punched into the phone.

The line buzzed four times and clicked over to silence. I strained to hear anything other than the pops and clicks of an outdated landline, but nothing came. No breathing, no background noise, nothing.

"Dr. Bismark?" My question was answered by a brief bubbling trill before the alchemist's voice came on the line.

"Mr. Smith."

"Dr. Bismark, I know you don't—"

"Don't bother speaking; this is a recording. Just for you, since we share the same nasty habit of surviving. Simply listen. I was quite pleased with your actions after our last meeting. It would seem that my death and several others were avenged considerably. Thank you for that; it was the very reason I entrusted you with the little cipher of my phone number. Considering your age, I thought you might enjoy the challenge."

I closed my eyes in a moment of pique. It had taken me months to even realize the numbers were a puzzle.

"Regardless, I'm sure you're calling me with yet another end-of-the-world scenario. Describe your problem and where you'll be in twelve hours' time. I'll see what I can do.

"And do take note, Mr. Smith: this concludes our business together. Should we meet again, our slate is clean."

The line clicked and beeped, recording, I assumed. I was succinct: "I need a weapon to fight a horde of vampires. I'll be at Majispin's before midnight."

CHAPTER 17

Within the hour, I was standing outside the Sweaty Magus, eying the streets for vampires. I needed to get all the way inside and stay out of sight. I didn't want my survival to be revealed to my enemies just yet. I had no idea who was aligned with the church and I wasn't interested in finding hornets outside of the nest right now. I had no reasonable expectation that the church didn't have operatives keeping eyes on the safe house. I had to be sure before exposing myself. I cursed the necessary waste of time.

Backtracking a block or two, I surveilled the building, picking out ways it might be watched surreptitiously. I didn't see anyone, but I could imagine a few vantage points to keep the Magus under observation. Scanning the edges of the roofline overhead, I knew I had to start up there. A number of the many alleyways in the Back Bay have iron fire escapes reaching down from fourth and fifth stories. I found one that looked sturdy enough and made the jump to the ladder. Hoisting myself over the top of the rust-coated railing, I recalled my first meeting with Maria. It had been nearby, and we'd eventually had an argument on a rooftop somewhere around here. I'd been impressed with both her fighting skill and her beauty. Irrevocably so. I passed by several emotions and hacked a direct path to anger. I'd have time to sort out remorse and the like as soon as I'd torn the church to the ground and recovered my daughter.

An airplane roared overhead as I reached the top of the fire escape. I hopped up and seized the edge of the roof and swung precariously into space. My grip was sure, however, and I was thankful the mortar didn't crumble through my fingers as I peeked over the edge. With no one in sight, I slipped over the edge, keeping as low a profile as possible. A low crawl across the tarred roof and a cautious look over the edge revealed what I wanted to see. One building separated me from the figure leaning casually over the edge of the next, looking down at the Sweaty Magus's door. Their back was to me for the moment, silhouetted by the light from the streets below, and I had to figure out how to take advantage of it.

I knew there was no unobservable access to the building on which my current nemesis perched. I'd cased both on my way to my present position. It was looking like this was going to need to be done the hard way. Something to make matters more difficult, of course. I should have expected it. I stayed low and retreated to the other end of my rooftop. About ten meters separated these buildings. It was going to be ugly and noisy. I hoped what little sound the sparse traffic provided would help mask my approach. Vampires have a less developed sense of hearing than shapeshifters, and that might work to my advantage as well. Maybe there was something else that could assist. I scanned the horizon, finding what I wanted, and waited. Soon, the passenger jet passed over, adding its roar, and I sprinted across the rooftop.

Every step felt charged as adrenaline and vile magic coursed through my veins. No whispers or tremors, static in my ears, or distraction of any sort. I had clarity when I launched myself into the space between buildings. I kept my feet close to each other as I landed hard, tucking and rolling, regaining my footing, speeding across the rooftop, intent on the next.

I cleared the next ten meters with my eyes securely on

the back of my target, his face pointed in the opposite direction, eyeing the street below. When I hit the rooftop, I was certain he'd hear it and turn. I rolled, as before, and came up running behind some HVAC structures. When I rounded the edge of the obstruction, I was pleased to see he'd looked but was startled to see me so close. He made the mistake of reaching into his jacket. Whether it was for a weapon or a phone didn't matter. Confronted with an assailant moving at a run, never waste time reaching for a weapon—deal with the immediate threat.

Without breaking stride, I drove a kick into the arm reaching into his jacket, knocking him backward. His arms flailed as he fell and I could see the gun as he lost his grip and it sailed away. Too far for either of us to recover.

He had a wide forehead with a long nose and short, brown hair. Handsome, really, until he hissed. His face elongated and his lower jaw dropped into his chest, exposing his fangs. Rather than acknowledge the aggressive display tactic, I treated it like the non-threat it was and drove a right hook into the side of his head, followed with an uppercut across his cheek and a kick upward into his crotch. Despite his eel-like pliability, it had the desired effect. When he gasped and nearly doubled over, I clapped my hands on his ears and drove my knee into the center of his face, breaking teeth and flattening his nose. In the movies, a knee strike like that would be the end of it; the target would be released to stumble away. Instead, I held on tight and slammed my knee into his face again, spinning him around and switching legs for another blow.

He finally reacted by twisting in a wild, tornado-like move that broke him from my grasp. He continued his spin and whipped a fist across my face, following with a roundhouse kick into my thigh. I was surprised and nearly dropped to a knee. He followed by slashing with elongated fingers at my face. I twisted away, but two nails raked across my cheek and forehead.

We stood facing each other. I was panting with the effort and he was stonily silent. He spat a blackened glob of blood into the tar between us and glared at me. It wouldn't be long before his teeth healed, so I decided to act first by rushing him. This time, he was prepared for the level of violence. He dipped and turned, evading my punches. When he countered, I did the same, except I stepped forward, slipping inside a slashing, roundhouse blow. My elbow connected with his pliable jaw, doing little damage this time, but I swiped my forearm across his face, distracting him and driving my other hand into the side of his neck.

Close combat tends to be uncomfortable for most unseasoned fighters. Without his fangs, I had no particular fear being this close to the vampire, and I pressed the advantage. He raked at the back of my head and neck, but I remained close, sticking one thumb into his eye and holding the back of his neck so he couldn't jerk away. He kneed me just below my ribs and I returned the favor with a more effective strike straight into his thigh, bowing his leg backward.

When I stepped through, he was off balance with his legs in a wide stance. I twisted around and down, sticking my free thumb into his other eye, driving him to the edge and throwing my weight down into the move. He made a strangled cry as I thrust into his brain, causing his body to spasm. He would heal from that in short order, however, so I flipped over to put my feet against his shoulders for leverage. Pulling from his jaw towards me, I removed his head in a burst of ichor.

The head passed through my fingers, liquefying hotly with the body into a puddle of foul-smelling carbon and water. I slid back and took a deep breath as a bullet ripped through the air, cutting across my shoulder and burying itself in brick and mortar.

I rolled away from the direction I thought the bullet had come from, reaching for my guns and realizing they were empty and mucked up, regardless. I was effectively unarmed. More shots followed and I glimpsed a figure behind the cover of an HVAC unit, firing in my direction.

One, two, three, four...

Another round burned hot across my body, this time cutting through the back of my thigh. I pulled one of my pistols anyway and pointed it in his direction. He flinched and his next two shots went wild.

Five, six...

I needed cover before I got shot to pieces. Gravel sprayed as another round came too close and in a dangerous move, I sprinted across his line of fire, attempting to keep the industrial unit between us and baffling a clear shot. I kept my arm facing the shooter wrapped around my head, desperate to avoid a shot into my brain.

Seven, eight, nine, te–

A bullet ripped through the meat of my back on the right side before another one cracked a rib and collapsed my lung.

Eleven, twelve...

I had cover, the firing fell short. My breath came and went in gasps. I'd been moving too fast for too long. Despite feeling energized from killing David and consuming his life-spark, the physical world had limitations. And I needed air to function.

I could hear my assailant's footsteps hustling around the structures on the roof and I strained to hear any of the telltale sounds of a slide being worked or the clatter of a magazine ejecting. The pain in my side sharpened and air surged into both of my lungs. The hole had knit, if not the entire wound. I still felt the electric strikes of pain. Then I felt an awkward tickle inside my chest, a need to cough. The bullet was still inside, and my body wanted to reject it. I pushed myself to a crouch, holstering my useless gun, and stifled the choking pressure to hack. The need for stealth dissipated when a silhouette turned the corner farthest from me and the muzzle flash of a pistol lit up the space between us. I spun away, turning the corner nearest to me as a round burned through the flesh of my buttocks. More followed.

Thirteen, fourteen, fifteen.

At the last count, I spun and charged the gunman as he dropped a magazine to reload. I scooped upward with both hands, grabbing the spent pistol and the hand that held it. The hot metal burned my hand and I had less than one second to recognize the surprise on his pale face before I slammed the pistol into his mouth once, twice, three times before he could react. When his eyes focused and he slammed a palm into my face in a panicked move to push me off, I kicked upward into his crotch and pulled to the side. As he went off balance, I reversed direction, twisting downward, and he flipped over hard onto his back. With no air to be driven out of his body, his immediate response was to thrash, kicking upward at me. I knelt down into his soft rib cage as he twisted like a snake to strike me, but I had his arms pinned down with most of his mass. In this position, I could free up my right hand. I envisioned the strike going through the rooftop and slammed my fingers through his skin, into his throat, just below the jawline. He gave an involuntary gargle, but when I grabbed his jawbone and ripped it out of his face; he screamed, ending in a sound like bubbling syrup.

The next time I reached in, the sounds stopped.

I sat back hard as the vampire's body bubbled away. I took deep breaths until I started coughing hard enough to feel nauseous. The bullet popped into the back of my throat and I spat it out. On the distant horizon, the sun began making its daily appearance. Tendrils of light slithered across the sky and I decided it was time to take a short break.

Leaning against the nearest HVAC unit, I calmed my breathing and watched the sun rise until it was full light. I hadn't seen the other sentry before he started shooting at me. I got lucky. Damn lucky. When my hands stopped shaking, I climbed down the fire escape to enter the club. It was early, but we'd just made a hell of a racket on a rooftop and I didn't see any need to stick around if someone came looking.

Benjamin, as was far too usual, stood behind the bar. Either I had the magical ability of showing up whenever he was on shift, or he had the magical ability of being there whenever I walked in. He opened his mouth to greet me, but what came out was a question.

"What the hell happened to you?"

I wasn't exactly pleased to be confronted, but his look betrayed his concern. "Why?"

"Seriously? After your last visit... You've been gone well past twenty-four hours and look like crap. Besides..." Benjamin pulled his long hair back from the side of his head, exposing the beginnings of the intricate, tattooed spell that allowed him to detect weapons. "You're setting this off and I can't see why."

"You know I'm carrying."

"It's not that. There's something—are those bullet holes in your filthy clothes?"

I waved him off, not at all interested in explaining the why of the matter—not that I fully understood. I was busy using timeworn techniques to bury the guilty memories, certain that the monster inside me wasn't going to steal this particular set of awful thoughts. It would let me have them to my last day.

I was operating at high clarity again, as if the Dragon had just buried the power's personality once more. The difference then was the absence of any background noise—and I had given up, letting the monster run loose in what was effectively going to be my suicide. This time, I felt as if I were inside the purring chassis of a Formula One racer, floating on an encouraging hum.

In response to the thought, the smell of David's blood filled my nostrils, sending a disconcerting tremble through my body. "Not now, damn it," I muttered.

Benjamin looked confused. "Come again?"

"Better question: why are you always here?"

Benjamin's face screwed up in skepticism. "I'm not always here."

"Whether I come in at night or during the day, there you are. I know you head up the bar, but it's like you live here."

The barkeep's teeth clenched and he looked sideways. "That's because I do. Lady troubles; I needed a place to crash. This was my best option."

Sometimes I forget there are entire lives being lived outside of my experience. I had no need to invade Benjamin's privacy and I regretted blurting out the questions that I had. Rather than apologize, I changed the subject. "I need to find someone. A friend of Ana's. He's a collector. Weapons. Is he here?" My guns clattered onto the bar top and Benjamin dug out a box and a chip while eyeing the dirty pistols with disapproval. I handed over the two pistols I got from the holy scumbags I'd ended, as well.

"Think you can find a use for these?"

"Ah." Benjamin handed me the chip and scooped the two extra guns off the counter before considering his words for a moment. Or perhaps he was appraising me. "When he's not doing whatever he does, he tends to be here. Probably in the rear lounge with his group. Portly, always wears black, thick beard, glasses, bald. They came in early this morning; I haven't seen them leave yet."

I hurried off, and whatever additional comment Benjamin was about to deliver died in the space behind me. He'd wanted to stop me, but I had to find this man. At the central portion of the club, I was careful to choose the detour around the dance floor, sure that I didn't want to pass through that room ever again. Not after the last time. Being swept away by spontaneous tribal magic wasn't an experience I wanted to repeat.

As I passed the private rooms, I wondered if any of the vampires inside the club and their self-sacrificial fetishists, the Faithful, were a part of the church. Plotting against me and everyone else. Again.

I scanned the rear lounge. It was roomier and adorned more warmly than the blue-themed forward lounge. Dark woods, mixed and matched sets of tables and chairs, knickknacks on the walls. It presented a space where larger groups of customers could ensconce themselves in relative privacy. There was a smaller bar back there, staffed by a young woman I didn't recognize. Her eyes lingered on me for a moment until the phone rang behind the bar. She stepped away to answer.

My thoughts drifted to Mark. We'd had our very first confrontation here. As soon as I'd stepped into the room, groggy from a relentless, wild magic, he'd punched me in the gut. It would set the tone of our relationship right up until I'd both wounded and healed him. We barely had the time to figure out what we were doing when I'd made us blood brothers and tied the pack together. He died the very same evening I had helped him smooth out the inner tumult he suffered, that had so often manifested in a coarse display.

Another strange thought leapt to the forefront of my mind, something I'd never considered or bothered to notice: when I'd been taken by the magic generated by the dancers, there'd been no pain, nothing to indicate otherworldly powers at work. It was something else I needed to track some other day. This day, I had a far more important *who* to track down.

At one of the larger tables, I saw what I assumed was my target. A table full of them. All heavyset, bald men with thick beards and glasses. They were a mix of ethnicities and had different features, of course, but to a man, they all matched the description. I stepped up to the table and their conversation died. They sat waiting as I circled the table. Frustrated that it would be impossible to pick out Ana's scent, I stood at the head of the table and waited for all eyes to turn to me. When they had settled, I realized I must be a sight. Most of my clothing was riddled with holes and tears, dirt and other things clung to me, smudged all over from my shoes to shirt.

"Ana needs your help."

A nervous glance on my left and the sour scent of anxiety drifted to my nose. The barest flare of nostrils and widening of eyes at my attention let me know who my man was. I looked directly at him and said, "That'd be you."

"Excuse us, gentlemen." My target heaved himself out of his chair, nodding to the table. They all eyed him warily; unasked questions hung tight in the air. He avoided eye contact with his colleagues and his fingers waggled nervously at his side as he walked a discreet distance away with me.

"You must be Alexander. I don't really know Ana. I've only met her a few times. In passing. The man you're looking for isn't here." He was careful to keep his hands in sight and use conservative gestures. I could smell his temperature rising. I was making him nervous, but I wasn't entirely certain why. It could be the aura or he could be hiding something. Either way, I could use it to my advantage.

"Where is he, then?"

"I can't divulge that—"

I stepped closer. A thin trickle of sweat formed at his brow and I could see the pulse thumping in his neck. He wavered, gamely resisting the urge to take a step back.

"I mean—"

"Shut up. I don't have time for this secret society shit. I don't care how you do it; I need to speak to this guy so he can help his friend, my…friend."

"But—"

"No 'buts.' You call him right now. If it'll make you feel better, let him decide for you."

The man swallowed the lump in his throat and dragged a phone out of his pocket. My gamble had worked. Humans dabbling at the edges of the mystic tended to be…skittish. He tried not to watch me as he dialed and waited for his call to be picked up.

He took the phone from his ear and clicked off. "There's no answer. It's early; he was…busy with something else last night."

"Try again."

"Uhm…"

"Try. Again."

"Okay, okay." He thumbed redial and waited for the connection. "Look, I don't think he's going to—oh! Hey, yeah, hey, it's me. Look, there's, uh—Alexander Smith is asking after you."

Great. *Everyone* knew too much about me.

The angle and the noise in the club prevented me from eavesdropping. He continued the one-sided conversation. "About Ana. Yes, he's standing right—"

I snatched the phone from his hand and he halfheartedly held his fingers out as if to take it back. "Listen to me: Ana is in trouble. You helped her out the last time with an artifact. The sort of thing I could use right now to help her. You're the only one I know of around here who might have what I need to get the job done."

On the other end of the line, a crackle of silence was the only response. I waited, fumbling for patience. Then his voice came over the line. "Okay. I'll help, okay? Don't...hurt anybody. We can meet right now." Ana's friend rattled off his address and said, "Can you put my associate back on the line, please?"

I cut the call off and handed the phone back. Maybe this reputation would come in handy again sometime. Although I'm sure that wasn't Majispin's intent when he'd spread the word about me, the sorcerous bastard.

One more quick matter to attend to. I headed upstairs to find clothing that didn't have bullet holes, river mud or death embedded in them. It reminded me that this was the second time I'd had to wear Mark's clothing after his death. Only this time, Maria was dead too.

I'd discard the jeans and shirt, then dump the shoes later. My jacket had a couple of bullet holes in it, but it could be mended. In the first room beyond the anteroom, there was a bathroom near the small library. I was certain that Maria had grabbed the clothing from somewhere very close to that. To the left of the door, there was another small room with a bench and slim lockers. It took a minute of rooting around to find where Mark's clothing was stashed. Perhaps it had fallen to Maria to empty Mark's locker and she'd left it be? No matter, I was fortunate that the clothes were still present.

There were a couple pairs of jeans and a stack of tee shirts on the shelf above them. The pants were oddly deformed, having hung in the locker unmoved for so many months, but they fit just as well as the last time. I stood there, staring into the locker at the stack of shirts, cool air raising the hairs on my back. My stomach flip-flopped and I waited for a wave of nausea or remorse or regret. Guilt I kept on ice, packed away for so long and so deep that the feeling passed through me on an invisible wave of greyed-out emotion. Regret was a constant but something I wouldn't allow to slow me down. That left remorse. And I never had time for that.

Instead, I trembled, fists clenched, my insides boiling. There were steps to be taken, vampires to be destroyed, friends to be avenged. Most important, I needed to find my daughter, and wallowing in emotions was a waste of time. That she had been taken from me in such a manner only fueled my determination. I snatched a black tee shirt over my head, slipped my jacket on, and pressed forward. I needed more than allies to make this happen.

Ana's friend lived in a crappy little nowhere strip between the South End and downtown Boston. Whenever I learned of one of her friends, I couldn't imagine how she met or maintained relationships with any of these people. I could never tell who was a friend or a victim. My little girl had a rich afterlife that I couldn't wrap my arms around.

It would have been about a twenty-minute walk if I hadn't run for five minutes to find myself in front of his building. I waited to the side of the stoop rather than use the buzzer. It wasn't long before a young woman walked out. I startled her by jumping halfway up the stoop and catching the door. She scrambled on her way and I went inside to find number seven. A glance at the mailbox nameplates showed an empty slot where my quarry was supposed to be.

On the landing, an otherworldly scent tickled my nose. I paused and took a deeper breath, trying to find anything familiar about it. The only memory I could come up with was the mishmash of scents on the dance floor at the Magus. The smell reminded me of the half-human hybrid disco scene whose dance had called a wild energy to them and ensnared me. This was worth a pause, but I didn't see any way around it. I clenched and unclenched teeth, hands, toes, and ass before pounding on the door.

"Hey, hello?"

"It's Alexander. Open up."

"I... Okay." He sounded surprised, exactly what I wanted from my unexpected appearance at his door instead of ringing the buzzer at the foyer. I heard a barely-there whisper and the shuffling of feet. An unnatural gait, attempting to tiptoe, faded into the background. A door closed and what I assumed was Ana's friend's heavy footfalls hustled for the front door.

The person who greeted me bore a marked similarity to the rest of his group: bald, portly, and bespectacled. He invited me in and led me to a small kitchen.

At a table for two, we sat and he eyed me warily while I watched him with what I hoped was a neutral expression. I kept my hands in my lap and he kept his on the table.

"Am I making you nervous?" I knew the psychic buzz that normally bleeds off me had been tamped to a manageable level for anyone with supernatural experience.

"I, uh, I'm aware of what you did this past year and...your acquaintance isn't...desirable in this city. So, I don't mean to—that is, I don't want to—"

I clenched my teeth and held up a hand for him to stop. "Okay, I get it. I'll make this brief. I need some ordnance and I'm willing to bet you can get your hands on it."

"What?"

"You gave Ana a flamethrower last year—"

"Loaned. And she didn't give it back!"

"Whatever. Look—"

"No, not 'whatever.' You don't understand what I do. What we do. That was an object with more than obvious value."

"It was a goddamned German killing machine."

"Precisely. You have no idea who it was used to kill."

"At least a dozen vampires."

"No! It's not about when Ana used it. During the first World War, that flamethrower was turned on—oh, never mind. I don't think I can—"

"Do. Not. Say that to me. Listen. She's missing. I need some things. You said you would help me."

Fresh sweat blossomed on his skin; he leaned back in his chair, chewed his lip and stole the briefest of glances down the hallway. Without thinking, I'd bled power all over him, gripped the edge of the table, and risen partially out of my seat. I sat back down with a slow, deliberate movement, trying to cool the situation off. This obviously wasn't working; the aggressive play shouldn't have been anywhere in my repertoire for this meeting. I reeled it all back in and tried again. This man was human, after all, and he needed to exercise caution when dealing with monsters. Especially the socially undesirable ones.

"Okay, okay, look, I'm not after you. What's your name?"

Hesitation, caution, trepidation—every circumspect emotion could be read in the pause before he answered. "Bracken." My face must have betrayed my reaction to the odd name, because he added, "It's Scottish."

It's a plant, overabundant like heather, but I didn't want to quibble. "Look, I was under the impression you were Ana's friend. You'll be compensated."

In a twitch, he narrowed his eyes and nodded, glancing down the hallway again.

"She's been...taken and I need to get her back."

In an instant, he shifted from cautious to surprised. "That...couldn't have been easy."

He really does know Ana. I nodded.

"Why do you care so much; who is she to you?"

Because of me, the full measure of our relationship was

out and I saw no need to be coy. "She's my daughter; I raised her."

Bracken sat back in his chair and dropped his hands into his lap. "I see. All right. What do you need?"

A rustle from the direction he'd been glancing came to both of our ears. We each leaned out and looked down the hallway. Considering what I'd learned about humans who dabbled in powers unnatural to them, I wasn't particularly interested to see who—or *what*—he had back there.

Instead, I answered his questions and we agreed to meet again later, just before dark.

I had several hours to kill before my next meeting with Bracken, and my apartment was at the nexus of a mass murder and a shootout, so it seemed prudent to head back to the club. Inside, there was a different bartender at the front. A tiny light flashed on an elaborate charm on her wrist as I closed the distance, and before she could ask, I placed my filthy weapons on the bar. She slid a chip my way and I stalked off without a word.

I smelled the bartender on the soft push of air in front of her as she came after me. I turned as she came within arm's length. Prepared to tap me on the shoulder, she stumbled to an abrupt halt.

"You're Alexander, right?"

I stared at her, my brow creased.

"Uh, Majispin wants to see you upstairs."

I smirked and brushed her request away, purposefully not going to see Majispin.

"Oh, wait! I'm sorry. He said, 'Please ask Alexander if he'd be willing to come upstairs and meet with me.' Sorry, he did say to be exact."

I shook my head and changed direction, knowing she

wasn't going to last long if she followed Majispin's orders in such a manner.

I wound my way back through the club, to the stairwell that would take me up to Majispin's private offices. "Offices" seemed inexact, considering that he had an anteroom, lab, medical bay, and who knew what else on that floor. I tapped on the first door and the magician immediately called me in.

I made one concise observation when I entered. "You look like hell, Majispin."

The owner, in satin pajamas that needed to be sent to the dry cleaner and tattered leather slippers, sat slumped in one of his studded wingback chairs, a full rocks glass of brandy in one hand, half-empty bottle in the other. He was disheveled, hair and face unmaintained. His cane lay carelessly discarded near the chair. Beyond the obvious visuals, whatever spell he used to scramble his personal scent remained.

He raised the glass in my direction, fingernails a bit long but still etched with runes. "And good day to you, shapeshifter; welcome to the Looking Like Shit Club. You've been gone a while. Any luck this past eve? Sit, please."

I dropped into a chair, my muscles taut, forearms on my thighs. "I found the church."

He sat up. "You were right?"

"I was. I saw Ana, too, but nearly got myself killed for the trouble. I came here for…help, but you seem hardly in any shape."

"Pfah! I value your daughter's acquaintance. She did help save my life, if not my leg. I'm staying out of sight to keep the local vamps from getting too rowdy around here. If they need me downstairs, they'll call."

I hummed in sarcastic agreement. There was one other matter. "I called Bismark."

Majispin's incredulity was obvious. "He's alive? Hah. I

shouldn't be surprised. I am surprised you were able to get in touch with him. How the hell did you know?"

"He sent me a letter. It contained an annoying little cipher of his phone number. I asked him for something to help fight a group of vampires, and he said it'd be ready by sundown."

"Really?" He set his drink aside, curiosity fully piqued. "And you don't know what it is he might be preparing?"

"No."

He paused in concentration before asking his next question. "How is he to get it to you?"

"No idea."

"Then—"

"I just told him where I'd be by midnight, Majispin! I didn't even get to speak to h—"

"Oh, shit!" Majispin thrust himself up out of the chair, nearly losing his balance but catching himself on the wingback. It wobbled precariously as he reached for his cane.

"What..."

"Come, come, come!" He hobbled past me and triggered one of the hidden doors. I followed him past the medical bay into his laboratory. "Here, here!" He indicated I stand on the other side of the steel table that dominated one side of the lab. "I dismantled the bloody thing."

"I don't know what you're talking about. Oh."

Majispin began slamming brass fittings onto the table. Then he cleared the center and handed me a pipe. "I have to put the mechanism back together again before he sends something through. The son of a bitch was supposed to be dead."

"We have a few hours—"

"How long would it take you to rebuild a car engine?" Majispin's eyes were wild with fear. "If he sends something through and this isn't together, the resultant backlash would obliterate a good chunk of everything on either side of the connection!" He paused, face pinched. "Well, maybe just this side."

"All right, let's do it, then."

He touched the pipe in my hands and said a word I didn't recognize. A nasty tremor shot up my spine as the magic came to life. "Hey, a little warning, Majispin!"

"Sorry. I need you to hold several pieces after I put them together. It's going to hurt."

"Why don't you ask someone else? Benjamin, one of your other human employees?"

"We're shorthanded here, if you hadn't noticed! Besides, the device will be too heavy soon. I don't have time to set up the pulleys and vises. I need your help."

My teeth still ached from the last jolt, but I nodded assent and Majispin set to rebuilding the device. It was more complicated than I'd imagined and the minutes passed into hours. Majispin moved with sure grace as he reassembled the pieces, some large, most small, the whole gaining mass by the minute. I was sweating, the clock was ticking, and stress thickened the room.

Well past the late afternoon, after he'd attached several parts to the pipe I was holding, he quickly cobbled together two other pieces approximately the size of watermelons. As he'd said, the weight was getting significant and awkward. I wondered when or if he were going to balance the thing. Where were the goddamned legs; why didn't he have legs for this device? A familiar feeling brushed my senses; the sun was setting.

"Where are the legs for this thing?"

"There are none." At my blank look, he continued. "The device basically exists in two places at once. It is neither here nor there, so it's not really resting in space once it's set. Can't have things accidentally being sent back and forth. Eh?"

I growled in response.

"Now, hold yours steady. I have to bring these three

together and set them."

"And by 'set them,' you mean damn near electrocute me?"

He grinned without conviction. "Something like that."

Majispin held his two pieces to the open ends of the curved pipe and began to chant under his breath, willing the device to life. The small hairs on the back of my neck rose with his voice and I struggled to avoid anticipating what was going to come. I had no real idea, of course, but I knew it'd be bad. Then I caught the glint of brass out of the corner of my eye.

"Hey, wait!"

"What?" Majispin was fully irritated at the interruption.

"Is that part of your damn machine?" I nodded at the piece on the floor, partially hidden by the table's leg.

"Shit!" Majispin scooped up the misshapen thing; it was about the size of large pen. Bent with a twist across its center. The magician stared at the piece.

"Don't you know where it goes?" My arms were starting to burn.

"I'm thinking!"

"Faster, damn it, it's getting late!"

"Shut up!" Majispin lunged forward and tinkered with one of the assembled pieces. It cracked open like a clamshell and he shoved his hand inside. Then he slapped the two halves back together and set the whole thing back to where it had been.

"Is that it?"

"I think so."

I rolled my eyes and snarled.

After a glare at me, he began his chant again. The air came alive; Majispin's voice hit a crescendo followed by an abrupt silence. Prickles of power stabbed the air, slicing through my skin. Needles, tiny attacks burned all over me, invading my mouth and ears, causing my eyes to ache.

Majispin whispered one word: "Connect."

The two pieces slid together magnetically and a short and blinding flash of pain drove me backward. I stumbled to the ground as if thousands of amps arced through me. I couldn't curse or react in any way other than to stiffen and black out. I think it was only for a moment, because when I opened my eyes, Majispin still stood in the same spot. There was a sharp collapse of air, the machine rattled ominously as it glowed and a paper package the size of a grapefruit settled on the brass platform.

Majispin laughed, full-throated and proud of his device and its successful completion. Then his eyes fell to me and he sobered. I would've choked his laughter off with my bare hands if I'd been able to move. As it was, I willed him to die with my eyes.

The magician hustled around the table and, struggling with his stiff leg, helped me to my feet. I fought to catch my breath. Once I had, I pushed Majispin aside.

"Don't be an ass," he snapped.

Ignoring him, I lifted the supposed weapon from the brass platform. It was light and warm, soft to the touch. I began unraveling the paper to find that it was smaller than expected, wrapped in several layers, and getting warmer as I peeled the paper away.

CHAPTER 18

Majispin held the globe—a glass orb a bit larger than a baseball—turning it over in his hands. At the center roiled a molten core. I wasn't at all certain how something like this would function as a weapon.

"I'll be damned." He passed the orb back and forth between his hands, avoiding the heat it was generating.

"What is it?"

"That crafty son of a bitch."

I snatched the globe and nestled it back in the paper it had arrived in.

"Careful with that! It's a piece of the sun."

"What?"

"A piece of the sun. He's an alchemist, a master of elements. I'm certain you break it and get a sunrise whenever or wherever you like. A little bit of sunburn for certain folks, I'd imagine."

I gingerly placed the package in my pocket, more than a little concerned about the miniature hydrogen apocalypse at my disposal. "I have to get going."

"Well, then, good luck."

I knew Majispin wouldn't be of much help beyond the walls of his club, but I felt disappointed nonetheless. The walk down the stairs felt longer than ever before and when I reached the bottom, I was anxious to collect the tools I'd requested.

At the forward bar, I could see Bracken perched on a stool. His leg jittered up and down so fast, it would make a hummingbird dizzy. I could tell he was sweating and his breathing came a little too fast; anyone could see he was nervous. His scent burned with volatile emotions. When he saw me, he slid off the stool, scooped up a heavy canvas bag, and motioned for me to follow. We both nodded at the bartender as we exited the room into one of the private areas. The collector wobbled as he moved, bracing the heavy bag against his leg while he hobbled ahead.

"Okay, here." Bracken made two attempts to heft the bag onto the table as I closed the door. I stepped up and put my strength behind the effort. The goods banged into the table decisively.

The zip seemed exceptionally loud in the closed space. His hand hesitated halfway. "No cops will be involved. Right?"

"That's right," I lied. I had no idea what might come of this, whether the call I'd made from Maria's would yield fruit.

"'Cause this is some real ordnance, acquired from neo-Nazis, used in some awful shit. Lucky for you, they had a kung fu fetish, too." He pointed out a couple of exotic weapons. "You mentioned something sharp for skirmishing? That's your pal right there. Easy to hide, quick to deploy."

"Uh-huh." I admired the weapon, knew little of how to use it, and started getting restless.

Bracken visibly relaxed, sliding into a zone he was far more comfortable with. He identified the guns in the bag, starting with a long, black shotgun and boxes of slugs. "This is an Italian make, strictly functional, holds eight rounds." He tapped the boxes. "This'd be thirty-two total."

Something noisy with power.

He moved the shotgun to reveal two submachine guns. "These are modified MP5s; they fire a 9mm round, thirty in the magazine."

Full-auto pistols or something like it.

"There are two because of this webbing." He pulled on a mass of elasticized belts and loops. "These go over your shoulders, around your torso, and the two weapons sit under your arms near the hips. You can pull 'em out, fire, drop 'em, and they'll slide right back into place. It's pretty cool."

Quick to deploy.

He'd remembered everything so far. "You remembered the cleaning kit?" My pistols had suffered long enough and I didn't want to spend time cobbling together an improvised cleaning kit of mineral spirits and 3-IN-ONE Oil.

"Side pocket, dude." He slapped a zippered compartment.

Bracken zipped the top of the bag closed and stood back with his hands up. "That's you, man."

I wrapped one hand around the bag handles and said, "This is very helpful, thank you."

He speared me with his odd, grey-green eyes and stared for several beats. "Yeah, I'd appreciate getting those back." Then he hustled his bulk from the room.

I hefted the bag with far more ease than its deliverer had and headed for the exit. Bracken was nowhere to be seen.

Outside, the sun's absence reminded me of the weapon I carried in my pocket. The night sky began overwhelming the warm light left on the city's horizon as I stood in front of the lone pay phone in Copley Square, unable to decide whether to call him again. I'd given him a heads-up from Maria's apartment, but I wasn't certain he'd be willing to help. I needed it. I needed someone who might be comfortable with this style of combat. I needed someone with tactical expertise who hated monsters.

I dialed the number and he picked up on the fifth ring. "Detective Roberts."

I hesitated long enough for him to begin saying his

name again when I blurted, "Detective, it's Alexander."

"Funny you should call after leaving that message earlier. Someone matching your description had a running shootout in the Fenway leading to a building where several people had been slaughtered. It's weird, but no one can locate the occupant of one of the apartments. No murders inside that one, however, just a couple couches, a table, missing-person bulletins. It looked like a serial killer's crash pad, straight off the TV."

Shit. I knew this would be messy; I was under no illusions that Roberts was going to jump right in on a plan like this. With that in mind, I cut straight with the truth, trying to be as sincere as possible. "I won't lie to you; we're under attack."

"There you go with that 'we' shit again. *We* are not under attack; you are. You had a small army gunning for you—we're damn lucky no one got shot—and it looks like they killed all of *your* neighbors. That, on the other hand, is now my problem. Now what the hell do you want?"

"Your help, and it is *we.*"

It was his turn to pause. "You have got to be kidding me."

"The same monsters who killed those people in my apartment building are responsible for the on-set murders and the missing family from the Back Bay."

He sighed, knowing his already awkward position was getting more difficult. He couldn't simply call in assault teams to take down vampires. The scope of this was well above his pay grade but not his experience. The real problem for him was that there was only so much he could smooth over. And I didn't bother to remind him of that. I needed Roberts on my side, or at least focused on a common enemy.

"Now, I can give you a location and you can meet me there, or we can part ways right now. You might not hear from me again."

"Threats again?"

"I might be dead."

"Fine."

I took a breath to think about his response and asked, "What's fine? My dying or giving you the—"

"Just give me the address!"

"Bring a rifle you'll be comfortable using."

"For what?"

"Sniper. Bring as much skirmishing ordnance as you can carry, in fact."

"Unbelievable." Roberts grumbled and we agreed to meet in two hours. I had my guns to clean and some new friends to load.

CHAPTER 19

"Those are all, uh, vampires?"

We watched from across the river as the occasional group of vamps made their way into the murk beneath the bridge and disappeared through the hatch. It was full dark and we'd met as planned. Roberts had listened to my thoughts on the situation and agreed to support what I was planning. He seemed to relish the idea of killing some of the monsters who'd been wreaking havoc in his city for the last few days and more last year. It appeared he'd redeveloped the fine-edged focus I hadn't seen since that last scrap. Whether or not he knew he was in for the long haul didn't matter anymore. Right now, the bulldog had a bone.

"Yes."

"How can you tell? They just don't look like anything special to me. Not like the last time."

"It can be…difficult…when they intend to blend in. In close proximity, there's something about us that doesn't allow hiding our true nature from each other. Not for long, anyway."

"That's not helpful."

I sighed in my thoughts. This was never easy. "I'd suggest looking for inhuman cues, like a penchant for stillness, unusual strength and speed, healing, pliability…"

"Pliability?"

"Yes. They can be as flexible as rats slipping under

doors. Or like an octopus. One moment solid and the next a bag of muscle. You might notice when grabbing someone, trying to cuff them, say, or—"

"Okay, I get it." Roberts never took his eye from the scope, preferring to observe the groups coming to the church. He'd fallen with completeness into a cold relentlessness likely learned on Marine Corps firing ranges. Or firefights.

"Where's your partner, Pepperman?"

Roberts adjusted the weapon at his shoulder. "Pep don't need to be involved in this mess."

"So he doesn't know anything?"

"Why? You gonna threaten to kill him, too?"

I let that comment slide. I was pleased I could let it slide. Pepperman certainly had as much experience with this madness as he needed. Still, Roberts had misunderstood and I endeavored to straighten him out. "I was wondering if you'd spoken to anybody. I figured if anyone, it'd be Pepperman."

Roberts sighed, still not taking his eye out of the scope. "I'll be fine."

I doubted it. "What can you tell me about the missing family?"

"Why?"

I wasn't sure. Maybe a lunge at basic humanity or fuel to add to the revenge bonfire. It had crossed my mind regardless, and I explained it that way to Roberts.

"Well, the father made most of his money in media. Loved Boston and moved his wife and daughter up with him from New York. They settled in the Back Bay and had two more children here. All the kids are teens now. According to friends and family, the couple wanted a small-city life away from the intensity of New York. I'm pretty sure this wasn't what they had in mind."

"The crew from the porn set, the family in the Back Bay. Was there any connection?"

"None that we could find. It doesn't make much sense. The Back Bay family was the most high-profile, but I bet there are other people missing."

I knew exactly who Roberts was referring to. There were millions of people off America's radar—whether they were criminals or victims. It was questionable whether current resources were up to the task of policing this country. What was not in question was that there was enough wealth here to do so, but the political will was missing. For now, it seemed, the majority of the population was content with unacknowledged class distinctions.

I had an inkling of what the connection between the families might be or, more likely, the lack of connection. "I don't think the two murders are connected in any conventional way."

"You see any convention here?"

"No. I mean, they're connected by the church, but weren't planned or executed by the same person."

Roberts looked at me with a skeptics glare. "That doesn't make sense. The MO was the same."

"That's probably because there were both perpetrated by vampires but under different agendas. I think Alexa was taken, just like the family in the Back Bay, but for different reasons."

"I don't understand."

"Let me simplify. On one hand: church, priest, pretty young thing. On the other..." I shrugged.

I hadn't realized that Roberts could be more disgusted with monsters. "Are you shitting me?" He shook his head and chewed his lip for a second before changing gears. "What's the surest way to kill a vampire?"

"Remove its head."

"That's it?"

"The real answer is to sever the spine. Removing the head is the most efficient way to do it."

"Since we ain't walkin' 'round with swords and axes,

would pumping enough bullets through center mass do it?"

"As long as one cut through the spine, yes."

"Or blow its head off?"

"Not the surest way, but yeah, that would do it in most instances if the brain pan is emptied."

"Is that the same with you?"

I was wondering when he'd get to that. "Yeah, it is. You sure you're up for this?"

"Uh-huh, I brought a few things." He patted his overcoat. I had noticed it hung tight around his neck and shoulders. He had weight in there.

Traffic to the church's entrance died down until nothing happened for a few moments. Then four figures slipped out and took up guard positions, one on each side of the hatch and two above, on the rails beneath the bridge. I'd hoped that security would be exposed in this manner since my previous visit. It also gave Roberts targets he wouldn't have to engage up close.

"It's time. You understand what I'm about to do. Right?"

"Yeah."

"You're ready for this?"

"Yes, goddammit; go."

"Head shots, Roberts. At this distance, you're good?"

He only grunted in response.

"And stay back."

Nothing in response to that. Well and good; if Roberts wanted to close with death, then so be it. He'd been warned. I slipped into the water at the muddy bank, wading through garbage and weeds. I had no desire to be back in the river that'd nearly been my grave, but it was the best option for a stealthy approach. I had the machine pistols strapped to my torso, my personal pistols in their usual holsters and the shotgun slung over my shoulder. I had given all of the weapons an extra coating of oil to keep them serviceable. It'd be slow going with the sluggish but strong current and that was fine. I needed to come in quiet.

As I crossed the river, I had unsettling thoughts of Ana and her grandsire, Graamvater. The name bubbled up again from the memories stolen when we'd been painfully linked. Nikolaus Graamvater. It meant nothing to me, sounded familiar in no way. More than the water began to chill me to the bone, knowing that he'd been inside my head as I'd been in his.

More than halfway across, I still swam in a slow breaststroke, mostly submerged. I held my breath until my lungs burned, then I took a slow breath before repeating the process. I could drown, like before, still needing oxygen—unlike my adversaries. This time, however, I was in control, and I did not fear water. My fingers began to brush thicker vegetation as I neared the opposite shore. The water remained an impenetrable murk when I hit the muddy end.

With deliberate, slow movements, I pulled myself forward until I could get my feet under me. Then I rose up from the river in plain view, climbing onto the footbridge.

"Hey!" The closest sentry spoke in urgent but hushed tones.

His partner looked to where he was pointing and started to come closer. The one who'd sounded the alarm, a dark-haired, lanky vamp, began to raise his weapon when the back of his head exploded and his body crumpled before he could set foot on the bridge. No movie-style flying backward from the impact; one moment upright and the next a heap dissolving into muck. I could hear the action of the weapon being fired, but I doubted they could. The second sentry snapped his attention to his fallen comrade and swung sharply in my direction before suffering the same demise as his doubly dead partner.

I walked along the loose boards and said, "Come to me, my children." With my hands raised Christ-like on either side of me, I waited.

First one, then the other vampire peeked down from the rusted rails. Then they dropped down on either side of me.

"What the hell's going on down here; where's Sta—"

I didn't hear any more from them. Roberts was clearly an expert sharpshooter and I wondered how long he'd had that particular skill.

CHAPTER 20

I worked the seal as I had before, pushing the hidden door open. The scent of wet concrete flooded my nose. The small, dirty foyer was empty. On the other side of the wooden door, I could hear Father Cauldwell's voice rumbling, working the congregation into a frenzy. He proselytized about the rightful place of vampires and their heritage.

As soon as I placed one foot into the foyer, I heard footsteps on the bridge. Familiar footsteps. They scuffled off and into the dirt. Roberts appeared around the side of the foundation.

"What? You knew I wasn't going to wait." He started climbing up to the entrance.

I shrugged. "Try not to shoot me in the back. We go in quiet. I need to find Ana before the shit starts."

Inside, Roberts hefted the rifle to his shoulder, keeping the business end a hair's breadth off of me. At the wooden door, I paused and turned to him. We could both hear the low moan of prayer. They did a kind of call and response, a few words from the pastor echoed by the congregation. Then they began chanting, a monotonous song, the words of which I couldn't make out.

Roberts's jaw looked like his molars were about to crack. He was starting to sweat and I could smell his stress. I locked eyes with him and he lowered the rifle to swipe at his brow.

"This is it," I whispered. "The church is set up pretty

standard, with two rows of pews and an aisle down the middle. This door is off-center, so when we go through, stay low and follow me. We're going right. Keep us covered, and remember: quiet."

He gave me the bird and shouldered the rifle again. I held up three fingers and counted down.

Three...

Two...

One.

I pushed the door slowly open. As before, warm light bathed the area and the cold, dead air of a roomful of vampires washed over us. I eased through the cracked door in a crouch and slid along the back wall below Cauldwell's line of sight. Roberts did the same, but I could still smell his tension. Vamps may not have the noses of 'shifters, but they could smell a human close by. If Roberts couldn't keep his mood in check, we were going to be found out long before I could circumnavigate the room.

As soon as that thought crossed my mind, the fresh scent of other humans met my nose. Roberts wasn't alone here. *The missing families and others.* Where were they?

On the dais, Cauldwell continued to preach, his cadence reaching a crescendo. I tried to listen to what he was saying as I looked for any sign of Ana.

"Jesus! My friends, Jesus was but the first lamb, the first to fall and rise under the beloved and overwhelming beauty that is our destiny. Never forget, friends, never forget. And it was Jesus in his rightful place as our lamb who said, 'This is my body, which is for you. Take this in remembrance of me.' And what did that mean? Know first that Jesus spoke to us—directly to us—and gave of himself for us, to ensure our survival. My friends, it's all right here. Right here in the good book, plain as night."

Around the church, various vampires said, "Ah'na," in response. The same as the pamphlet. The sermon continued like that.

"In context: 'For we received from the former Lord what I also delivered to you, that Jesus on the night when he was brought took bread, and when he had given thanks, he broke it, said 'This is my body, which is for you. Take this in remembrance of me.'

"Some of you may wonder: why? Why now? Why not, say, always? Our lamb knew, my friends, he knew we needed time to grow, to prosper, to connect with each other. To be protected until we could see his words in full, decipher the hidden message right under humanity's nose!"

"Ah'na!"

"And who is our Lord, our Protector? He remains, as ever, unfathomable, but remember, friends, remember, he gave us Jesus and Jesus loves us, wishes for us to ascend to the place we have been ordained for, a place thousands of years in the making. There are but two obstacles: the lambs and the dogs.

"The lambs, we claim now. We teach them daily what their place in the True Order is. They'll come around; they always do."

"Ah'na!"

Cauldwell's matter-of-fact statement gave me pause. I was at the corner of the rear pew, looking for a way to sneak forward a few rows and slip behind giant draperies covering the crumbling walls.

Sneaking a glance at the dais, I saw Cauldwell motion delicately to his left. A line of human beings began stumbling onto the platform, herded by two armed guards up the short stairs. Disheveled, stunned people, horrified in appearance, their faces locked in fear.

Cauldwell pulled the nearest one to him in a gentle, almost loving embrace. With one arm draped around the woman, he smoothed back her hair and spoke again to the assembled congregation.

"These are among the first of our lambs—the dogs, we

have begun dispatching. The first of which was a follower of that human fool, Majispin, in his downtown atrocity. 'Neutral territory'! Please, spare us this nonsense, my Lord. There is no neutral territory; there is only truth! The others will follow her to oblivion soon; tonight, we rise and shift the balance back to its rightful order! A place where we may begin our true ascension!"

"Ah'na!"

Cauldwell's face contorted and with the speed of his monstrous kin, he buried his face in the woman's neck. She gasped as he sucked at her throat and gulped once, twice, before releasing her. His lips, deep red—a striking slash in his otherwise perfect face—began to call the faithful forward.

"Who will sup of the body of Christ? Who among you enters this sacred pact?"

Multiple voices rang out and the faces of the vampires began to twist, showing their true nature. Fangs dropped into place and their bodies vibrated with need. Somehow, Cauldwell kept them in place, seated until called.

"Who, I say?"

A cacophony thundered forth: "Me! Me! I will! I believe! Ah'na!"

At that moment, I made the connection. *Ah'na*. Ana. My daughter. My body went cold and a crease of pain lanced my temples. How had this happened? *Graamvater*. Why would he do this, unleash this kind of madness? *Just to draw us out.*

On the opposite side of the dais, partway in shadow, obscured by errant tapestry, Kelsey stood staring. Not at the bloodletting scene in front of her but directly at me. I couldn't read the look on her face, but I could tell she was watching me and doing nothing to let Cauldwell know I was there.

I stole a glance at Roberts, expecting to see disgust and horror. Instead, I saw pure rage. Hatred at these creatures who fed on humanity, who insisted on a class hierarchy that he could not abide. He stood up, hands steady, and brought the rifle sights up to his eye.

CHAPTER 21

"Roberts…" I hissed, trying not to draw any more attention than a sniper in plain sight would.

"This is too much; I can't allow this…" His finger tightened on the trigger and I reached for him.

"Behold, brothers and sisters!" Cauldwell pointed at us, stepping behind the woman he'd just bled. "They work against us, the feeble *others*!" Then the preacher's eyes narrowed, recognizing me, and more than theatrical bluster crossed his features.

The guards on the dais stepped forward, but the congregation rose to its collective feet, all eyes on us, effectively baffling the guards' approach.

Roberts wavered. "I don't have the shot."

"We have bigger problems, Detective." I snapped the shotgun up, racked a round into the chamber and blew a hole in the nearest vampire.

The party started in earnest.

Roberts, to his credit, didn't flinch when I started firing, merely began pumping rounds into the crowd. They fell back, the bullets doing little to kill them but surely causing more pain than they were accustomed to. When they fell back, the detective began picking his targets more sensibly and vampires started going down for good. He efficiently dropped a magazine and rammed a fresh one home.

This chaotic advantage wasn't going to last, however; neither of us had an infinite amount of ammunition and we'd be sitting ducks soon, unable to reload or do much else surrounded by this many monsters.

Kelsey's once-again-familiar face appeared, square in my sights, unaffected by the fact I was pointing a shotgun at her. She wasn't surging forward like the others; her feet remained rooted to a spot not ten feet away. I spotted Charlie's blond head in the crowd, trying to move in the opposite direction, and I redirected my attention. The back of his head splattered with the slug's impact. A selfish and foolish decision on my part, but satisfying.

Kelsey's face swam between sorrow and anger, back and forth. The crowd around her reflected only rage and began to push forward around my wayward girl. We locked eyes and the corners of her mouth twitched up once as she floated backward against the flow of the crowd and faded into the chaos, lost again. I had to remember to find her, but there sure as hell wasn't any time at the moment to take a memo.

I racked the slide and pulled the trigger to a loud click. I'd not been using any firing discipline, being more concerned with spotting Ana, and the vampire I'd targeted surged forward to wrap her hands around the barrel. When she tugged, I simply let go of the weapon, reached to my torso, and pulled the machine pistols into firing position. They burped sharply, cutting her torso to pieces, and she dropped, shrieking. Well behind the fallen vamp, I caught a glimpse of a familiar face. *Ana.* In the adjacent corner, Kelsey's blond hair flashed and disappeared around a stack of broken stone.

Ana was dragged out of view behind a drapery, her eyes unfocused and jaw slack. I didn't see who had her, but I could guess. I had eyes on Cauldwell, who was desperately directing his last few guards toward us. Graamvater had Ana and we were due a family reunion.

I trained the pistols on the crowd in front of me, cutting a path with Roberts at my back.

The pistols clacked on empty and a brave bloodsucker stepped toward me. I reached to my belt and loosed the whip sword around my waist. In an awkward motion, I slashed my own arm and removed the vampire's head at the same time. The flexible blade curved around my shoulder from the arc of the blow.

"What the fuck?" Roberts cried. "Hey! Watch that goddamned thing!"

I heard another magazine clatter to the floor, and Roberts rammed a third home. The whip sword wobbled in my hand. I hadn't handled one of them in decades and I'd never been proficient with it. I tucked my left arm in before I cut it off and began weaving a pattern in front of me, trusting Roberts to keep our backs clear.

A now-familiar metallic thunk on the stone floor was followed by the mechanical slap of a bolt driving home. "Last mag!" Roberts growled.

"I saw her!"

"Go!"

The whip sword tangled in a tight space between vamps and the crowd surged. I twisted, using the weight of those around me to redirect the surge as I pushed forward, reaching for the tapestry. I heard Roberts yell something incoherent and furious that was followed by a deafening boom. A glance confirmed that the detective was now holding a huge revolver, one shot of which tossed a vampire backward into two more.

"Come on, motherfuckers!"

A slender pair of pale hands reached out with fuzzy speed to seize Roberts's head. Rather than the wet crunch I expected to hear, Graamvater spoke instead.

"He's mine. Stop this now."

Sweat poured out of Roberts's hairline and his face stretched into a rigor of terror and pain. Blood trickled from his nose and his eyes locked open. Both of his arms froze at his sides.

I ground my teeth, angry at needing to make this decision, and turned to yank apart the drapes. There was nothing there.

"See here, Alexander, my granddaughter is by my side, where she belongs. And your human pet is here as well, in perpetual terror as I flood his mind with the truth of his puny existence in my world."

Graamvater leered at me, his face crooked and demented. He had the look of a man who'd rather fight a platoon with one arm tied behind his back than casually drink a glass of water. Cruel, horrifically capable, and calm. His dark pupils swam in a blood-clotted mess, the whole of his appearance combining to provide a disturbing visual message that Graamvater was not to be trifled with.

"Thank you, Savior! This dog has brought nothing but chaos to our doorstep—"

"Shut your mouth and kill him, Cauldwell."

"Yes, Savior." Cauldwell shouldered his way to the front of the crowd, his guards coming around him, sighting on me.

The faint rasp of gunmetal was followed by a sharp blast and Graamvater bellowed, dancing backward as Roberts tumbled forward, gasping. The detective had managed to pull the trigger and blow off half of the terrifying vampire's foot.

For a moment, everyone's attention turned to Graamvater. With the tapestry from the wall still in my hand, I produced the alchemist's globe and slammed it on the ground as I dove for Ana. I held the tapestry out, wrapping it around her, protecting her with my body. The temperature rose sharply and the air in the room became like hot mud. A flare followed shortly thereafter, the brightest sunrise I hoped I'd never see again burning hotly at my back as I covered Ana. She screamed, struggling against my efforts, raging against everything, coming back to her senses.

The vampires fell back in a concentric wave, toppling and dissolving in flaming puddles, leaving Roberts upright and dazed. A howling, two-legged fireball cut a swath through the crowd for the door, splintering it. Here and there, a lucky few were mostly protected by their compatriots taking the full-frontal brunt of the burn. Like Cauldwell. He struggled out from underneath one of his guards melting atop him. His extremities and half his face were severely burned as he levered himself to his knees, one good eye wildly scanning the room. His perfect hair and half his face were ruined, burned beyond recognition.

I looked to Ana, my daughter, my little girl. She took in my eyes and coiled around me tightly. I soothed her as best I could, speaking Kainai, our first language. "I love you, Little Crow; I'll always come for you. *Always.* Everything for you, my dark bird." As I stroked her hair, I noticed that she'd been slightly burnt by the alchemist's weapon. I knew she'd heal, her physical form would endure, but I couldn't speak for her mind. Graamvater had been there, held her like an ornament for days. Anger lanced through my veins, a pure rage at the escaped monster. Cauldwell was here, however, so he would have to do for now.

I gently pried Ana from me, whispering that I'd be right back, that I wasn't going far. When I turned to Cauldwell, fear trembled in his one good eye and he tried to move, cast about for a weapon.

The nearest pew, covered in vampire death, cracked beneath my fingers and I tore a ragged piece away. In a few strides, I was standing over Cauldwell. His charred mouth moved and throat constricted as he tried to speak, and his fingers struggled to grasp a rifle nearby. I shoved the makeshift stake directly down his throat, burying it up to my knuckles. He gagged and convulsed, making wet sounds, and toppled over. I commenced to stomping on his neck, trying to drive my foot through the solid stone floor. I felt the wood in his throat snap, followed by his spine.

I didn't stop until he was a puddle of blackened filth bubbling into the cracks of the masonry.

CHAPTER 22

With Ana back in my arms, I jumped when a sharp boom thundered. Roberts stood over a rapidly melting vampire. He strode calmly to the next survivor and repeated the process. Between kills, he notified the freed humans of his status as a Boston police detective and instructed them to exit the area and wait together outside for medical attention.

"Roberts."

Boom.

"Detective!"

Boom.

He paused and spoke to me. "That motherfucker's horror show was nothing but the usual shit I get to see around you. At this point, you need to leave."

"Are you going to be okay?"

"No. Is that woman the preacher bit going to…"

"No, it's more complicated than that."

"Get out of here." He met my eyes and nodded. "Take her. Just go."

I didn't respond except to collect Bracken's weapons and carry Ana towards the exit. Roberts was dealing as best he knew how. Behind me, I heard the rattle of a cylinder and spent shells scattering on the floor. It was followed by the clack of a speedloader dropping fresh bullets into place and the snap of the cylinder going home.

Boom.

I carried my shivering little girl toward Majispin's after

stuffing the canvas bag with the guns. It was the only place I knew of for her to get a fresh and cooperative supply of blood. She'd need it to get through this. I didn't know when she'd last fed or what Graamvater had been doing with her. She wasn't talking and I couldn't bear to ask, to force her to relive it. She needed to be safe. I needed to get her somewhere safe, away from Graamvater. Still, he'd managed to find her once before. How? How long had he been looking and why?

The monstrously powerful vampire was still an enigma. He'd escaped the conflagration at the church—I knew that much. It was clear to me that he was still alive somewhere. But his rationale was unfathomable. His very presence generated questions I couldn't even imagine the answers for. He behaved as rationally as any sociopathic fiend I'd encountered, but he seemed bereft of the madness that should plague a monster of his age. The connection to Ana was murky as well. She was born of his lineage, but I had no clue how or why she was the way that she was or what Graamvater's plans for her were. The creation of this church—was its sole purpose to root her out? He didn't strike me as simplistic as that. The structure of the church would roll on without him, if needed. It was the nature of such things. So, he must have plans for that as well, but what?

Nothing reasonable came to mind and I focused on putting one foot in front of the other. The streets were middle-of-the-night-Boston empty. Nothing was open, no people wandering about, and only the occasional pair of headlights passed us. Carrying Ana and the bag of weapons like this was awkward, but I didn't see any easy alternatives. No cabs, and modern cars weren't easy to hot-wire. Another few minutes and we'd be there. She hadn't stopped shaking since I'd scooped her up, and that added a keener edge to my worry. She couldn't die. Not like this, not on my watch, in my arms. Not before me. Just a few more blocks; one foot in front of the other.

I smelled his burnt clothes before I heard his footsteps. A guttural howl, and he was nearly upon us. Graamvater had been blackened by the portable sun, cooked nearly to death, and he was on his feet, overtaking us.

"She's mine! Mine!"

Since Graamvater and I weren't on level speaking terms, I didn't bother to answer. When you're being chased, don't look back; focus on more important matters. Like surviving. Graamvater was clearly more powerful than any vampire I'd ever encountered. I had been fortunate to be able to injure him so severely. If we survived this, I owed Bismark serious thanks. I increased my pace and he matched it. We blazed through the streets, closing on the club at what I could muster as top speed. He snarled and spat at my heels, more animalistic than anything else. I'd treat him like a wild animal as soon as I was able. I needed a plan to get Graamvater off our backs long enough to slip into the club. Between myself and Majispin, we were sure to finish this monster.

We needed space; I had to slow this bastard down. To Ana, I said, "I'm sorry, sweetheart, stay tucked."

Graamvater was practically on my back, so I let myself go down to the ground, rolling over Ana and letting her go as the vampire stumbled over us, sprawling ahead on the sidewalk. I rolled once more, reaching for one of my pistols and came up in a two-handed stance, on one knee. Graamvater sprang to his feet, arms protecting his head.

At close range, the .45 round is like a high-velocity bludgeon. The bullets were designed for close-range killing, fat rounds that slammed hard into whatever they hit and rarely produced exit wounds. I put four shots into Graamvater's chest, flinging him backward, stumbling into the street and onto his back. He snarled and spat, flopping there like a sick bug. The gun reports were incredibly loud on the empty sidewalk. I holstered the weapon, scooped up Ana and the canvas bag in one motion, and made a beeline for the door of the Magus. I could feel the anger at my back as I stole a glance over my shoulder. Graamvater flopped in the street like a fish out of water, blood spraying from his charred mouth. He flailed a final time before the vampire made a catlike flip and hoisted himself to his feet to give chase again.

Six feet from the steps. Two. We were up the short flight and I flung the old, red door open. We spilled down the stairs into the first bar, and I ducked my head and stumbled with Ana. We hit the bottom of the next set of stairs and were met with chaos.

CHAPTER 23

Gunfire sang sharp in close quarters, punctuated only by the steady boom and slide action of a shotgun. A blue cloud, smelling sweet and burnt, hovered in the space from all the spent ammunition. I could see three gunmen facing the bar, trying to stay under cover as they fired wildly. Benjamin, bloodied, wielding the shotgun, dark hair clinging to his neck and forehead, wet with sweat and blood, hunched down. Around them, an assortment of customers curled underneath booths and tables, looking for an escape.

Bullets pinged off the bar, shattering tile and cracking the aquarium. The great white worms quivered in their tank, agitated by the assault around them.

Benjamin clicked on empty and the gunmen rose up, reloading their weapons, to finish the assault. The barkeep sprang forward and rounded the bar as quickly as he could manage, holding the barrel of the shotgun in a two-handed grip as he roared.

Graamvater clattered down the stairs behind us and I had no choice but to move forward. I drew my second pistol and shot one of the agitators point blank in the base of his skull. He crumpled, melting. Benjamin, hands burning on the hot barrel, brought the stock down hard against the glass of the massive, cracked aquarium. Remnants of vampire mixed with the water that blasted out across the floor. More customers scrambled for safety as the worms spilled out and uncoiled.

Benjamin leapt onto the bar and shouted for me to get off the floor. I didn't hesitate, rolling onto a table by the wall and turning to fire at Graamvater. He fell back against the stairs in a rage. With an awkward motion around Ana, I managed to snap my final magazine into the pistol.

The worms undulated into the feet of the remaining two shooters, wrapping around their legs. They both screamed as they collapsed like man-shaped balloons devoid of air, their skin deflating and wrinkling like raisins before they and the worms winked out of existence with a pop. I could ask about that later, if I remembered.

"Benjamin, where's Majispin?"

The bartender looked from the bar to me, his hands held in a manner that showed they were clearly in pain. Then he looked at Graamvater; the vampire huffed, spat, and growled before rising to a sitting position on the stairs. Benjamin's eyes widened and he placed his hands on the sides of his head, reeling a bit.

"This way!"

He rolled off the bar and I followed, noting that the blood on him was coming from a wound somewhere high on his side. His exposed skin was covered in scratches.

The last remaining customers sprang to their feet and streamed for the exits, the exact opposite to the direction we were going. Frightened screams behind us reminded me that Graamvater was still chasing us. The red dance floor was empty as we scrambled across it and into the back lounge. I heard a sound ahead of us, too loud for a standard weapon. Another crack, like the world was breaking, made me hesitate.

"What the hell is that?"

Benjamin glanced over his shoulder. "It's Majispin! Don't stop!"

We slammed the doors open and the air itself assaulted us. Benjamin sprawled to my right, Ana and I tumbled to the left.

Majispin stood at the center of the room, his cane held high and steady in his left hand while he made complex gestures with his right. Vampires struggled to reach him as another bolt of lightning assaulted our senses, blasting the room with light, sound, and heat. Another member of the assault team boiled away. A swirl of power circled above the magician's head. His eyes were closed and I had no idea if he was even aware we were in the room. The cyclone kept the attacking vampires clinging to whatever they could to maintain their balance.

Benjamin crawled behind the bar. I could see the female bartender from earlier back there as well, one hand to her neck where blood had overflowed her fingers and coated her breasts. I couldn't tell if she was dead or alive.

I pushed as far into the corner as I could with Ana and watched the door. Graamvater burst through seconds later, red eyes scanning the room. Before he could spot us, I surged forward and fired a round at his head. He ducked at the same moment and lunged for my shooting arm. I slugged him across the jaw and his head spun as he stumbled, but he quickly recovered. An uppercut drove him backward into the wall. I intended to crush his head any way possible, but he dodged again, allowing me to slam my knuckles into the concrete wall. He wrapped one scarred and deformed hand around my wrist and seized my neck with the other. When he stabbed himself into my brain, his fingers coiled like a boa constrictor, and another lightning strike provided further disorientation as all of my perceptions fractured and fell away. He had me again and I swirled, lost but aware of the passage back toward Graamvater. I dove for it, but he was ready this time and we met in a shower of mental sparks.

Another second locked like this, ravaged with pain and confusion, before I realized that I couldn't breathe. He was strangling me inside and out. I was getting weaker as he surged anew. I had no physicality to work with, nothing but instinct and an oncoming darkness. Rage served nothing; clear thought had no purchase here. Though we were both in pain, I was losing badly. Another flash of blinding brilliance and I slid further away, failing Ana, failing myself, silence and cold closing the door on my life.

I came back to my senses, gasping and stumbling onto my ass as Graamvater stood struggling at nothing, eyes spinning wildly. His elongated fingers twitched and began to fold in on themselves. The action didn't stop there as his hands folded into his arms and they crumpled inward. His head lolled grotesquely to one side and his knees started to buckle.

Ana leaned awkwardly against the wall and focused on her grandsire. She used a telekinetic blanket of pressure, pushing and folding him down. "You. Can go. To Hell!" she managed through clenched teeth, resisting as Graamvater pushed back. Blood began to seep from her eyes, her nose—anywhere it could escape her body, as she began to waver.

Another lightning strike pulled my attention to Majispin. He'd turned and had cornered the last few vamps, but he looked weary, older. Stooped and exhausted, he struggled to maintain his spell.

I called desperately to Majispin, my voice slurred, thick with fatigue, as Ana struggled with Graamvater. The master vampire twisted toward her and managed to reach out.

"You will...come with me...granddaughter. Scores of years spent looking for you, searching the world, concocting this fool church to draw you out and guide the hordes, will not go to waste. You will come with me and I will peel the secret of your existence from you molecule by molecule, if I must."

Somehow, he managed to reach her across the space between them. She screamed and swooned, held only by her grandsire's hand. Graamvater sprang back to his full height.

"You are the key, granddaughter, the key to creating vampires without the foul influence that monsters like your adopted father have dealt with and lost to. Only I have been strong enough to eat my possessor! I am your master and none of you can resist me!"

The world around me spun and I saw double. With a snap, everything came back into focus and I pointed my pistol at his distracted head. The remaining six rounds punched through his brain until the slide locked back, magazine empty. Ana collapsed, unconscious, as Graamvater turned toward me like a broken toy. His remaining eye was locked wide and his jaw hung broken and slack. A ragged chunk the size of a grapefruit was missing from the side of his head. Rotten brain and viscous fluids dribbled from the traumatic wound. I rocked to my feet, ignoring the nausea and vertigo as best as I could, and began striking him with the weapon in my hand, using the metal to tear him to pieces and sheer malice to communicate my feelings with a jackhammer's abandon.

Bone cracked and fluids spattered my hands and face. I wanted to drive him into the ground forever; Graamvater became the focus for everything I hated. Still, he reached for me, fingers trembling with malicious need.

"Alexander, get down!"

For once, I didn't ignore Majispin's command, and dropped to the floor. A crack of lightning seared through the space I'd just been standing in. The hair all over my body snapped to attention and the air was sucked away. A sickening boom followed and Graamvater flew from the room as if he'd been unmoored from the world itself. In the gloom across the red dance floor, through spots in my eyesight, I saw him peel what was left of his splattered self from the wall. I wasn't sure if I imagined it, but I thought I could hear the monster gibbering as he slithered up the wall and squeezed through the conical vent in the roof.

We'd see the bastard again, one day; there was no doubt of that.

CHAPTER 24

Benjamin had been shot twice. One bullet remained buried in his shoulder, a souvenir, and the other in the wall after it grazed him. While the forward bar was rebuilt, he spent a great deal of time as Majispin's personal assistant after the *second* assault on the safe house in as many years. Both attacks involved me, somehow. I didn't get around to asking Benjamin about the worms, certain that I didn't want to know anything more about them.

Bracken was very pleased to get his weapons back. With change. If thousands of dollars could be considered change. Both of us considered the deal square. With Ana back, he was even willing to be more forgiving that she'd destroyed his antique flamethrower. When he'd checked the bag, he babbled something about their value being intact since I'd only used them to shoot vampires. The details behind that comment were not something I wanted to be overly familiar with.

I made one follow-up phone call to Roberts. He seemed much more stable but still tightly wound. He briefly described how he'd managed to deflect the truth behind the vampire church as a clutch of pretenders who'd managed to convince the people they'd kidnapped that vampires were real. With no additional human casualties, little evidence, and the captives' stories too bizarre to believe, Roberts was as far in the clear as he could get. At least he was seeing the situation clearly and how he fit into it. I knew it was a lot to take in, and I resolved, as before, to simply let him be. I wasn't sure how he was going to deal with Pepperman, but that was entirely his problem.

Near as I could discern from Majispin, the safe-house coalition considered the assaults of the past year to be an aberration fomented first by the sun-seeking conspiracy and followed by the bizarre vampire church that was now assumed to be irreparably broken. Stupid, in my opinion; ideas never die. Unless they could mysteriously crush belief in this madness, it'd be a problem again one day. Graamvater, I'm sure, was going to prove them idiots. Using religion to control people never got old.

It took precious little time to find one of the Faithful fetishists for Ana to feed from. Until she'd been presented with fresh blood, she remained unresponsive and near rigor. Majispin needed a wheelchair at that point, but I hardly noticed his discomfort where Ana was concerned. A peppering of white now spread through his dark hair and a few more lines accented his face. Controlling the environment itself had cost him dearly, it seemed. He allowed her to stay in one of the windowless rooms upstairs. I stayed despite his protestations.

Nursing Ana was a disorienting experience that reminded me of her childhood, the main difference being people willing to donate their blood to her. The first day was awkward, getting fresh blood past her lips until we settled on a direct line from the Faithful's neck to her mouth. Then it was a problem keeping her from draining someone like a milkshake.

Once word spread amongst the Faithful, they began coming around on a schedule. Ana seemed to provide a unique pleasure, something for them to savor when she fed. They remembered what it had been like and remained loyal. While she was barely conscious, she provided nothing but need. Still, they came.

My little girl *was* something unique, more so than I had ever suspected. She was special enough that she'd inadvertently inspired an insane monster to devote decades to tracking her down for an as yet unknown purpose. He wanted her as a figurehead for his ersatz church and as a source for new vampires. The idea that Ana could be free of the deteriorating influence the rest of us suffered had never occurred to me until Graamvater had mentioned it. He'd also implied that rather than his power consuming him over time, he'd consumed it instead. What kind of human monster had he been before that he'd been able to turn the tables like that? I suspected that the Queen of Dragons held some answers, but I'd rather not speak to her ever again. But there lived empty hope.

The time that Ana lay nearly inert afforded me an unusual amount of time to think. Kelsey remained top of mind and an unsolvable problem. Was she a problem? Somehow, I knew I'd see her again and that question would be answered once and for all. I owed that girl and it would come time to pay one of these days. She was the one that started my decline from humanity, however inadvertent. My involvement in her life was a spiral I'd only just begun to recover from. She deserved better than I had. I'd have to see to it, if I could. Kelsey had a disturbing ability to stay off my radar when she didn't want to be found. Now that she was a vampire, she'd be even harder to locate. The way things were going in my life at the moment, I wondered how much time I had left before someone finally put the scissors to my thread.

When this line of thought threatened to drag me down into depression, I cracked open the book Pat had sold to me. It was a wreck, barely surviving its travels with me. The book posited several theories on the origins of shapeshifters and vampires. Most of which Majispin had provided a synopsis for in his arrogant way. There were some details here, however, bits and pieces that jibed in disturbing ways with my experiences of the last year and a half. Armies and gods and punching holes in other dimensions. Cosmic stuff I wanted nothing to do with, but *it* seemed determined to involve me. If the explanations were true, then there would be a reckoning for us all in the future, an inevitability that no once-human supernatural could avoid.

A new sense of foreboding threatened my quiet time and I set the book aside, determined to do nothing but wait for Ana. And think.

Late one night, as I dozed near Ana's bed, she began a conversation I didn't want to hear.

"Da."

She'd been lying so still, I was somewhat surprised when she spoke. "Yes, sweetheart?"

"I never knew..."

She took several breaths and the muscles in her jaw worked tirelessly. I didn't want to encourage or interrupt in any way. Whatever she had to say was going to come entirely of her own volition.

"I didn't know what it was like to be afraid like that. To be completely stripped of my own free will. I don't... I don't know what to do."

For the first time in over a century, Ana looked her age to me and it broke my heart. "You move forward. You already proved to yourself that you're capable when you fought back as soon as you had an opportunity." Offered without hesitation, it was the only solution I knew that had kept me alive for so long.

"I know, but—"

"There's no 'but' there." I moved from the chair to her bed. "You fight; you move forward. The price they pay must be as high if not higher for coming after you. You have friends—more than I—and you have family. He has *nothing*. You have my love and my trust."

She hugged me then, hard enough to hurt my

shoulders. As ever, she was as strong as she needed to be.

"He… He wanted to use me as a figurehead."

She said nothing more for a minute or two until I asked, "How?"

"The time I was with him, he was combing through my head, tinkering with my beliefs. He wanted to unmake our relationship and replace you in my head. I don't think he expected it to be as difficult as it was. Given more time—"

"Which he didn't get and he never will." I was uncertain, but as a father, I couldn't help but be confident that I would do whatever it took to protect Ana.

"Is that all he wanted from you?"

She shook her head and searched the room for words. "When he picked through my mind, I could get glimpses from his."

"I had something similar happen. When he does that, there's an opportunity to dive into his mind. It's painful."

"Oh." She looked disappointed.

"It was a reckless move on my part and it seemed like I could only do it once. I hope there isn't a next time."

She nodded. "Everything's changed now."

She was right about that. "We know he's out there now. Something we were completely unaware of before. As hard as he worked this time, he's going to need to try much harder if he wants to surprise us."

"What we know has been compromised. Our familiar patterns have to change."

"You're right about that. I'm going to have to abandon every place I have in reserve."

"And I have friends I need to warn."

I tapped the notebook in my lap. "I think there are some people I should contact, as well."

We sat silent, considering the enormity of the task ahead, what changes needed to be made to keep Graamvater at a distance.

"Someday, we're going to have to track him down."

She didn't look at me, only stared at her hands.

"Only when we're ready." I reached out and engulfed her smaller hands in mine.

She nodded and grinned briefly. "I got something for you before all this started. I had one of my 'fans' bring it over." She handed me a mobile phone. "My number's already in there. You can text me."

"Poppa don't text."

"Poppa needs to learn how; I can't have my father making embarrassing and awkward phone calls to me."

I smiled and tucked the device into the waterproof bag I kept my notebook in.

Ana looked sad for a moment. "I need to get going again."

"I know." And I did. Ana roamed; she had her own life. It's where she drew her power from as much as—if not more than—her relationship with me. "When are you going to go?"

She smiled and lay back in the bed. We sat like that for hours until I dozed again, thinking of Maria, remembering her scent, the smell of her home, the feel of her skin. When I next opened my eyes, Ana was gone. It reminded me of the last time she'd disappeared while I slept, and a pang of worry rumbled through my belly. It passed—more that I shoved it away than a natural acceptance. Where would I go now?

The bag with my notebook remained in my lap. I opened it up to my entries on Kelsey. It took about half an hour to update it. I wasn't sure what, if anything, to do about her. It'd be a difficult puzzle to find her again, I was sure. There was no guarantee that, even if I did, I could fix our relationship or, to be honest, create one. I sat in silence until a metallic rattling came to my ears. Followed by quick footsteps.

I heard Benjamin ask, "What's it doing?"

"I don't know!" Majispin snarled in return.

"Why's it shaking like that? Is it going to explode?"

"Of course not! Maybe. I'm not sure…"

They were in the lab. I hustled from the room and made my way there. The brass contraption rattled above the table, beginning to glow. I could feel the temperature in the room rising.

"Is something wrong?" I had to shout, the rattling had been joined by a keening whine.

"I don't kn—wait! I think someone's trying to hack into the stream. Damn, they must be using a lot of power to do this." Majispin's face fell calm as he became lost in his little boy's curiosity about magic. "But how…? No. Who? Who could do this? Why?"

We stared a moment longer as sound and heat accelerated. I tapped Benjamin for his attention, only to see that we were clearly on the same page. He pulled Majispin's chair backward and I followed suit. We scooted out of the room just as the device began to flare, sucking the air out in a rushing flow.

Then silence.

We three looked at each other, baffled. With deliberate caution, we peered in, where all was quiet. A sudden burst displaced the atmosphere at us. We covered our heads, instinct squelching inquisitiveness.

Both Benjamin and Majispin stared at me through their arms. I gave them my best dissatisfied look and peered into the room again. Nothing appeared to have exploded; the machine was still intact. On its pedestal, a single white envelope lay. In a humiliating move that reminded me of the Three Stooges, we tried to enter the room at the same time. A brief stumble put me at the front, staring down at the envelope…with my name on it.

"That's not from Bismark," Majispin said with gravitas.

"No shit." I swallowed, feeling serious trepidation as I watched the envelope, waiting for it to attack or for demons to fly out of it or something else bloody and dreadful. In the end, my mantra guided me as it always had.

I picked up the envelope and slid the packet open. Inside, there was a single rectangular item. A printed piece of slick card stock, perforated across its shortest length. The name of a city peeked out, just at the edge of the opening. I ground my teeth at recognizing it.

Benjamin looked around me and into the envelope. "It's a ticket."

"What? Let me... Please." Majispin took the paper envelope. Glanced at it, grunted, and handed it back to me. "It's warm and it certainly has your name on it. There's a note inside."

I took the envelope back and slid the letter out. The paper was indeed warm and a humid scent floated out, along with mineral rich soil and reptiles, some wax and cotton textiles and a few drops of...cognac? All smells that reminded me of New Orleans, a town I hated and never wanted to see again. It was the heart of the state my father had fled for his life, seeking freedom from slavery, up the Mississippi River until he'd reached Canada to find opportunity and my mother. He'd never spoken fondly of the state or the city, and the first and last time I visited, I found the area distasteful as well. Every nook and cranny was imbued with enough blood and history that raw magic floated in the air, burning my every pore.

Folded inside the letter was a small square of cotton. The patch was its natural color, bereft of dyes, frayed at the edges, and it smelled of spicy oils and very old memories. As it sat in the palm of my hand, I read the handwritten letter on crinkled vellum:

Dear Mr. Smith,
My daughter, Sera, of late a mere ten years old, is still missing and I know it is only you who can find

her. The Loa have told me so, for rather than guide me to my little girl, they have brought me to you. Whatever situation has waylaid you in Boston, I beg that you put it to rest. I also ask again that you come and I have provided for your transportation as a sign of my desperation and faith. I do apologize for whatever may come next, but I have no other recourse, no other hope but you. My gods have spoken to me and my faith lies in you now as it had before.
Sincerely,
M.M. Lespiaux

My eyes traced the precise lettering, a perfect cursive form, every letter inscribed with purpose, it seemed. And the name. Comically close to the historical Voodoo Queen of the city's past. Then I reread the destination on the ticket. New Orleans. According to the departure time indicated, I had less than six hours to catch the train. Despite my distaste, I determined to go. The effect was all-encompassing, like a powerful sedative, a seductive force, compelling and insistent. My curiosity was piqued, bringing a placid clarity to my mind and I knew it was possible that I was being manipulated, but I didn't care—couldn't. There was nothing at stake but the journey, my immediate goal. Ana was on her feet and back out in the world. Why not help this woman find her daughter?

Benjamin's voice came to me through a formless barrier of air and wishes, his voice muffled by my disinterest in anything but getting ready, heading to the train station, and traveling. He called my name once or twice and I looked at him but had no desire to respond. Then I looked to Majispin who said something like "well" or "what the hell" before I wandered towards the exit.

Somewhere in that fog, I mumbled, "New Orleans. I was on my way before I met you."

CHAPTER 25

I hardly remember packing a bag. When I'm on the move, I don't bring much with me; there isn't much I need. I tend to avoid most public interstate transportation. Buses are best, because the others use scanners and such. There's no way I'm getting on an airplane. The train would be tough but not impossible. The guns were the worst part. Having to break them completely down and baffle the parts required tools, and I didn't have much time. To hide even a small amount of ammunition was a pain in the ass. I worked as quickly as possible and got my traveling kit together, hailed a cab, and hustled to the station.

It was a particularly beautiful and sunny afternoon. Light splashed artfully on the hundred-year-old architecture of the station. Despite the smell of diesel in the air, my nose felt clear and potent. The platform was less crowded than I had expected and I was grateful for that. I still felt a kind of subdued euphoria, a pleasant and positive feeling about where I was going. Which was strange, considering my usual opinion of New Orleans. When I was last in the city, it seemed the air itself was out of phase and difficult to breathe. This time would be different, though; I could tell. A few days relaxing on the train and everything would soon be in order.

An unusually short porter examined my ticket and gave me a brilliant smile before imploring me to follow him to my assigned compartment. The ticket provided privacy in one of the sleeper cars, the preferred method for long train rides and the safest for someone like me.

We stepped into a car with very little foot traffic while several times as many people crushed themselves into coach. They would spend the duration of their trip sitting upright, shoulder to shoulder with other passengers. I was looking forward to stretching out, reading my book, and watching the world go by.

The porter stopped, smiled again, and slid open the door of my room. Inside, an elegant pair of lightly toasted legs reclined in plain view. Her feet were bare, but her toenails were painted with what looked like solid gold. Here and there, sparkles adorned her bare skin where it showed, spilling out of a luxuriant silk wrap that appeared to be spun from precious metals. A light mist boiled out of the room.

The Queen of Dragons leaned forward, looked into my eyes, and said, "Come in, Alexander, have a seat."

I looked at the porter, and it was her attendant, smiling brilliantly, as usual. He bowed and gestured, bidding me to enter. My initial terror ran short against my new, positive attitude. I smiled at her and entered the room as her man closed the door. After stowing my small bag, I sat facing her, our knees less than a foot apart.

She stared at me curiously. Her eyes, inhuman and diamond-like, slowly closed until they were mere slits with an occasional sparkle slipping between them.

Her bare foot slid up the inside of my calf.

"Rub my foot."

My hands slid automatically to the sides of her feet and caressed them once from heel to toe. Her skin was as unreal as I remembered, both human and something more. A pleasant hum vibrated along my fingers and into my body. I began working the muscles and tendons, stretching each toe in turn as I massaged her foot.

We sat like that for an indeterminate amount of time. I began to feel the weight of her intense scrutiny. The cloud of positive feeling around me began to dissipate and the more familiar buzz of cynicism grew. My hands slowed in accompaniment with the shift.

After a few more minutes of this, the Queen smiled, showing one fang, and the sparkle in her eyes flashed brighter. "You're welcome."

"What was that?" I took my hands off her, but she kept her foot in my lap.

"You were enchanted."

"Enchanted?"

"Yes, compelled to be here, on this train."

"When, how? I didn't feel any active magic, no pain."

She smiled again, giving me that unnerving feeling of being in the sights of a predator. "Well, it's clever. Isn't it? None of the magic I've done on or around you has caused pain, has it? Your enchantment was old, subtle, laced with...old friends."

Old friends of the Dragon's were none I'd ever want to meet. Frustration boiled. *Lespiaux did this to me.* I wasn't sure what to do next when the train lurched and we were on our way. All of my trepidation about New Orleans surged anew. "You broke it, took it away?"

"Only temporarily; I wouldn't want to alter your journey. Now we have some time to talk freely. Rub the other." She switched feet.

"Beg pardon?" I'd heard her quite clearly and feared where this was going.

"Rub. The. Other." She punctuated the statement by prodding me with her toes. "It's rather enjoyable. I'm not often human and comfortable."

I froze, my hands raised about chest height. *She calls this human?*

After a dramatic sigh, she said, "If it at all matters, the contact helps me to keep the enchantment off of you. *Now rub.*"

Her eyes flashed and a seriousness equivalent to the

weight of the train settled in her voice at the last. So I rubbed and she smiled, draining what tension she could out of the compartment. To her credit, the grin didn't make me think she wanted to eat me.

She watched and waited while I worked her foot, and took her time before speaking again. "You're going to repay your debt to me soon."

I froze again, not sure this time if I'd heard her correctly. She wiggled her toes in my crotch until I started rubbing again.

"The situation you're walking into is part of a bigger problem. If you unravel things properly, you can consider your debt to me repaid. Consider that information incentive for getting the job *done*."

"What is it that needs…doing?"

"There are rules, Alexander, some that even I can't break. You get there, you get involved, and you fix it on your own."

"You're not going to tell me, not even a hint? Are you sure you want whatever this is to be done?"

"Mmmm. What if you fail, you mean? Then you'll still be beholden to me and whatever joys come with it. The rest is none of your business."

I ground my teeth. "That doesn't make any sense. Either you want this done or something else. Which is it? Because I don't want there to be any misunderstandings on this. I don't want to owe you anything."

"Nothing, Alexander? There's not a thing you'd like to give me?"

"I think it'd be better if, uh, we gave each other some space."

Another smile from her, but this one devolved into something else. She regarded me with the kind of hunger a man would normally welcome, but coming from her, it made my guts shrivel with the cold memory of being driven and out of control. The Queen of Dragons placed her opposite foot on my knee with the delicate touch of a butterfly. Her silken wrap slid down her thighs as they separated, revealing what I could safely consider the source of my fear.

Her feet slid off me and she pitched forward. I believe I flinched but it was difficult to tell from the rising numbness through my chest. She hovered over me as the uncontrollable need within me slammed against my apprehension. I could see how her skin seemed to be made up of tiny, iridescent scales that shimmered through the spectrum. She smelled unearthly, foreign, and delicious all at once. Her eyes twinkled—not from mischief, but because her pupils swam in pools of sharp glass. She nuzzled my cheek and paused the barest inch above me, her lips hovering above mine.

My hands, almost of their own volition, gripped her hips and trembled in place.

She sighed. "This is not satisfying at all."

I must have relaxed visibly when she sat back and pouted. Then she took a deep breath and when she exhaled, Maria sat across from me. Her scent flooded the small room, every detail I could see or smell was accurate. Right down to her eyes.

"Is this better?" She asked in Maria's voice, using my dead lover's typical direct inflection.

I licked my lips, trying to relax. "In some ways."

She made a small, pouty sound while pursing her lips—Maria's lips, full of hidden promise. "'In some ways.' Okay, let's try this, then. Louisiana is pretty close to Texas. Right?"

I nodded, a sadness pulling at my chest as I watched my dead lover, fully reanimated, seemingly alive, and wanting to tell me something about New Orleans.

"I been there, been to New Orleans. I know what you're dealing with."

"So?" I was starting to wonder if this were the Queen

talking of her experience or some mystical amalgamation of Maria's history gleaned from who knew where.

"Ass." A curt judgement that was typical from Maria. "'So.' I might could help you out with some background; that's what's 'so.' To hell with it if you don't wanna know; just forget about it." She stood up, narrowly missing the bunk rail overhead, and laid her fingers on the door handle.

I put my hand over hers before I knew what I was doing. "No. I...I'd like to hear what you have to say."

That touch sparked something. I felt the familiar tug and burn of our auras reacting to each other and pulled back. She seemed to feel it as well, pausing and looking from her hand to me once. She sat and resettled herself. I took in her scent again and her body. From the copper-tinted curls right down the curve of her neck into the exposed hollows of her collarbones above muscle and breasts that—

"Up here. Focus."

I gulped, losing myself in the moment, trying to focus on her words instead of the loss I felt. *The desire.* There had to be a way to weather this spell, to maintain a connection to reality. *This couldn't be real; Maria was dead.*

"Okay. Fine. You know there are other...places, other dimensions—like the Twilight Zone. Right? You know how Faeries and all them other people show up at Majispin's club near the dance floor? What's happening there is what comes naturally in Nola. The barrier is rubbed thin there. It's a weak spot. The whole place is dirty with weird magic. It's somewhere other stuff can slip in—some things more than others."

"Some more than others?" This was a clue, some roundabout way the Queen was telling me something. *This was not Maria, could not be Maria.*

"Yeah." She settled back and put one foot on my

armrest. She was still dressed in the same clothes the Queen had been wearing, still barefoot.

Still bare in that dangerous place, I remembered with an ache. Maybe I could rattle the cage with something here. "That wrap looks better on you than it did on the Queen."

Maria's eyes met mine and not even a quiver of pique crossed her face. She smiled slyly with none of the serpentine promise I'd become used to seeing from this being. "You think so? It's a little snug." She shimmied the silks demurely down her thighs a bit and I came undone.

"Yeah, I think so." My hand caressed the top of her foot and I could feel the familiar sparks beneath my fingertips, the odd power surge that I shared with Maria when we were close. The kind that could start a fire.

Maria's other foot slid up the inside of my calf and I bolted upright. She met me halfway and our lips crushed together before our mouths parted and wrestled for dominance. The wrap came away easily, but my conventional clothing took a bit more convincing. Maria tore my shirt and paused to examine the damage.

"You owed me one or two, anyway."

That bit of personal history sent me further over the edge, any hesitation I might have felt steamed away in an instant. With our skin loosed from clothing and our minds turned to exploring, I was able to verify that this was indeed Maria right down to any details I could access, inside and out.

We wrestled for position, nipped, pushed, pulled and encouraged for I don't know how long. There was a scratch or two or more, a few bites, and a great heat generated by both our physical bodies mixing with the energy that sluiced between us. And when we finished, it wasn't long before we began anew with a reduced vigor and an increased tenderness.

Raw and spent, we curled uncomfortably on the

squared-off loungers that doubled as a bed.

"I'm sorry," I said.

"For what?"

"For not getting to you in time, for not talking to you sooner—so many things."

She caressed my chest, letting the words linger before answering. "We all make decisions we regret; you can't hide from it and you can't be sorry all the time. Sometimes we gotta do things that we don't want so that others don't suffer as bad as we have. Or as long."

"I haven't forgotten about your son."

A sadness soiled her face even as she smiled. "You better not." She prodded my stomach with one playful jab. "But I have to go."

She began to pull herself away from me and I clung a bit longer than I should have.

"I won't soon forget you, Alexander. Our business may conclude, but we're connected in ways that you have yet to understand."

The feel of her skin shifted beneath my fingers and I was holding the Queen of Dragons—something I wouldn't willingly do for long. She slipped away, clothes re-dressing her as if they were sentient, and with the same fluid motion, opened the door. She stopped in the doorway and spoke over her shoulder.

"This wouldn't have been possible if you didn't love her." And then she was gone, a wisp of vapor curled on the floor.

I folded into myself with nowhere to go and no one to blame. My thoughts crumpled to the simplest emotions and I melted, ragged and alone, determined to remain in my room until the train made New Orleans and I had no choice but to exit.

Hunger and harassing whispers bid me otherwise.

Errick Nunnally was born and raised in Boston, Massachusetts, and served one tour in the Marine Corps before deciding art school was a safer pursuit. He enjoys art, comics, and genre novels. A designer by day, he earned a black belt in Krav Maga and Muay Thai kickboxing by night. His writing has appeared in several anthologies and is best described as "dark pulp." His work can be found in *Transcendent, Monarchies of Mau: Tales of Excellent Cats, Protectors 2, Nightlight Podcast, The Final Summons, Lamplight,* and the novels, BLOOD FOR THE SUN (The first Alexander Smith novel), and LIGHTNING WEARS A RED CAPE.

See more of his work online at erricknunnally.us